BACK TO BEFORE

BLAIR BRYAN

Copyright 2021 by Blair Bryan

All rights reserved.

This is a work of fiction. Names, characters, businesses, places, events and incidents are either the products of the author's imagination or used in a fictitious manner. Any resemblance to actual persons, living or dead, or actual events is purely coincidental.

To every mother who is asked to navigate the path of addiction and treatment with a child they have loved since the moment of conception. You are stronger than you realize.

Love is not the cure for addiction.
Just ask the mother of an addict. —Addict Chick

ONE

Mothers of teenage boys never sleep well, and Holly was no different. But that night in May, she thought she had hit the single mother jackpot. The coincidence of both Chance and Dillon having sleepovers at a friend's house on the same night had never happened before. She was giddy at the thought of having a night completely to herself.

Finally, the stars have aligned for me. It's about time!

The prospect of a nice warm bath and opening a fresh box of red wine without worrying about the ever-watchful eyes of her two sons, who had been deeply affected by her ex-husband's alcoholism, seemed like a dream. She savored it, not knowing it was the last time in a long time she would feel completely peaceful and free.

She piled her coffee-colored hair that was getting its first streaks of white cream on her head, slipped off her clothes, and dipped her mom bod into the hot water. A few stretch marks like tiger claw marks streaked down her slightly too wide hips, and there was a subtle softening around her tummy. Evidence of the two pregnancies her body had sustained left their marks, but she worked out and tried to stay in decent shape. Holly was down to the last fifteen pounds, knowing that someday, eventually, she would want to get back out there and date. Just not now. Her life was too full and over-scheduled as it was; to add a man to the mix wasn't even on her radar. She'd take a solid eight hours of sleep over a roll in the hay any day.

Brown eyes closed, she sipped the boxed Merlot slowly, letting it roll on her tongue and coat the back of her throat. The Epsom salts worked their magnesium magic to loosen the ever-present tension in her shoulders. She forgot about the calls she would have to make to two of her students' parents. Since moving to the most affluent neighborhood just outside of Indianapolis a little over a year ago, she thought things would be better, that they would be easier. She had told herself that serving students that weren't as economically disadvantaged wouldn't be as stressful. Turns out, it was actually *more* stressful, but in weird ways. First-grade parents already vying for college acceptance tracks held 'emergency' conferences with her to discuss why she wasn't including Chinese Mandarin in her lesson plan. They were too intense with too much time on their hands, and their helicopter parenting style had been a huge adjustment.

Later that night, still warmed from the bath and fuzzy from the glasses of wine, she read part of a romance novel until her eyes got heavy. If you asked her, she could never tell you which one, since they were all the same. Happily ever after squeezed into under three hundred pages with a colorful cover that looked pretty on her nightstand. The novels were about as far from real life as it gets, but it was her only friv-olous escape and fed her hopeless romantic tendencies. She fluffed the pile of pillows, stretched her strong legs, and relaxed into her down comforter. Sighing contentedly, it was the one splurge she had allowed herself when she moved into her new townhouse, and she smiled as she drifted off. Her dog, Murph, a rescued ball of pure white fluffiness settled into her knee pits and began to snore. Completely carefree and relaxed, she fell into a hard and deep sleep. Her cell phone, a sentinel, stood guard on her bedside table, just in case her boys needed her in the middle of the night.

The nightmare began with a text message sent at two a.m. from Chance's best friend. Her ever-mothering hyper-vigilant ears heard the delicate text notification, forcing her to pop up and rub her eyes. A slight headache pinched her head from the wine. She grabbed the phone, held it at arm's length, and squinted so she could make out the words. She was on the brink of needing reading glasses, but she just wasn't ready or willing to admit that yet. On her to-do list, things she needed were always buried underneath the needs of the kids.

Blake: *Is Chance ok? I am scared.*

She felt a chill go through her. On high alert, she immediately responded. Fear took up residence in her throat, a thick lump that choked off her air supply and made it hard to breathe.

Holly: What? He's supposed to be with you.

The incoming text bubble blinked and blinked, adding more tension.

Where could he possibly be at two o'clock in the morning?

Blake: He's not here. Heard he was at Triangle Park with Angel.

Angel? Who the hell was that?

Holly racked her brain, searching for that name, and came up blank. She ran to her closet and threw on a sweatshirt over the old running t-shirt she had worn to bed. Grabbing the keys from the lavender-colored dish, she raced to the car, not even stopping to put on a bra. Pure panic, sharp and hot coursed through her, and her heart hammered as she drove to the park in complete darkness. She made two wrong turns before she got there. New Hope wasn't even that big, and she was slightly embarrassed she still depended on GPS to navigate to places. A reliable voice guiding her turn by turn was how she preferred to maneuver through life instead of finding her own route on a map.

"Dammit," she cursed. Mad at herself for the delay, she hit her hands against the steering wheel. Slamming her foot back on the gas, she turned the final corner, and the red flashing lights made her stomach drop to her feet. Parking the minivan, she ran past a merry-go-round toward the red lights, her breathing shallow as beads of sweat formed on her forehead. She slipped on the wet and muddy grass in her purple crocs, twinging a muscle in her back. Her hand circled to the spot, rubbing it as she started to run faster.

An ambulance. A stretcher. A body lying on it. Pale, lifeless, small.

She let out a yelp, and her hand flew up to her mouth to cover it. Holly froze in terror. Her hand itched to touch him, to smooth the long wavy brown hair away from his brow. She ached to brush her thumb across the cleft in his chin he hated, but she adored. It was her favorite place to kiss when he was an infant, and the first day after they brought him home from the hospital, she rubbed that soft little dent so much, she thought a blister might form. He was so pale and so still, he looked like he was sleeping.

I always loved to watch him sleep, especially when he was a baby. His face was always so sweet and tender, wrapped up in his crib. Safe.

She clutched the metal bar of the stretcher as the EMT worked on her son, monitoring his heartbeat and hooking him up to monitors. An oxygen mask was placed over his mouth and nose. A smear of dirt on his jeans and those stupid Osiris shoes, bright ass green with the fat tongues that had rubbed blisters on his shins for weeks. Shoes that she had used to bribe him to wear the first days at his new high school. Footwear was suddenly so important, so critical that it leaked onto his ten-year-old brother, Dillon, who made the same demands and chose an equally offensive color. They were shoes she really couldn't afford but were one way she could assuage the guilt she still felt from the divorce.

"Ma'am, please stand back," the ambulance attendant said, pulling her focus back to the stretcher.

"This is my son!" Holly cried her voice tense and shrill. "What happened?"

"Appears to be an overdose. We found two Xanax bars in his pocket."

"Xanax?" Holly said, dumbfounded.

How does a fifteen-year-old get his hands on Xanax?

"His breathing is stabilized. His vitals are good. But with his age and weight and not knowing how much he ingested, we're going to transfer him to the hospital for observation."

"Okay," Holly said weakly.

"You're welcome to ride with us, but I'd recommend you follow in your vehicle instead."

"Yes, of course. I'll follow."

She climbed back into her old but reliable minivan recognizing that her night of freedom had instantly become dark and nightmarish. The panic finally subsided enough for the first tears to surface. Hot and warm they fell down her freckled cheeks, running down the tracks of her laugh lines and spilling onto her hand. Her chest heaved as she turned on the headlights and followed the ambulance to the hospital.

What she didn't know was that nothing would ever be the same. That this was the beginning of her slow descent into hell. That she was going to wish that she could go back to before this moment. Back to before this night, when everything she thought she knew and everything she believed in had unraveled. The ugly truths hidden in lies and misdeeds would be soon exposed. A truth so painful that she would never recover from it. She would never be the same.

Before she was a newly divorced single mother. A beloved first-grade teacher starting over in a new town. Before, she was filled with hope; the name was half the silly reason she decided to move to New Hope in the first place. An affluent town with beautiful neighborhoods and expensive houses with planned parks and open green spaces. Filled with designer dogs with curly hair that got to exercise with other doodle dogs in poshly appointed dog parks. New Hope was swimming with privilege and opportunities. At the time, she had told herself she would be giving her kids a much better life, that they would have extraordinary opportunities in music and art, things both her kids excelled at. Creative classes that were first on the chopping block at their old school when the budgets needed to be balanced. She was doing this for them. She was sacrificing for them.

They didn't get it yet, but when they graduated, when they went on to live productive lives and be successful, then she would get her thank you. Then she would get their appreciation for her sacrifice. She knew what was best for them. That was another ugly lie that would soon be exposed because it turns out, she really didn't know at all.

TWO

Holly sat in the hospital room, listening to the beep from the monitors and the blood pressure cuff that would tighten mechanically every five minutes, punctuated by the ticking of the clock. It was a medicinal symphony that gave her déjà vu. The sterile nothingness of the stale hospital air was suffocating. She clawed at her throat wishing she could leave, glancing at Chance and the clock and willing time to go faster.

Hospitals always made her anxious after her father had died in one when she was fifteen. He had taken a high-stress job as a traveling salesman when she was thirteen. Two years and four bleeding ulcers later, he had a heart attack and died instantly, leaving her fatherless.

The day he died, she went to the hospital with her mom like she always had, knowing in a few days that he would be on the mend and get to recuperate at home like he had before. Holly would make him doctor-approved poached eggs and turkey bacon, and they would work on crossword puzzles together until he was strong enough to go back to work.

After a successful surgery, she sat and waited for him to

wake up. He had smiled, his eyes crinkly and warm, but his skin was gray and smelled sickeningly sweet when she bent down to hug him.

"That's my girl," he said. "I'll be home in a jiffy, and you'll get so sick of me being around all the time, you'll beg me to go back to work." She remembered reaching down and snapping the robe together on his shoulder.

"You missed one," she said, smiling at him.

"What would I do without you, sweetie?" he joked weakly, squeezed her hand, and closed his eyes. Two days later, he was gone. A fatal heart attack inside a hospital and nothing could be done to save him.

That night, she wished she could wake up from this nightmare and find Chance asleep in his bed at home. She wished she could be anywhere but here. Hospitals were where people died.

She had been distracted and busy filling out paperwork and finding insurance cards when they first arrived. But now she was sitting alone in the room with Chance. Waiting. Waiting for toxicology results and desperate for him to wake up. The waiting was the hardest part.

The toxicology report would be back soon. Then she would know the full scope of what she was dealing with. She reached out to stroke his hand that was losing its childlike softness, stretching out with longer fingers and rougher fingertips. His hand was almost as big as hers now, not the tiny hand she'd once grasped to lead him across the street when he was little.

When did that happen?

She reluctantly made the mandatory phone call to Chance's dad, not surprised at all that Mick didn't pick up.

Asshole is probably passed out cold.

She felt a small twinge of hypocrisy at the four glasses of

wine she drank but then recovered. The difference between the two of them was Holly would have a drink maybe once a week. Mick, on the other hand, would have a drink maybe once an hour.

A soft knock at the door and a middle-aged nurse entered pushing a rolling desk with a computer. She smiled thinly, taking in the old sweatshirt and crocs in one judgmental glance. "I need to ask you some questions." She turned toward her computer. "How long has your son been using drugs?"

The question was a shock to the system. Her son didn't do that. Her son had dutifully watched three seasons of *Intervention* with her and then submitted to her lengthy question and lecture period after the shows.

"I-I…" She stammered. "I don't…" She traced her thumb on the back of Chance's hand. Soft circles. Pinching between her eyes to quell the tension forming there and tried to think.

"Does he have a history of mental health problems? Or substance abuse issues?"

"No." Tears filled her eyes, making the nurse's face blurred and distorted. "This is a shock to me. I had no…"

"What about family history?" she pressed. "Any mental health or substance abuse diagnoses in his parents' or grandparents' histories?"

"Um, yes," Holly mumbled. "His father is an alcoholic."

"Any history of suicidal thoughts or ideation?"

"Not that I know of," Holly answered, feeling like the little boy who used to bring her fistfuls of dandelions had somehow turned into a stranger. Living a secret life in plain sight, right under her nose.

I'm not sure I even know who he is at all anymore.

"Where do you think he got the Xanax? Do you have a prescription for it?"

"I have no idea. His best friend, Blake, said he had been hanging out with someone named Angel."

"Do you know who that is?" she asked.

"I have no idea."

There was an audible *tsk* that the nurse barely concealed.

Chance stirred, and Holly's breath caught in her chest. His dark eyes fluttered open. Seeing his mom's face, he smiled and closed his eyes. Then his eyes popped open wide, taking in his surroundings, and he started to cry. He visibly crumpled and tightened his body, making his form contract so he took up even less space on the gurney.

"I'm sorry, Mommy," he slurred. "I'm just a piece of shit," he sobbed, getting more and more upset. "I promised you I would never do drugs. I am nothing, I am garbage."

Holly's heart broke open. "Garbage? No, honey, you are not garbage. You made a mistake."

Chance was inconsolable, his thin frame shaking uncontrollably.

"I am garbage," he cried, his entire body shaking, his mouth agape in a silent scream. A string of spit crossed it, making him look even more vulnerable.

"Can we have a blanket, please?" Holly asked, wanting to take away his pain. Needing to do something to make him feel better, to stop this agony from spreading and swallowing them both up whole.

"I promised you, and I broke my promise, Mommy. I am so sorry."

"Shh," Holly soothed him, smoothing back the wavy hairs on his head. His asymmetrical skater cut was one of his most recognizable features. He never called her Mommy anymore; his high had reverted him back to his three-year-old self. The word ripped through her heart. His pained mental state cast an anguished pall on the word now.

The nurse brought back a blanket and was joined by a police officer holding a clipboard.

"Normally in this situation, I would write him a ticket for possession and public intoxication. You should know we also found a vape in his backpack, so he should be issued a citation for that."

A vape?

The officer turned toward her son. "Chance, since this is your first offense, I am willing to give you a warning and just the fine for the tobacco use if you can tell us who was your hook-up."

Stunned, Holly mumbled, "Thank you." She jiggled Chance's arm and widened her eyes, nodding at the officer, urging him to comply.

"Tell him," she said sternly.

"I don't know who's it was," Chance squeaked out. "I found it."

"Angel was a name I heard," Holly offered.

"Angel," the officer repeated. "Yes, we have heard that name before." He wrote it down in his notebook.

Chance shot Holly a defiant look, then burst into tears again. He was so unstable, it was unsettling. Shooting from pain to anger to sadness in seconds, she was on edge and didn't know what to expect next.

"Obviously, this is the beginning of a problem that could really escalate if you don't take things seriously."

"I understand," Holly resigned. "I promise you I am taking this very seriously."

The officer looked straight at Chance. "We don't want you to have a record, so we are going to issue you a warning. Just this once."

Holly was relieved.

"Don't make this a habit," he stated. "The next time I see

you in this state, there will be major consequences."

Chance's thin lips pressed together.

"Thank you, officer," she said. "Chance, what do you have to say?" she prodded.

"Thank you," he repeated in a tone that made Holly wince from the insincerity.

Three long hours later, they were back in the car with a thick pad of paperwork that included referrals for a substance abuse evaluation and a psych evaluation. The sun was coming up, and Holly grabbed her sunglasses to diffuse it, grateful to have them to hide behind.

Chance, settled into the seat next to her, was quiet and his eyes were closed. She had a lot of things she wanted to say, but now was not the time. Holly was exhausted and needed to get them home and settled before Dillon was dropped off at ten. She was desperate to hide the truth from him to protect her younger son.

Dillon idolized his brother. He copied nearly everything Chance wore or did, even growing his hair out and begging for the same hairstyle, much to Chance's somewhat flattered annoyance. Chance usually put up with it in his joking good-natured way. But now she was afraid. She was afraid that Dillon would follow down this path, too, and for the first time, she longed to keep them separated and safe, and she didn't like the way that felt at all.

THREE

Holly looked down at the phone in her hand in frustration, knowing what a waste it was as a communication device when it came to Mick. Phone calls, emails, and texts all went unanswered, every damn time. She had finally driven over there, knowing the only way she was going to get in actual contact with him was to pop in unannounced.

She banged on his front door hard, bleached from the sun and dirty from neglect, knowing the chances of Mick still being in bed at eleven am were astronomically high. Her hand was turning red as she hit it over and over. She pumped the doorbell impatiently with her index finger and then went back to pounding on the door until she finally heard heavy footsteps stomping through the house.

"What in the fu…." Mick yanked the door open, his eyes squinted into the sunlight, and then seeing it was her, rubbed a hand across his face in frustration. Bare-chested and ruddy complected, his long rocker hairstyle was wavy at the ends, just like Chance's. In his mid-fifties, he still had a thick head of brown hair that was turning white with long streaks which seemed to multiply every time she saw him. Once in perfect shape, time and the booze had caught up with him. He was becoming pudgy around the middle and his wrinkled khaki shorts sat under his beer belly slung low over his hips. His watery, red-rimmed eyes used to be a piercing icy blue, and his obvious irritability was a tell Holly knew by heart. He was hungover. As usual.

"I wouldn't have to do this if you would just pick up the phone like an adult," she snapped.

Mick stepped out onto the porch and immediately lit a cigarette. "What do you want?"

"I want you to pick up the phone when I call!" she exploded.

"Take it easy, honey."

"You don't get to call me that anymore!"

He ignored her bait and pulled up an old deck chair, then offered her a dirty seat on the other one. Holly wiped at the dirt and leaves and then just gave up and sat down on the edge.

"Something has obviously got you all worked up, so you might as well lay it on me."

"Chance overdosed last night," she blurted. Hearing the words outside the confines of her mind made them seem infinitely more real.

Mick leaned toward her. "Jesus. No shit?" Stunned, he ran a hand through his hair, a gesture that seventeen years ago would have brought her to her knees. But now, she felt nothing, just numb. He sucked on the cigarette hard, like it was the only thing keeping him alive.

"Xanax. Marijuana." She started to cry, forcing herself to speak the words she wished didn't exist in her vocabulary. Words that didn't belong associated with her son's name.

"So, he's okay?" Mick asked.

"Definitely not okay. We were at the hospital all night. He's home now, sleeping it off."

"That's such a relief."

"A relief? Are you kidding me?" She shook her head flabbergasted at his cavalier response. "It's far from a relief. Our son is doing drugs."

"Calm down." He exhaled another cloud of bitter smoke. "It's pot, Hol. You're overreacting."

"Are you serious right now?" Her voice was taking on a screechy quality she couldn't control. "Pot *and* prescription drugs. I am not overreacting."

"How did he even get it?" Mick asked and drew another long drag on the cigarette. The smoke was making Holly nauseous.

"He started hanging out with a kid named Angel. Do you know who that is?"

"Well, you have to admit that is really ironic."

"Jokes? At a time like this?" She shot back. "I knew I could never count on you to respond like an adult and take me seriously."

"You need to chill out or this conversation is over."

Completely incensed, Holly wanted to shake the man, to scream in his face. *See, you piece of shit? Like father like son!* But she didn't. It took everything in her to keep those words from crossing her lips.

"So, what do you want to do?" Mick asked after a long pause.

"Get him evaluated. Get him the help he needs."

"Okay, good." He stood and crushed the cigarette with his dirty sandal. "Anything else?" Thinking the meeting was over, he turned toward the door, his hand eagerly resting on the knob.

Holly was enraged at his obvious lack of interest. The

heat spread across her face, flushing her cheeks. "Sorry to have bothered you with the details of your son's overdose," Holly shot at him sarcastically.

"What is your problem? Why do you have to make everything so bloody dramatic all the time? So, he experimented a little? Every teenage boy does. It sounds like you've got it all handled, so what am I missing here?"

"You're a piece of work," Holly snapped. "I guess this will fall on my shoulders like everything else when it comes to the boys. You're worthless."

He recoiled from the insult. "I think you should go. Tell Chancy I love him and I'll see him Sunday."

"Do it yourself," Holly spat at him. "And there is no way in hell they are coming here anytime soon."

"You can't keep my sons from me."

They shared custody. She did the heavy lifting, and Mick had them every other weekend. He was a functional alcoholic and had convinced the judge he had life under control. Because there was no evidence of DUIs or other charges, he got what he wanted. He got to call himself a father every other weekend. Mick was the fun dad, the one who was laid back and took them on adventures. Holly got to take them to the dentist and show up for parent-teacher conferences and hound them about their homework. It wasn't fair, but it was what it was. Holly accepted her role, but on days like today and after conversations like this, the fury grew. Mick was never expected to mature or be responsible and was incredibly adept at shirking responsibilities.

She strode angrily to her car while mumbling under her breath. What did she expect? That he would somehow morph into a real parent overnight?

He watched her leave and then shook his head wryly and disappeared back inside. Holly drove back to her house. Her road rage was in full effect, transferring her anger to the elderly drivers she got behind who seemed to have all the time in the world, dawdling toward their destinations at a snail's pace. Pulling into her neighborhood, she drove past houses where normal dads were washing the family cars in the driveway and loving fathers were getting ready to take their family on bike rides. She was consumed with jealousy. Jealous of kids that actually had two healthy parents. Jealous of husbands that actually contributed to the household duties. She was so angry and hurt and ashamed; she had been as long as she could remember and that was the worst part. She didn't know how to feel anything else.

———

The next morning, Holly was so grateful it was Sunday, the only day of the week she got to sleep in. The night before, she turned off her alarm, turned on her ocean sounds app, placed her sleeping mask on her eyes, and after taking a half-dose of sleep aid finally drifted off. The phone on her nightstand made her jump at 7:42 am the next morning.

Cursing under her breath, Holly felt for the phone and pushed the mask up onto her forehead. Squinting, she could barely make out the number, but she saw the name. Anna Leighton-Blackwell. The busiest of the busybodies in her over-privileged neighborhood. The afternoon Holly moved in, Anna softly knocked on her door, put a perfectly manicured hand in hers, and offered a wicker basket of tastefully gift-wrapped muffins with a cascade of long curly lengths of sparkly ribbon. Boldly declaring with a perfect white smile, "It's pronounced Ah-nah." Holly's eyebrows rose, and she had to choke back her laughter.

Of course, it is.

Hyphenated named women were the worst. That extra little line wasn't the only thing extra about her. Impeccably dressed, routinely Botox-ed, and completely connected, she was the town resource for everything. She was tall yet curvy, a testament to her incredibly skilled plastic surgeon and the discipline of her gym regimen. Never a perfectly blown-out hair out of place, it hung dark and silky down her back or was occasionally confined to a high ponytail. She never left the house without a full face of makeup.

Probably sleeps in it in her coffin. Energy Vampire.

Holly rolled her eyes and longed to let the phone go to voicemail but knew it was better to just bite the bullet.

"Oh, Holly," Anna said. "We are all just so worried sick about you and Chance. When I heard the police scanner, I was terrified. We called the phone tree and posted on the Facebook group, but no one had any details. Then Zach said he heard it was Chance on Snapchat."

Stupid Snapchat.

"Thank you for your concern, but he is doing okay and is recovering back at home. We have a plan set up in place." Holly tried to be dismissive and was ready to end the call, but Ah-nah continued.

"Is there anything, and I mean *anything*, we can do for you during this difficult time?" Her voice purred thick with condescension. "We are all on pins and needles worried about you and your little family. How is Dillon?"

Actually, there is. You can hang up this phone call and quit pretending you give a rip. I know this is just a fact-finding mission to fan the flames of neighborhood gossip.

She exhaled and chose her words carefully. "Dillon is doing fine. He's not really sure what is going on."

"You're going to want to fill him in before he goes to

school on Monday. I mean, kids *talk*. If he doesn't already know, he will on Monday."

"I know they do." Holly pressed on the space under her eyebrows where tension was starting to fill. "Is there anything else you need? It's been a very long couple of days, and I'm so incredibly tired."

"How terrible of me. Of course, you are, dear. Bless your heart. Reach out if you need anything. I'm only a phone call away. I can put together a dinner train on google events for you, just say the word."

"Thank you, but it's not necessary."

"Single mothers truly have the most difficult job on earth. I tell Clayton all the time how lucky we are."

Barely able to resist the urge to vomit, Holly hung up the phone, cursing herself for answering it in the first place. Knowing the second she ended the call, Ah-nah would be on the neighborhood phone tree and Facebook board spreading the story like wildfire. The secret would be too salacious to keep to herself. Anna relished a nice long gossip session and would drag anyone into it who seemed remotely interested. The weekend's events would keep her mouth jabbering for a nice long time. The neighborhood hive bustled around the queen bee and her perfect family. A son and a daughter. Both headed to big ten schools. With an anesthesiologist husband, she projected the perfect image of success and privilege.

The most difficult decision she makes every day is where to have lunch.

Holly was envious of the ease of her life. She wasn't proud of it, but it was the truth.

"Is there anything, and I mean anything, we can do for you during this difficult time?" Holly repeated to herself, mimicking the nasal quality of Ah-nah's voice.

"No, Anna." She answered herself and pronounced it wrong on purpose. "Bless *your* heart."

When she first moved to the neighborhood, she was so proud. Her little townhouse was in the best school district and the only one she could afford there. It had felt like such a win when everything came together for her to own it, but the clique-ness of the ladies in the neighborhood felt too much like going back to high school. She forced herself to go to a Bunco night, but twenty minutes into it, she found herself alone in the corner with her fake smile pasted on while consuming fistfuls of cherry balls. Each minute of that evening was more unbearable than the last. She literally had nothing in common with these women. When the game was over, she immediately walked home with a hostess gift tucked under her arm and the rest of the cherry balls hidden deep in her purse, vowing to never return to Bunco night ever again.

FOUR

"Why do we have to go?" Chance whined. His remorse had been short-lived and quickly transformed into teenage defiance. Dragging his feet, thinking he could wiggle out of it by begging, he stayed in his room all weekend, sullen and irritable. He was hard to be around, only surfacing for food. Holly let him stew in there, wanting to wait until after the evaluation before serving up his consequences, but his attitude was getting tiresome already.

"Look, dude, it's not optional," Holly stated. She held out one hand and then the other. "Actions... it's time to meet consequences. I had to take a day off work for this. It's not exactly how I wanted to spend my personal day, either."

Chance was silent on the ride over, and Holly turned up the radio just to have something to fill the void. The heavy silence was always there now like another passenger in the car. Singing was a form of meditation for her; she did it in the shower, in the car, anywhere without an audience. She hit the high note, occasionally destroying lyrics, and ignored Chance's eye rolls and shifting in his seat.

Music was something she and Mick both loved and was

the matchmaker that brought them together. One random night nearly twenty years ago, she went with friends to a local bar to hear live music, and there he was. He'd been charismatic, older, and fun. Holly was infatuated with his energy from the start. In the crowd of tipsy females vying for his attention, his gaze had somehow settled on her. She fell hard and fast for the guy. In her limited experience, it was hard not to. He was magnetic, pure energy, and she wanted to feel something, anything that filled the void that her father's death had left. He lit her up for the first time in her entire life, and now that she was older, she could see it for what it was. A naïve little girl with daddy issues, trying to be a woman, starved for male attention. The craving had been so deep and ravenous that anything would do.

She glanced over at Chance, who continued to stare out the window, his leg always jiggling up and down lately, quiet rage endlessly bubbling just under the surface.

He followed her dutifully into the office where she checked him in and started to fill out the thick stack of paperwork. Then she sat down and felt a little stab in her heart when he chose a seat two seats away from her, desperate to put some physical space between them.

That hurts. He's acting like I am the enemy.

Holly sat filling out line after line on the never-ending questionnaire and finally having completed it she returned it to the desk and purposefully sat down in the chair right next to Chance. He shifted as far as he could away from her, leaning on the opposite arm of the chair like he couldn't stand the thought of actually touching his mother.

Chance was never sick, and she rarely needed to bring him to the doctor's office. A memory fragment popped up of a well-child check-up appointment when he was six months old.

His soft, round baby face and huge, brown eyes were framed in thick black lashes. Sitting on her lap, he bounced and rocked. His wispy fine baby waves that she couldn't bear to cut wrapped around his ears and poked out from his neck.

He was such a pretty baby.

She sat with him nearest the exit door, and each time a patient or a nurse would sweep through the swinging door, it would send Chance into a fit of full-on belly laughter so loud and so long that the rest of the waiting room laughed right along with him. His sweet, uncontrollable baby laugh was joy personified, pealing and rippling into the room, spreading happiness like a virus. Holly saw people elbow each other and point at them with huge smiles on their faces enjoying the show. Then Chance would calm down, but a few minutes later, the door would whoosh open again. The fresh burst of air would send Chance into another round of uncontrollable giggles so loud and so long that Holly started to giggle too. This went on and on until their name was finally called for Chance's immunizations.

Looking at Chance now, that wispy baby fuzz was replaced by thick wavy hair that he'd kept in a skater cut since last year. It hung long and greasy, tucked behind his ears and kissing his cheekbones. She couldn't remember the last time she heard him really laugh. Sullenly sitting next to her, propping up his chin with his hand, he was leagues away from that sweet little baby that made everyone crack up at the doctor's office.

The door swept open, and a nurse called out, "Chance Simon?"

Holly jumped up, grabbing her bag. "That's us." She followed her, with Chance finally hoisting his slight frame from the chair with an exasperated sigh and shuffling into place behind Holly.

The nurse settled them both around a round golden oak table.

This was probably chosen on purpose, subtly making no one feel superior. Sending the signal that we're all equal.

The door swung open, and in walked a heavily tattooed, giant of a man. He instantly commanded the room, and Holly and Chance both stood up reflexively. He pumped Holly's hand like a politician and then Chance's, and indicated they should have a seat. With a thick black beard, multiple piercings, and a deep booming voice, he stood well over six feet tall. "I'm Matt." He opened a manilla folder with a stack of paperwork, pre-filled with Chance's name and barcoded. He took a long moment to read the paperwork thoughtfully.

"Okay." He sat back in the chair that seemed a little too small for him. "We're going to do an evaluation today and determine the course of treatment Chance needs." He punched down the plunger on a ballpoint pen, licked the tip, and then began with the questions. "How old are you?"

"Fifteen," Holly answered.

"If you don't mind, I'd like to hear from Chance," he said gently.

"Oh, I'm so sorry. Of course." Holly shuffled her chair back a bit from the table to give them more room.

"How tall are you?"

"Five-foot-one."

"Weight?"

"One-hundred and eleven pounds."

"Do you smoke?"

"No," Chance said dully. "I vape, but that's not the same."

"Do you vape with nicotine?"

"Sometimes."

"Then that is a yes." Matt checked a box on his form.

Holly was speechless as she watched Chance roll his eyes.

"You tested positive for Xanax and Marijuana. Have you used any other recreational drugs? Sorry." He glanced at Holly and then continued, "I have to read all of these." He rattled off a long list of substances. Holly's stomach filled heavy with lead listening to all the options, some of them she didn't even know existed. Detached from the conversation, she heard Chance's responses and wondered if he was being truthful or not. Holly sat there silently. Focused on a deep scratch on the table, she rubbed her finger across it.

How many other moms have sat in this exact same chair and had to learn the ugly truth about their own child during an interrogation from a complete stranger?

She listened to his questions quietly.

"Any mental health issues?"

"No."

"Anxiety?"

"No."

"Wait, he's been biting his fingernails since he was six years old. I took him to the doctor, but he just said it was a bad habit and told us to try deterrent sprays and band-aids," Holly offered.

Chance let out a sigh and hid his hands under the table. They were still bitten to the quick, including the skin around the nails. His hands always looked rough and sometimes bled.

"Depression?"

"Impulse control?"

"Trouble concentrating?"

"Do you engage in risk-taking behaviors?"

Chance answered, "No. No. No. No."

"Wait." Holly held up a hand. "Um, remember when you did a backflip off that bridge last summer with your friends?"

Chance rolled his eyes.

"ADHD?"

"No."

"Meaning, you've been screened and it was negative?"

"No, he's never been screened," Holly offered. "I asked the pediatrician once, and he discounted my worries and so I didn't pursue it further."

Matt turned to a filing cabinet and pulled out a thick wad of papers. "I'd like you to give these questionnaires to four of Chance's teachers."

He handed her the screening paperwork in triplicate, and Holly added it to her pile. She was getting overwhelmed.

"Cutting?"

"Setting or playing with fire?"

"Wait. He did when he was six." She turned to Chance. "Remember, you set off the smoke detector with that ball?"

"Jesus Christ," he muttered.

"Chance!" Holly chastised.

"You have to be truthful, give him all the information or he can't help you," Holly insisted.

Matt cleared his throat and shifted in his chair. "Let's continue." He was getting to the end of the questionnaire, and finally, he turned to Holly. "Did you have a normal pregnancy and delivery?"

"Yes," Holly said simply.

"Is there a history of substance abuse in his family?"

"His father is an alcoholic and addicted to sleeping pills."

"Is he in treatment?"

"Not to my knowledge."

"Okay, I think I have everything I need. Dual diagnosis is incredibly common with teenagers. Having underlying untreated mental health issues will push someone to pursue methods to self-soothe. Teenagers don't have the life experience to make the right choices and will usually find themselves experimenting with substances to alter how they feel or escape pain they don't want to deal with. They just want to feel normal. Feel like everyone else."

Holly studied Chance and was shocked when the last comment struck a nerve and a tear spilled down his cheek. He wiped the evidence of it away quickly and turned away from her, shrugging off the hand she put on his shoulder to comfort him.

"We're going to start him in outpatient treatment. He will come here four days a week from five to nine pm. He will have to submit to random weekly drug tests. If he succeeds, then after the first thirty days, we will step him down to three days a week, and then eventually wean him down to graduate the program, provided he stays clean. He will be assigned a counselor, either myself or one of the others in my department for weekly one-on-ones."

Matt handed Holly a brochure. "You and his father will have to come to mandatory once a week family therapy and participate in Ala-non meetings. We have resources for Chance's brother as well."

Holly flipped through all the paperwork and brochures. The weight of what the next month required from her felt heavy on her shoulders.

This is really happening. I can't believe this is really happening. This is my new life.

FIVE

New Hope Charter Elementary was a beautiful new facility financed by the hefty property taxes collected in her neighborhood. Filled with light and wide-open spaces and color-splashed walls that had been tastefully chosen by an award-winning architect, it was the most beautiful school Holly had ever seen. It boasted state of the art technology and a charismatic superintendent that looked like a descendant of JFK. When she was offered the contract, she celebrated her win with the boys at a Japanese Steakhouse. It seemed like everything was finally coming together for her, and she was the happiest she had been for years.

Nearly a year later, the joy had worn off, the perfect patina was starting to show some wear, and she discovered that there was a darker underbelly in the charter school. An underlying sense of competition and fakery that flooded everything. Parents continually tried to one-up each other, going to great lengths to engineer experiences for their precious trust fund babies. Even in elementary school, everything was a contest and carefully measured. Down to the token scholarship children of color they admitted to back up their commitment to diversity claim.

It was still dark when she got to school on Tuesday morning. On auto-pilot, she didn't even remember driving to work, although the urge to burrow deep under the covers that morning and shut out the world was hard to ignore. She hit snooze five times before finally getting out of bed. Running so late she had to rush out of the house while clutching a cup of coffee, a granola bar, and shouting at the kids to get in the car.

Driving in a trance, she felt shell shocked and traumatized from the weekend and the evaluation. Her emotional skin was paper-thin and so sensitive now like a burn victim who was covered in third-degree burns over her entire body. Every little word or action hurt. She had hidden at home locked away with her boys over the weekend, but now she was thrust back out into the world. A very different one than the one she inhabited only three days prior. Everything hurt and took an immense amount of effort, but she knew she had to compartmentalize and put on her teacher hat. She would be expected to do her job well and to maintain the standards of New Hope Charter without skipping a beat. It didn't matter what bomb had detonated in her personal life.

She checked her mailbox and grabbed another cup of coffee at the fully equipped teacher's lounge, trying to dodge the box of fresh doughnuts waiting there. The high-end espresso maker was bubbling and steaming, a transparent bribe from one of the kindergarten parents.

"Screw it," she said and then grabbed a maple frosted one and took a big bite, closing her eyes when the sugar hit her bloodstream.

"Looks like you might need a moment alone with that, woman." Stacey chimed in. Stacey was her sweet, bubbly friend whom she had instantly clicked with when they were paired together to co-teach a section of first-grade mathematics. Her thick blonde hair was defiantly curly and held back in a ponytail. Stacey's giant blue eyes were fringed with generous black eyelashes, and a pair of reading glasses hung around her neck from a lanyard. Dressed in her normal workplace uniform, a green cardigan and a navy maxi dress with tanned leather flats, she was comfortable and just professional enough. Stacey studied her weary friend with concern. "Are you okay?"

"I'm looking that good, huh?" Holly teased.

Looking down at her feet for the first time, she noticed that she was wearing two different shoes.

"Oh my god." Holly pointed at her feet. "I can't believe I left the house like this."

"Now you are really scaring me." Stacey eyed her more closely. "You look exhausted."

"I am. It's been a crazy weekend."

"Oh yeah?" Stacey winked and shimmied her shoulders.

"Not like that, silly. Something happened with Chance."

"Oh no! Is he okay?" She stepped closer, speaking more quietly.

"I don't... He..." she stammered, scrambling to find the right words. Tears brimmed at her bottom lashes. Stacey's eyes filled with worry, and she put an arm around her friend.

"Take a breath. Then tell me."

Holly exhaled. "Chance overdosed on Xanax last weekend, and now he's in treatment."

"Oh, God, Holly! I am so sorry to hear that. I can't imagine."

"I had no idea. Apparently, he's been experimenting for weeks. Coming home high. I was clueless. He was using right under my nose. I feel like such a fool," she cried. "And with his dad's history, you would think I'd know the signs, but this just came out of nowhere."

"You can't blame yourself. Raising teenagers is brutal."

"I need to suck it up. Dr. Remington will be in the office soon, and I can't let her see me like this."

"Yeah, she's an ice-cold bitch. What size are you? I think I have an extra pair of shoes in my classroom."

"Eight? I think."

"You're in luck. I'll bring them over during our planning period."

"You're a lifesaver."

Stacey gave her one more squeeze. "If you need anything, call me. Okay? I'm right next door."

"Thanks, girl," Holly said and shuffled out the door, walking down the hall to her bright and cheery modern classroom. When she got the job in this school district, she thought it would be a piece of cake. Her class size was a very manageable seventeen. She loved first graders since they were a little more used to the system than their unpredictable kindergarten counterparts. Her kids in her previous school faced bigger problems. Getting three meals a day was a challenge for most of them. Parent involvement was stretched thin with most households working multiple jobs to still end up below the poverty line. Here at New Hope Charter Elementary, anxiety was the bigger demon, usually brought on by unrestricted access to technology. She was shocked to see Apple watches on the wrists of most of her first graders.

By high school, the over-indulgences got even more pronounced. Every kid had the latest iPhone in their hands, walking to the cars at parent pickup like zombies. Chance had begged and begged for an iPhone for his birthday last year, and she wouldn't even begin to entertain that idea.

A thousand dollars for a phone for a teenager? Um, thank you, but no.

————

"Okay, friends, let's clean up and get ready for lunch," Holly said. The kids in her small class were perfectly dressed in comfortable and adorable outfits that were completely coordinated. The girls' hair was lovingly braided with giant bows. Holly noticed the more affluent the family, the larger the bow. Bows were becoming a benchmark of wealth in the Midwest. The kids were groomed so immaculately, with fingernails that were brightly colored with something called "accent nails," a phenomenon that Holly had never heard before, where the third finger on each hand was painted in glitter.

"Callie is being a good leader," Holly said in her teacher's voice. It was a sweet but firm voice that she never knew existed until a guy she dated pointed it out.

Immediately, a few of the other girls fell into line and started helping pick up the pieces of the game they were working on.

"Voices need to be a level zero," Holly reminded them. The kids made quick work of putting the rest of their supplies away and made a line near the coatroom.

"We will not go to lunch until all your voices are off. Miles is making good decisions," she pointed out, and the rest of the class calmed down quickly.

"This isn't the kind of line I expect, friends." The kids immediately corrected their line after her sweet chastising, lining up perfectly with near military precision.

She grabbed her mug of water and walked out into the hall, her kids starting to get louder the further they got from her classroom. She stopped abruptly. "Level zero, friends. Walking feet. We will stay here until you are at level zero."

They calmed down again, and she walked the class into the lunchroom before she left and headed to the teacher's lounge.

Holly opened up the refrigerator and pulled out her lunch box. Inside was a note on a pink post-it that instantly made her tear up. "You're the best mom in the whole world."

Oh, Dilly-dilly.

Her sweet boy was always the peacemaker, always wanting to spread love wherever he could. He was incredibly intuitive at ten. She had been a walking zombie all weekend long, and he had obviously noticed.

I need to spend some time with him this week, just the two of us.

"Aww, that kid is special." Stacey swept into the break room, grabbing her own lunch from the fridge.

"He is."

"If only they could stay like that forever."

"Then we'd never want them to leave. It would be detrimental to the circle of life."

"Yeah, they have to become jerks so it's easier to kick them out," Stacey mused. "I love mine to death, but I'm up for parole in eight more years and there will be no empty nest syndrome over here!"

"And this is why I love you." Holly laughed. "The bluntness. The honesty."

Stacey chuckled. "I am who I am." She warmed up her leftovers and sat back down next to Holly. "Do you want to talk about it?"

"Not here," Holly whispered. "It feels like all the walls have ears."

"That's smart." She took a bite of her rice dish and then a

sip from her water bottle. "If you need some back-up, bring Dillon over anytime. He can hang out with Sarah and take the dog for a walk."

"I might have to take you up on that. There's a bunch of hoops to jump through right now, and you know Mick."

"Yeah, I know Mick," Stacey said wryly. "Only concerned about Mick."

"Some things never change."

"You're not alone, honey," Stacey said. "I can help you."

Holly's eyes filled up again. She was always on the edge of tears now. Every mood was elevated. Even the sweetness of Stacey's offer was almost too much to bear. "You're the only one I can count on."

"You'd do the same thing for me," Stacey admitted. It was true, Holly would. She loved Stacey like a sister. But Stacey's life was so thoughtfully put together and healthy that she never got a chance to reciprocate. "And don't you dare feel guilty about it."

Holly laughed. "God, you know me so well!"

"That I do." She pulled a tiny Snickers from her bag and slid it toward Holly.

"So well!" Holly said again, smiling. "Thank you. For everything." She nibbled the chocolate and exhaled. The tiniest glimmer of hope remained. It was incredible the support a fierce female friendship could bring to your life.

SIX

That night, the first battle was waged. "This is bullshit," Chance protested. Holly was running around the house doing a few little errands before she had to take Chance to his orientation at treatment.

"You do the crime, you do the time," Holly threw back at him. "It's non-negotiable. Please watch your mouth in front of your brother."

Dillon came racing around the corner. "Where are we going?" His blond hair was thick and hung in his eyes slightly as he tried to grow it out to become a carbon copy of his brother. He jerked his head to the side to clear the long bangs out of his eyes. It was a gesture he was doing so frequently Holly wondered if he could get whiplash from it.

"Your brother has a meeting, and we have to drop him off. Get your shoes on."

"I can't find them."

"Try harder, mister, and quit looking with your guy eyes." Holly immediately jumped up and started searching for his shoes, even though Dillon sat down and started watching YouTube on his kindle. Scared they would be late, Holly ran all over the house, and finally, under his backpack, she pulled the shoes out and waved them in the air.

"Ah-ha!" Triumphant, she declared it a win and pushed away the irritation she felt when Dillon had stopped looking. "Get in the car."

Chance was silent, but at least he stopped fighting. He yanked open the door and slammed it shut, nearly catching Dillon's fingers in the door jamb.

"Watch it. You almost hurt your brother!"

Chance grunted.

"Yeah!" Dillon shouted. "You almost hurt me!"

"Sorry, Dilly," Chance mumbled. Holly was relieved to see that at least his anger was only directed at her.

The drive was twenty minutes of tension-filled silence, so she turned on the radio to fill the void.

"Ooh, I love this song," she said to herself and turned it up slightly, singing along.

Chance immediately leaned forward and pressed a button to change the station. "Not feeling it."

Holly shot him a look. "That was rude. My first graders have more manners than that."

"My first graders have more manners than that," Chance mimicked, mocking her voice, twisting it up into a disrespectful harping tone.

Pick your battles. Discuss this later. Not in front of Dilly.

Finally, she pulled up in front of the building where his meetings were held: Promises Care Center.

"Is Chance sick?" Dillon asked, picking up on the tension and reading the sign on the building.

Holly didn't know how to respond, so she ignored it for a second. "Go check in. We will be here at nine."

"Whatever," Chance mumbled and got out, slamming the door again.

"Can I sit up front?" Dillon asked.

"Honey, you don't weigh enough to do that. It's against the law."

"Dad lets me."

Of course, he does. I guess I will just add that to the never-ending list of failed parenting expectations we need to rehash.

"It's not safe," Holly restated. "We need to fatten you up. How about some Chinese?"

"Orange chicken?" Dillon perked up immediately at the mention of his favorite food.

"Well, duh!" She finally relaxed her shoulders that had been unconsciously squeezed up to her ears. Making Dillon happy was so easy.

She pulled into the Chinese restaurant, and they walked inside.

"We get to eat inside?" Dillon was shocked. Holly was legendary for always opting for takeout.

"Yes." She laughed at his excitement and the way his cheeks flushed at such a small thrill.

The waitress brought their platters covered in freshly battered and crispy fried orange chicken. The vinegar tang and red chili flakes stung her nose and made her mouth water. Fat, tan egg rolls sat on a tiny white plate stuffed with cabbage and sausage with a hint of Chinese five spice. They ate quietly for a few minutes before Holly worked up the courage to broach the subject.

"Dilly, I need to talk to you."

"Is it about this weekend?" he asked as he dragged an egg roll through the orange duck sauce.

Of course, he picked up on something.

"Yes. Chance made some very bad choices, and now he has to pay the consequences and he's angry about it."

"What kind of bad choices?" He speared his last chunk of orange chicken on his fork before stuffing it in his mouth.

"The scary kind." Holly's eyes filled with tears.

Dillon's enormous brown eyes locked onto hers.

"You know how sad you guys were when I told you that Daddy and I weren't going to live in the same house anymore?"

"Yeah," he said cautiously, his eyes panicked and unwavering on hers searching for answers. The pain he suffered that day was permanently seared into his memory forever.

"Well, he didn't deal with that very well. Chance is sad and angry and tried to do something to escape his feelings instead of talking about them."

"Tried what?"

"Drugs."

Dillon was silent. He pushed his empty plate away. "But we promised you we would never do that."

"You did," Holly confirmed.

"And he broke that promise."

"He did," Holly agreed. "But that doesn't make him a bad person. It just means he made a mistake, and now he has to go to meetings a few times a week where they can help him fix it."

"Okay," Dillon said solemnly.

"Come over here." Holly patted the cracked burgundy vinyl seat next to her. Dillon walked around the table and slid into the booth.

"It's going to be okay, buddy. I promise. He's meeting with people who can help him." She squeezed Dillon into a side hug. Holly kissed the top of his head, breathing in his slightly sweaty and sweet little boy scent, and was glad he couldn't see her eyes welling up with tears again.

SEVEN

A few days later, Holly dropped Dillon off at Stacey's house to participate in mandatory family therapy. She was a bundle of nerves driving Chance there. He clutched his red treatment folder to his chest and was seeming to accept and comply with the program.

"How are things going?" she asked, trying to connect with him.

"Fine," he said curtly.

"Anything happening that you'd like to share?"

"Nope."

"Want to listen to your music?" She offered. Holly never allowed his hip hop around Dillon and hated it, but she was just searching for a way to connect and to soften him and was willing to put up with raunchy lyrics if it would help.

He grunted and turned on his Bluetooth, playing his favorite playlist. Holly concentrated, straining hard to pick up the mumbled lyrics, hearing words like "popping pillies," and "fucking hoes" glad that Dillon wasn't around to hear them.

This can't be helping, can it? Filling his ears with this insanity?

She parked the car and shut off the ignition, grateful to finally be able to shut off the offensive music. She felt dirty listening to some of it in front of him. He opened the door and ran willingly into the building, making her chuckle sadly.

He'd rather go to therapy than spend one more second with me. I. Am. Killing. This. Mom. Thing.

She sat in the van for a second gathering her thoughts. Tired from the long day at school, all she had wanted to do was take a bath and get in her pajamas, but here she was, fulfilling all the obligations that Matt set in front of her, thinking this is how we fix it. This is how we fix him.

She walked into the meeting five minutes early and was shocked to hear Mick's voice.

"Hello, Holly." He flashed his smile at her. It didn't work anymore, but she briefly acknowledged his ruggedly handsome face. She noticed his scruff that needed to be shaved and his shaggy haircut as he worked the room, weaving his spells over the people gathered there. It was easy to fall in love with Mick Simon. He was undeniably the most charismatic man she had ever encountered. Once, she had been powerless against him, but now, she saw through the façade. She knew he was really just a weak man who would do anything for attention.

"Hello, Mick," she said evenly and pulled out a chair, feeling like the outsider of the group already. Mick told one more joke and reveled in their laughter like the court jester he was and then pulled out the chair next to her and sat down.

It was a small group of tired and worn looking faces. Each person ravaged by their own child's personal battle with addiction.

"Let's get started. I'm Nancy, and we are glad to have you join us for family therapy.

Not like it was exactly optional, Nancy.

Nancy looked to be nearing sixty, her long gray hair was pulled into a loose braid, and she wore an ankle-length, modest, long sleeve dress and dirty Birkenstocks. Her deeply tanned skin was a road map of wrinkles and worry lines.

"Addiction is a family disease, and so we have learned that in order to be successful, we have to treat the entire family unit. Let's go around and introduce ourselves. Over the next several weeks, we are going to get a chance to really get to know each other. Why don't you start?" She waved a hand at Holly.

"I'm Holly, and you've met Mick. We are here to support our son Chance. His use included pot and Xanax."

"You can't really count dope," Mick said dismissively.

Holly wanted to throttle him but was glad she didn't have to because Nancy jumped right in. "Actually, that is a common misconception, Mick. It's detrimental to a young teen's brain to become dependent on any substance because their brain is still developing. The substance is not the focus. It is dealing with the underlying issues that drive our kids to use in the first place. What are they trying to escape?"

"Come on, Nancy. What do they really have to escape?" Mick interrupted ignorantly. He laughed, making eye contact with all the other parents like a politician on the campaign trail, trying to build rapport with the rest of the group. "These kids are living the dream. No responsibilities, access to everything they could ever want. Life really doesn't get any better than this. Am I right?"

Holly stifled the urge to roll her eyes and shifted in her seat, finding it ironic that Mick accused the kids of having no responsibilities when he was a master at shirking them himself.

"They have more than any generation before them, that is true," Nancy agreed. "But has it really helped?"

The group mumbled in agreement.

"Mental health statistics are alarming. Suicide rates are tripling. It is becoming an epidemic, and more kids than ever are turning toward escapism and drugs," Nancy stated. "This is the reality of the world they are living in." She turned to the next couple and nodded to encourage them to introduce themselves.

"We're Julie and Abe. Our son Marcus brings us here. This is our third time through family therapy." They looked exhausted and beat down by life. Average, normal people, plainly dressed in jeans and t-shirts. Obvious life-long smokers telling from the fine lines around their lips and eyes to their yellowed fingernails.

"Addiction is a relapsing disease," Nancy chimed in. Her tone was so matter-of-fact, bordering on chipper that it was like they were talking about the weather.

"This group has given us a lot of support," Julie said.

Three times. Heartbreaking.

The next man introduced himself as Tim, wearing a police officer's uniform. "I'm Tim, here for my daughter Nicole. I live a very high-profile life, Chief of Police in Indianapolis." He was cleanly shaven and bald. His smooth head shined in the light, his eyes wary and tired. He radiated authority and made Holly's pulse quicken from leftover anxiety toward the officer the night of Chance's overdose.

"This is a good time to remind you that everything said here is confidential. That it is not okay to speak of things disclosed here in any public setting. If we see each other in real life, it is best to ignore or keep things simple and vague," Nancy chimed in.

"Thank you." He nodded at Nancy's comment and then continued. "I just don't understand her. I don't know how to fix this."

"The truest answer is that you can't," Nancy murmured. "It is not your problem to fix. Nicole needs to fix herself, and my hope is that, through this group and Al-anon, you find the resources to support her in a healthy way."

"That's the hardest part. When your child is in its clutches, this disease will make them say and do unspeakable things. Reconciling that in your head is the hardest part. That little girl she used to be, so full of life and happy, to the angry oxycontin addict she has become." He wiped a tear from his eyes, and Holly felt her own well up in response to seeing this strong man brought to his knees by his daughter's addiction.

The final couple was Chad and Amanda. Amanda did the speaking. "We are here for our daughter Max. She's been in and out of treatment for several years, with a dual diagnosis. It's even harder now that she is legally an adult. We can't get any information pertaining to her care without her express written permission." Amanda squeezed her husband's hand.

"I am to blame. She is gay, and when she finally came out to me, I couldn't accept that." He broke down, the guilt overwhelming him. His crew cut hairstyle had a military familiarity to it. "I wish I could go back and react differently. I wish I could take it all back."

"She always was a daddy's girl," Amanda agreed, not as an insult just a statement. She looked down at her lap. Her brown hair was cropped short, her thin fingers nervously spun the rings on her knuckles.

"I thought it was a phase, something she was trying on just to get my goat," he explained. "It created this divide."

Holly gently nudged the box of tissues toward Chad. "Thank you." He pulled a tissue from the box and scraped it across his eyes and continued. "We used to be so close. I just don't know how we got here."

Me neither.

"Tonight, we are going to watch a video on co-dependence," Nancy started. "The dynamic in your households needs both patterns to continue. The addict has one set of behaviors, and as their caretakers and family members, we complete the other part of the pattern by the actions we take."

The lights darkened, and Holly numbed out to the video. It was like a 1990s after school special gone wrong. Cheesy actors, bad dialogue, and canned parental responses. She studied Mick sitting in front of her, noticing his phone lighting up under the table, his head down. Texting through the entire movie.

What a tool. Selfish bastard. Can't be bothered to actually participate in therapy in a meaningful way. He is supposed to sit and endure this poorly produced educational disaster like the rest of us.

An hour and a half of torture later, the lights came back up, and Holly rubbed her eyes.

"We will see you all next week." Nancy stood and shut off the TV.

Holly stood up and walked to the front office, looking for Chance as Mick trailed behind.

His eyes lit up when he saw his dad, and a huge smile broke out across his face as Mick scooped him up in a hug.

"How was it, Champ?" Mick ruffled his hair and squeezed his shoulder.

"Boring as fuck," Chance answered.

Holly's shoulders tensed. "Language," she chastised.

Chance rolled his eyes. "I think if you look at where we are at right now, Mom, language is the least of our concerns."

"He's got a point," Mick agreed, taking sides with Chance, as the boy smiled triumphantly.

"I don't care. It's disrespectful and not something I want

to hear in my presence. You save that stuff for around your friends."

"Okay, Holly." Chance insulted, pushing his luck.

"No, that's not okay either. You can call me Mom. Using my first name is disrespectful."

"Always the disrespect lecture with you. Doesn't it get old?" he snapped back.

"When you graduate and move out and live your own life, then you get to decide how you conduct yourself. In front of me, you will show me the respect I deserve."

"C'mon, buddy," Mick finally jumped in. "Be nice to your mama."

"Whatever," Chance mumbled, finally understanding that he needed to stop digging his hole. "Can Dad give me a ride home?"

"I guess, but bring him straight home, Mick."

"Yes, ma'am!" Mick mock saluted her.

They walked toward Mick's truck, shoving each other into cars playfully like immature teenagers and laughing like two friends hanging out.

They are both children. I had my children with Peter Pan. No wonder we are here.

That day, she had no idea the lengths Mick was willing to go to in order to be a friend instead of a parent, but soon she would.

EIGHT

A week later, Holly got home from work, carrying in bags of groceries when one paper bag ripped and spilled the entire contents out onto the stairs. A jar of tomato sauce hit the ground and cracked open, sending a shot of red marinara to her legs.

Shit. Can't catch a break lately.

She gingerly picked up the shards of glass, wiped things down, and then grabbed a soda out of the fridge. Enjoying the carbonated bite that hit the back of her throat, when she noticed the red folder Chance took with him to treatment lying on the table. He had doodled all over it, a habit he'd had since he could hold a pencil. She remembered finding his name written on everything when he was three. The walls, his toys, his leg, everything was branded in his baby handwriting with backward A's. Holly stared at it for a long time, wondering if there were clues inside to help her understand what Chance was going through in treatment. He was so sullen and silent lately; she didn't know what he was thinking anymore. Desperate for information to help her put the pieces together, she pulled it off the table.

She paused, hating that to find out how he was feeling she was resorting to invading his privacy. It felt wrong, but she opened it anyway and pulled out a thick printed stack of daily assessments. Composed of poor quality copies printed on thin copy paper, she leafed through the pages that were filled out in Chance's practically illegible handwriting. Each day had a new sheet, with a cramped date stamp, and on it, he rated his desire to use, how he was feeling, but most important at the bottom of every page he was required to "List five things I am thankful for today."

Page by page, she scrolled through them. They varied a little from day to day. He was like a typical teenager, only putting minimal effort into it, recycling the same eight things in a slightly different order. More often than not, on the list of things he was thankful for, Dad was listed, Dillon popped up regularly, too, and the dog. But not once on any of the worksheets did she see her name. It was like a stab to the heart. Each worksheet was a little slap to her face, his way of rebelling against the effort she had been putting in to help him. The sting of never being acknowledged tore through her, and the hurt manifested as anger.

She slammed the folder shut and threw it across the room and then crumpled against the wall and slid down it. Gathering up her legs into a ball, the tears finally came. Murph whimpered and walked over to Holly, his too-long nails clicking against the hardwood floor, and he nudged her hands with his face. Pushing into her personal space, he lapped at her tears and tucked himself in-between her legs, trying to comfort her. She tugged on his ears and stroked in long, slow strokes, watching his eyes half close as he blissed out to the sensation. She smiled wryly, remembering a pin she saw on Pinterest. "It's important to own a dog when you have teenagers. Then you will always have at least one creature at home that is happy to see you."

She was tired of always being the bad cop, the parent who laid down the law. Holly shouldered all the responsibility and allowed Mick to be the Disneyland Dad. He never had to step up and make any of the difficult decisions. Because he never did any of the heavy lifting, he could sit back and relax, knowing that she had everything handled. She was on top of everything with the kids.

A few minutes later, she got up, put the papers back in the folder, wiped her eyes, and placed it back on the table like nothing had ever happened. Then she started to make dinner, complete with a vegetable the kids would push around their plates with a fork but never eat.

NINE

Holly sat in her van in the parking lot with seven minutes until she had to be on the clock. She tilted her seat back, cranked up her radio, and closed her eyes. These precious few minutes were the only ones she got all day.

A determined knock on the window startled her. She sat up quickly, staring into the narrowed eyes of Dr. Remington.

She turned away, deeply sighing, and then grabbed her backpack and opened the door, forcing a smile on her face.

"Everything okay, Holly?"

"Didn't sleep well last night is all," Holly said in a cheery voice as she walked with her boss to the front door, thankful that her shoes matched today. Dr. Remington was a severe woman. Her dark hair was forced into a dark bob, routinely colored and cut so she looked identical every day. She bordered on robotic. Emotionless, data-driven, and logical, even her grooming regimen was carefully executed.

Dr. Remington stopped abruptly at the door and said, "I've been meaning to talk to you. I've heard through the grapevine that your son got into a bit of trouble and wanted to see how you're holding up."

"Oh, um, yes." Holly flushed red. "He's getting the help he needs, and we are working hard to get him back on track." She stood awkwardly at the door, her face burning in shame.

"I am glad to hear that," Dr. Remington stated. Her hair lay against her head like a helmet. Her pale skin was completely covered in a brown pantsuit, the sensible heels on her feet the only hint at her femininity. No makeup, no jewelry except for the American Flag lapel pin she always wore. Just the basics. Her time was too valuable to waste any of it on foolish things like her appearance.

She pulled the door open for Holly. "Single mothers really do have the most difficult job in the world. I hope you can get things straightened out at home and that this personal incident won't affect your ability to teach our students."

"Of course not," Holly managed. Her chest constricted; the words were heavy like dead weights on her shoulders. "I assure you I have it all under control."

"I have no doubt." She smiled curtly and walked toward her office. "My door is always open." The words were oozing obligatory empty sentiment.

Holly walked into the teacher's lounge to coax a strong espresso from the fancy cappuccino machine. When it first arrived at the teacher's lounge, Stacey had to give her a lesson on how to use it since the machine had so many buttons and settings. The interaction with Dr. Remington made her long for the ancient garage sale Keurig at her old school and the cheap dark roast off-brand coffee pods that were stacked there.

———

Sitting at her desk, she opened her email to answer the millions of questions lodged there about the upcoming field trip, turning down seven parents' offers to chaperone. The families of these kids were deeply involved. Just sending out one request for supplies or volunteer requests always generated a torrent of emails into her inbox.

She sipped the espresso slowly, savoring the calm before the storm. In two minutes, her students would start flooding through the doors and she would get lost in another long day of shaping their young minds, a welcome distraction to what was happening at home.

The kids poured into the classroom, chattering away, and she smiled. Things were so simple in first grade. Hearing snippets of their conversations was always entertaining and helpful to gauge how the day was going to go.

Some students lined their colorful little bento boxes up on the lunch box shelf, and others found their popsicle sticks, indicating their choices for the hot lunch options.

"Okay, friends," she greeted in her teacher's voice. "Gather round and grab a carpet square. Criss-cross applesauce on your square and not too close to your neighbor!"

The kids jumped up to follow her exact directions. Except one. "Tanner? Are you listening, friend?"

He turned toward her and then moved sluggishly toward the pile of carpet squares. Pulling one out slowly, he finally plopped it down on the fringes of the group.

I need to keep an eye on that one.

She sat down on the chair in front of the class. "Let's talk about being a good neighbor, class. Who has an idea to share on how to be a good neighbor?"

"One time, my mom paid for the car in front of ours at Starbucks when I got my Cotton Candy Frappuccino."

"Yes. That is a good example."

Holly called on another child. "When I let my friend use my iPhone charger when hers is dead at a sleepover."

"Yes, that is good too." Holly stopped for a moment. "How many of you have an iPhone?"

All the hands shot up except two.

Sweet Jesus. These kids are so out of touch.

"One time, when my daddy took me shopping, there was a guy taking a nap on the street, and he had a cup with money in it, so I tried to put a quarter in it," one of the blondest little girls with a huge white satin bow piled on her head revealed. "Daddy said people like that are garbage and would just waste my money, so I should keep it for myself."

Your dad is an overprivileged dick passing it on to the next generation.

"Sometimes, people need help. It's best to be generous in those situations. I am so proud of you for thinking like that!" She praised the little girl, watching her sit up a little taller with her words.

The first few hours of school passed by quickly. "Friends, it is time for lunch, so let's get your books put back in the bins. Cold lunch, grab your boxes and get in line. Today, I have a new way to reward one lucky leader. One of you gets to eat lunch with the teacher."

The kids scrambled to line up and then raised their hands, desperate to be chosen. "There are so many amazing leaders here today," she said, looking up and down the row of little cherub faces. "But, this week, I choose Tanner."

Tanner's blond head popped up, and a small smile crossed his face. "Tanner, you will lead the class to the lunchroom and then come with me to the secret office for lunch."

Some of the kids moaned their disappointment, and Tanner straightened up tall and walked to the front of the line. "Level zero," Holly said and held up her hand. The rest of the class immediately raised their hands, too, making a circle with their fingers and thumb.

A few minutes later, Holly and Tanner sat at the table in the empty resource room. "So, Mr. Tanner. How are you doing, friend?"

"Okay," he mumbled and pulled out a sandwich with the crust cut off and a Tupperware container of sliced kiwi and grapes.

"Can I share a secret with you?"

"Yes," he said sheepishly. Looking at her, his brown eyes were wide.

"I have a secret power." Holly leaned forward and rested her chin on her arms, getting closer to the boy. "I can see people's feelings, even if they try to hide them."

"You can?" He was inquisitive. "How?"

"If I told you how, then I would lose my powers."

He nodded slightly, buying her story.

"I can see that you are sad."

His eyes widened and blinked.

"I get sad sometimes, too," she whispered. "But the worst thing you can do is keep all that sadness inside. Because it just makes it worse. And sometimes, the sad turns to mad."

He looked down and put a grape in his mouth, chewing slowly. Considering her words.

His eyes were filling up. Holly knew she hit a nerve. He bit the side of his cheek. "What's on your mind, Tanner?"

"My mommy doesn't love my daddy anymore." He started to cry. "Daddy had to move out of our house."

His little shoulders started to shake. "I heard them yelling, and I tiptoed to the stairs and listened."

'That must have been very scary for you."

"It was," he agreed. "She called him bad names. Bad names that start with the letter 'F'." His eyes got huge. "Ms. Simon, what does addict mean?"

Stab me in the heart. This poor little guy.

She made a mental note to reach out to his mom. "It's when someone can't stop themselves from doing something." Holly was afraid to elaborate more, knowing the fallout from a parent right now could kill her already precarious position with Dr. Remington.

"Why is she so mad, if he can't help it?"

"That's a really hard thing to explain," Holly stated. "Have you talked to your mom or dad?"

"No." He took a bite of his sandwich, chewing it thoughtfully. "I don't like it when things change. I just want things to go back to the way they were before."

You and me both, buddy.

"I don't either, Tanner." She took out a bar of chocolate and broke him off a nib. "If you find yourself feeling sad again, come see me. And we will get the sads out before they become the mads."

She broke off another piece of chocolate and handed it to him. He gobbled it eagerly, the small sugar rush perking up his energy.

"When you feel bad, it's important to breathe. Let's take a big breath together, okay?" She breathed deep in with him, but his little face was so serious, she opened her eyes wide, acting goofy like she couldn't stop inhaling and didn't stop until Tanner started to giggle. "See?" That's the fastest way to get rid of the mads. Giggles are their kryptonite."

"What's kryptonite?"

"Their weakness. Haven't you ever seen Superman?"

"No."

"Ask your mom about it. Now, let's finish our lunch before you have to go out for recess."

TEN

Three weeks of intensive treatment had rushed by yet dragged slowly at the same time. Every day was exceptionally long. Crammed into the minivan, Holly's life had become a constant taxi service, shuttling the kids to appointments and eating greasy suppers from paper bags. There was treatment, family therapy, school, and the grocery store, and then closing time dollar store runs for last-minute projects that always required poster board. Each night, she collapsed into bed only to get up and do it all over again the next day. It was grinding her down to nothing.

Mick was absent from all of it, which made her even angrier. He never worked a traditional job, instead piecing together gigs that paid him under the table. When she asked for help, he either outright ignored her or didn't answer her texts until it was too late. He showed up for his court-appointed weekend visits, scooping the boys up for overnights that included trips to the drive-in theater or jam sessions in his basement with the never-ending string of musicians that always showed up at his house. But during the week, he couldn't be bothered to help out. He was just "too busy."

Late one night sitting in her bedroom, Dillon walked in and plopped face-down on the bed next to her, burying his face in her pillows and sighing loudly. "What's up, Dilly?" She scratched his back in big loopy circles, something he'd loved since he was a baby.

He said nothing and didn't move. "Hey." She tried tickling him. "I'm talking to you."

"I need to have you sign my conduct demerit," he moaned, his voice muffled by the pillow.

"What did you get one of those for?"

"Evan said his sister heard that Chance is a druggie." More syllables she had to strain to comprehend mumbled into cotton.

"What? Sit up!" Holly urged. "Look at me." Dillon sat up on the bed obediently, his hair askew from the pillow. His heavy eyes met hers. "When did he say that?"

"At school today, and I pushed him and told him to shut up. Mrs. Stall saw me and sent me to the principal's office."

"That is not okay, Dillon!" Holly chastised him, and he immediately hung his head. "We do not ever put our hands on another person in anger."

"Dad said you have to put bullies in their place."

Of course, he did. When did he manage time to impart that nugget of wisdom? When he was picking up the slack by driving Dillon to school last week? Oh yeah, that never happened.

"Who do you live with, Dillon?"

"You."

"Who sets the rules?"

"You," he mumbled.

"Look, buddy," she sighed and started to explain, "I know this is hard, and it's even more difficult because you are paying the price of Chance's bad decisions, but it is never okay to physically push someone. Even if you are angry, and even if they lie."

"I know," he answered.

"Next time, you tell an adult what is happening. Let them handle it." She squeezed his forearm and continued. "Chance made a bad choice, and he is getting help to learn to make better ones. It's okay to be mad at him, but we all need to work together to make the right decisions from now on."

"I know."

Holly ruffled his hair. "Go get your sheet. I'll sign it, but you're going to need to clean out the van this weekend as your punishment."

"What did Chance get for his punishment? It must have been something huge." Dillon's eyes were giant in his pale face.

"That is not for you to worry about, but trust me, he is not loving his life right now."

Holly scribbled her signature on the paper and then walked to Chance's room. Loud, driving base was rattling the walls. She knocked and waited. No answer.

"Chance!" she yelled, banging harder on the door with no answer. Finally, she gave up and grabbed a toothpick from the kitchen to jimmy the lock open. She jiggled it in the lock, and the door swung open to reveal Chance sitting in his old bean bag chair exhaling from a vape. Floored by his audacity, she watched the white cloud cover his face, filling the room with a sickly-sweet cherry smell. "What in the hell do you think you are doing?" Holly yelled at him, enraged. She walked across the room and yanked it out of his hand and then strode back to her bathroom and buried it deep in the garbage can. Hands shaking, Chance followed behind her too closely, all keyed up.

"That was mine!"

"Not in this house. You are fifteen! It is illegal for you to have any kind of nicotine delivery device. I cannot believe you would do that in my home! What the hell are you thinking?"

"Relax, it's not that big of a deal."

"It *is* that big of a deal. This is my house. I make the rules."

"Maybe I don't want to live here anymore then."

"And where else do you think you would live?"

"With Dad!"

"Your dad is a mess. He can't even take care of himself, let alone you."

"No wonder Dad left you. You're such a bitch."

"That is enough. You will respect me in my home."

"Then I don't want to be in your home." He ran down the steps two at a time, opened the front door, and slammed it. The portrait that hung next to it---of a younger and happier Dillon and Chance, with their arms wrapped around each other smiling widely at the camera---fell to the ground and the glass shattered.

"Mom? Are you okay?" Dillon ran downstairs, hearing the commotion.

"Stay up there. There is glass everywhere." Holly walked to the pantry and grabbed a broom and dustpan, and tucked Murph into his crate to protect his feet. He whined and clawed at it.

"Everything is okay," Holly said, but looking at the photo on the ground, with the red gash across Chance's cheek from the deep scratch to the photograph's emulsion layer, she knew that it was anything but okay.

"Where'd he go?" Dillon was anxious. "It's late and it's dark outside, Mom."

"It's okay, Dilly. You need to go to bed. You have school tomorrow."

"So does Chance," Dillon insisted.

Holly was losing her mind. Her patience was paper-thin and jagged. She was on edge again. "Enough! Dillon! Go to bed! Now!" She shouted too loudly and too roughly.

He yelped, and she heard his footsteps run up the stairs and away, and then his door slammed shut.

Two for two. I am really on a roll, parenting the hell out of these kids.

She swept up the mess and set the photograph in the garage. Not wanting to throw it away, but not able to put it back on the wall. She freed Murph from the crate, who then acted like he had been imprisoned for years, excitedly jumping up at her vying for attention.

Holly pulled a fresh tray of Oreo cookies from the pantry shelf and a bully stick for Murph and sat down on the floor next to the soft pile of white dog. Murph held the stick in his paws and bit at it eagerly, devouring his favorite treat while Holly devoured hers. Six cookies one after another, she chewed and chewed through her feelings, waiting, weighing, deciding what to do about Chance. Finally, she decided to just wait him out. Sitting in the living room, she watched TV until she fell into a light sleep on the sofa and then bolted upright when she heard the front door open. She rubbed her eyes and studied Chance. He was tired and thin, the fight worn out of him.

"I don't want to talk about it," he muttered and started the hike up the stairs without waiting for a reply.

"That makes two of us," Holly called after him, relieved that he was finally home. She locked the door behind him, turned off all the lights, and walked up the stairs to her own bedroom with Murph on her heels where she struggled to fall asleep for the rest of the night.

ELEVEN

The events of the night before hung thick and unspoken between them. In an effort to have one regular night, she took a break from putting down the hammer on Chance and decided to make his favorite dinner, Pasta Carbonara. She grated up the parmesan on the bamboo chopping block. It was a meditative act she usually loved. Her bare feet on the cool wooden floor, she hummed to the music and let her mind drift. Tanner popped into her thoughts again. He was getting quieter and more withdrawn. She needed to reach out to his mom again. After their lunch meeting, the phone call with his mother had been agonizing. She remembered how the woman's voice had cracked when Holly described the conversation, and even though she had said all the right things, she felt like she should check in again. Just to make sure. She cracked two eggs into a container and scrambled them, only half-listening to the radio station on Alexa.

A robotic female voice cut in, "Here's a station you might enjoy… The Broken Hearts Club."

"Alexa, you're an asshole," she said out loud in her defense, as though she was having a real conversation.

The water finally boiled on the stove, sending billowy clouds of steam to the exhaust hood. She turned on the fan and salted the water. A gust of warm air hit the back of her legs, and then the door slammed and she jumped. Seeing Chance and Dillon, she forced a tight smile on her face. "Hi, honey, I'm making your favorite," she said to Chance who ignored her. Dillon walked over to her and wrapped his thin arms around her waist, lingering.

"Hey, sweet boy," she mumbled into his hair, hugging him with her forearms, careful to keep her dirty hands away from his shirt.

Chance opened the refrigerator and pawed through the contents, looking for something. "Dude, I'm cooking. Don't spoil your appetite," she warned.

"Food doesn't make everything better, Mom," he said dully and shut the door.

"I like Carbonara, too, Mom!" Dillon chimed in, eager to smooth out the tension.

"Thank you for saying that, buddy. Why don't you wash your hands? We'll be ready to eat in a few minutes."

He ran to the bathroom to wash up. Lately, Dillon seemed so desperate to keep her happy, to make things easier, to undo the damage Chance was starting to do on a daily basis.

"After we eat, you can drive us to treatment," she offered to Chance.

"It's such a waste of time. I hate it there. Everyone is always complaining about everything. It's a non-stop bitch fest."

"Well, tough, mister. You're going to have to get through it until you are released from the program."

He sat sullenly at the table, shoveling in forkful after forkful of pasta into his mouth. His hair spilled over his cheeks when his chin dipped forward. Both his elbows rested on the table as he scooped it in quickly, his cheeks bulging with noodles.

"How is it?" she asked, fishing for praise.

Chance grunted and continued to chew.

Dillon smiled. "Dee-licious." A spot of sauce hit his chin and stuck there.

Holly pushed her sticky noodles around the plate. The tension was making her tummy queasy. The heavy sauce was too much to handle, and Chance was so ungrateful she regretted spending the time making it for him.

"Chance, it's your turn to do the dishes before we have to leave."

He grunted and put in headphones and set out to do the task, while Holly wiped down the table. She studied him, lately so cold and so angry.

What does he have to be this angry about? His life is cake. Just go to school, get decent grades, and help a little around the house.

Now, anytime she asked him to do anything, he carried on like she handed him a rusted butter knife and asked him to saw off one of his limbs.

She watched him as he worked, the occasional smile spilling across his face from the YouTube video he was watching. Smiles from him were so rare lately, only the reckless idiots on YouTube seemed to bring them out.

How did we get here, where this kid is someone I barely recognize?

He finished and grabbed the red folder and walked out to the van.

"I hate driving this thing. It's such a piece of crap. It's so embarrassing, Mom."

"I know it's not your dream car, but we have to get you some experience so you can pass driver's ed."

"I know, I know." He put the van in reverse, backed out, then eased into traffic.

Holly felt her blood pressure creeping up. "You're speeding."

"I'm only five miles over."

"The driver's ed teacher is not going to accept that as an answer. Slow down."

"Okay." He stomped on the brakes in defiance to comply with her request, sending Holly reeling forward. The seatbelt was the only thing stopping her from hitting the windshield. He chuckled to himself.

"Seriously, Chance? That's dangerous. You could have hurt me."

"But I didn't," he spouted matter-of-factly.

The light turned green, and he slammed down the gas pedal. Nearing a construction zone, Holly's heart was in her throat.

He's out of control.

"You're getting too close to the cones."

"I know."

Wham. He hit a cone with the mirror. "Oops." He laughed.

"Pull the car over now."

"But we're almost there."

"Now!" She shouted at him.

"Fine." He slammed on the brakes again, and the car behind them honked loudly, narrowly missing their bumper.

"Pull over onto the shoulder." She insisted.

He rolled to the shoulder and then nonchalantly got out of the car and strolled to the other side to switch places with her like he had no cares in the world. Holly's heart hammered in her chest enraged and her face flushed with anger as her fingers gripped the steering wheel. She drove the rest of the way to the center silently while Chance stared out the window, ignoring her.

Finally stopped in front of the door, he jumped out and grabbed his folder, running into the office ahead of her. Holly parked the car and turned the rearview mirror toward her face. She ran her fingers over her cheeks and then up the back of her neck, trying to dispel the tension headache that was building there. Then she grabbed her purse and walked slowly into the building, dreading her visit to family therapy. Over the last few weeks, she had dutifully shown up at the assigned time. She had gotten to know the other couples well and was sad that this shared hell is what brought them together. In another life, she would have never crossed paths with a single person in attendance. Tim was the easiest to talk to and the one she most understood.

She took a deep breath, bracing herself to meet Mick's treatment persona, the world's greatest dad-slash-comedian, a part he played flawlessly that made her want to bash his head in. Since the day they met, Mick had other people eating out of the palm of his hand. In small doses, his dad of the year act held up, but under closer scrutiny, he crashed and burned. It was one of the reasons his friendships were so superficial.

She walked into the family therapy room and filled a glass of water from the cooler just to have something to do.

"Holly, how is it going?" Tim asked, pulling a paper cup from the dispenser.

"I'm having about as much fun as I can stand." She smiled wryly. "How's Nicole?"

"So far, so good. Treatment always keeps her honest. It's when she gets out that the real work begins."

"Yeah, nothing inspires sobriety more than knowing that you could be asked to drop a sample at any moment."

He shook his head sadly at her as Mick sailed in the room,

acting like he was being asked to give an encore at a gig. He breezed around the room shaking hands.

Holly sighed, observing Mick's performance as Tim piped up. "I know the type, can see right through guys like that. He's an addict, right?"

"How'd you guess?" She looked at his eagle sharp eyes. "Yeah." She breathed out a resigned sigh. It felt good that one person could see through Mick's bullshit.

"Good golly Miss Holly!" Mick joked and dropped into place next to her.

"Mick." She greeted him woodenly.

"How's Chancy?"

"Honestly, he's being a giant asshole. He took off last night for a few hours after I found him vaping inside my house. Why don't you bring him home tonight, maybe talk to him about respecting his mom's rules?"

"Women and their respect, am I right?" He tried to elbow Tim conspiratorially, who moved out of arm's reach at just the perfect moment and sent Mick stumbling. Holly covered her lips with her hand to hide her smile. It was childish, but she loved seeing the cop set him off-kilter, causing him to trip over himself.

"No. You aren't right," Tim corrected bluntly. "Sounds like he could use a good chat about boundaries and rules. You have to be on the same page, especially since you're raising him in two different households. Kids will use that against you to manipulate you into giving them what they want. You can't send him mixed messages, especially now."

Holly smiled at Tim, thankful for his response and enjoying how it made Mick backpedal and fall all over himself to get back in Tim's good graces.

"You're right," Mick agreed. "I tell Holly that all the time, you know. A united front."

Sure you do.

Mick seemed relieved when Nancy rolled the TV into the room and the session was started. Holly chose a seat next to him, but as far away as she could possibly sit, without sitting on the lap of her neighbor.

The video droned on and on. Statistic after statistic. Relapse rates that completely crushed any hope of this likely being a one and done situation. Holly sat and listened and tried not to think about what her life would have been like if she had not gotten pregnant by the man child sitting next to her, who nodded off immediately when the lights were dimmed, sleeping through most of the video.

When the lights came on, he stirred and rubbed his eyes and then winked at Holly. The gesture repulsed her, and she shook her head in disgust.

He never takes anything seriously.

———

Afterward, she walked to her car alone. The smile that lit up Chance's face when he saw his father hurt more than she wanted to admit. He was always scrambling for Mick's attention. Learning to play guitar when he was seven, desperate to have Mick's eyes on him, determined to please him. They walked to Mick's truck, joking and laughing, and Mick peeled out of the parking lot, burning rubber as he went.

Tim watched them leave. "I think that was for my benefit." He hooked a thumb at the black line of rubber that stained the parking lot now.

"He's an immature asshat," Holly confided.

"I see guys like him in my line of work all the time. They think the rules don't apply to them." Tim paused briefly before continuing. "Look, it's none of my business, but you are in a trust but verify situation at home. Unfortunately, I can see that you are going to have to be the jailer. You will have to toss his room, go through his phone, invade his privacy to make sure Chance is being truthful. It's going to suck, and he is going to hate it. But you cannot give him too long of a leash right now because the consequences could be deadly."

A tear welled up, and she wiped it away quickly. "The stakes are so high. I feel like I can't relax anymore."

"That's a totally normal reaction. I was so used to being in control, of having everything handled. But when you have a kid that is experimenting and pushing boundaries suddenly, you discover how little control you actually have."

"Tell me it gets better. Tell me it gets easier and that he can recover."

He looked down at his shoe and folded his arms across his chest as he carefully chose his words. "I don't think I can honestly do that. It gets different." He met her eyes again and palmed the back of his head as an exhausted exhale reverberated through his lips. "Parenting becomes the check-ins and the drug tests and all of this." He circled his hand at the building, indicating treatment. "But you have to keep going and keep doing things to try to turn this around because the other alternative is much worse." He hesitated. "It's so hard to accept that addiction is a demon our children will face every day until they die. A beast has been awakened in them, and there is nothing we can do to stop it. All we can do is try to keep them safe and hope that something changes. That something learned here sticks."

"That must hit you awfully hard in your line of work."

"It does. I became a cop to help people, and it turns out I can't seem to help the one person I love most."

Holly reached out and squeezed his thick forearm. "You are a good father. I can see that already."

"Not good enough," he said sadly. His blue eyes moistened.

"Don't tell yourself that lie." Holly went on, "It's brain chemistry and biology and genetics. Any kid from any family can fall down this hell hole."

He nodded gently and said, "Goodnight, Holly. Keep an eye on your other son. He's going through a lot, too. Addiction affects the entire family unit. Take care. I'll see you next week."

She drove home hearing the words "A beast has been awakened," and it rang so true that it gave her goosebumps.

Time to slay the beast.

TWELVE

Chance's room was an obnoxious tangerine orange they'd painted together the week before she moved into her home. It was so bright it was hard to look at. When she rolled that first line of color on the wall and cringed, she asked Chance, "Are you sure? It's not too late to change your mind."

"I'm sure." He laughed and dipped his roller into the paint pan right next to hers, evenly covering the roller in bright orange paint and then snickering as he rolled it up Holly's thigh and onto her bottom.

"Hey!" She laughed. "On the wall, not on your mom."

That day felt lightyears away, yet had happened only thirteen months prior. The time warp of the events of the last year contorted in her mind. The stress had elongated everything, stretching mere months into lifetimes.

She opened the drawers to his dresser, hearing Tim's voice in her ears. "Toss his room. Trust but verify." So far, the hunt had been blissfully uneventful. Nearing the end of hiding places to check, she yanked open a drawer in his TV cabinet and felt around in the darkness. Her fingers poked into a crumpled ball of paper, and she fished it out, opened it, and smoothed it flat. Handwritten in Chance's scrawling handwriting were a series of digits she instantly recognized--- all of her credit card numbers. The shock of seeing them in black and white and written in his penmanship took her breath away, making her gasp for air. Trembling at his audacity, her heart clamored in her chest. She felt around again inside the cabinet and found the spare key to her van that had gone "missing" months ago. Time slowed down. In shock, it was hard to think a clear thought. Her mind struggled to piece together a valid reason for what she had found. Trying to conjure up possible plausible explanations as to why he would have these things hidden in a cabinet in his room. There were none.

She felt dirty and violated. In disbelief, she stared at the crumpled paper in her hand. The key fob burned in her hand. She sunk down in defeat on his bed, unable to comprehend as tears welled up in her eyes, and when she clenched her fists into balls, the key cut into the palm of her hand. She stood and walked to her office and pulled up her credit card accounts to report them all stolen.

At least he hasn't used them yet.

It was a small relief, but tempered by the massive betrayal of trust. It was hard to celebrate that minuscule win when he had crossed a major line by reaching into her purse without her consent and writing them down on paper in the first place.

Feeling nauseous, she returned to his room and pulled everything out of the closet, where she found a shoebox full of vaping instruments and refill juice tucked behind a stack of old shoe boxes.

Outraged and exasperated, she yanked the sheets off his bed and lifted up the mattress, her hands shaking with fury. She dropped the corner of the mattress when she heard the door slam, and seconds later, his feet were running up the stairs two at a time. She braced for the coming confrontation. Squaring her shoulders, she wiped the tears from her eyes dismissively. Each step closer made her heart pound faster.

Seeing the current state of his bedroom, Chance froze and yanked out his headphones.

"What are you doing?" His words shot out. "You had no right." His eyes flicked to the cabinet where she found the paper and the key and then to the closet where he hid his stash in a panic.

"I have every right. This is my home. I own every room in it."

"You are such a bitch. Controlling everything I do! You're pathetic!" She ignored the insults and waved the wrinkled paper with her credit card numbers written on it. "What is this?"

"Nothing. I didn't do anything."

"This is *not* nothing!" Holly's blood was boiling. "This is stealing. Taking something that isn't yours!"

"You build everything up bigger than it has to be, Holly. You're such a fucking drama queen."

"Chance, that is *enough*!" Holly yelled at him. I am your *mother*, and you will address me as such when you refer to me. It is a sign of respect, and you will not disrespect me in my own home."

"Every man you've ever met leaves you. Even Dad couldn't stand to be around you."

"Enough!" She crossed the room and slapped him hard. He was startled and recoiled. Shame flooded her cheeks, staining them blood red. Her broken heart hammered deep inside her chest, and her palm was feverishly hot and pinked where it had connected with his cheek.

Where did that come from? This was a kid I never, ever spanked.

Seething rage and shame filled her. Chance rankled and charged Holly to intimidate her, so riled up his outrage sucked all the air out of the room.

"Do that again and I'll call the police and tell them you're abusing me," he hissed. Defiance twisted his face into an almost unrecognizable disguise. Holly felt a few drops of warm spittle land on her cheek. Their eyes locked on each other, stuck in this twisted power play.

Can he do that?

Chance finally backed down, ran to the closet, and pawed through the contents spilled on the floor, instantly incensed when he noticed his vape stash was gone. "Where is it?"

"Are you looking for this?" Holly held up the box and shook it in her hands, the bottles rattled against each other.

"That is mine. Give it back!" he screamed and lunged at her, the vein in his neck throbbing. He goaded her again, threatening her, his anger shrinking her into tiny pieces, making her feel small and afraid. It was the first time she realized he had gotten strong enough to overpower her physically, and that knowledge was deeply unsettling. The first slivers of fear walked up her spine.

"Not so loud. Your brother is home."

"Give me my shit!" he screamed again. The blue vein pulsed.

Holly closed her eyes, trying to summon the tiny bit of self-control she had left in her wheelhouse. She focused on her breathing.

In through the nose, out through the mouth.

Her eyes opened. "Wrong again, Bucko. Everything in this house is mine. It is illegal for you to have these items, so I will dispose of them for you."

He roared, and the windows rattled and vibrated, the sound reverberating through the space. His frustration was building, Holly froze, cognizant of a subtle alarming change. There was a shift in the air. Electric and snappy, an uncontrollable quality that was terrifying. Chance roared again, swung hard, and punched the wall. Holly bit her tongue to control her initial reaction, and through her teeth growled, "You break it, you will pay for it."

He bellowed again and punched harder. This time his hand went through the drywall and connected with a stud. Chance yelped in pain, and a sliver of crimson stained the broken drywall.

"You are going to pay for that," she said calmly and walked out the door with the box, hearing him slam it behind her as he continued to scream.

Holly locked the vapes in her closet and then checked on Dillon. Hearing muffled crying, she looked for him in his bedroom, but he was not there. She crouched down and looked under the bed.

"Dilly!" Panicked, she listened, trying to figure out where the sound was coming from. The silence was punctuated by Chance's faint screams. Finally, she noticed a sliver of light under the door in the walk-in closet. She opened the door and found him on the gray carpet, sobbing into his forearms, cradling himself into a tight little ball. He rocked back and forth, trying to self-soothe. Dillon ignored her completely, rocking and crying. Chanting over and over, "I want to be a happy family again. Why can't we just be a happy family again?" It was devastating.

Holly dropped to her knees, sweeping the boy into her arms. He was shaking, his hot tears staining her jeans. "Shh," she whispered into his sweaty hair. "I've got you."

More muffled screams came from Chance's direction,

making Dillon curl himself tighter and deeper into Holly's arms. "Why is he always so angry all the time now?"

"I don't know, sweetie," she admitted. "He just is."

"It's like he's turning into a different person."

"I can see why you would say that," she agreed. Finally, he had stopped crying, but he was having a hard time catching his breath. She scratched his back while she held him, and after a long silence, he finally was able to relax.

"There, that's better." Holly pulled back and leaned against the wall with her legs crossed while Dillon mirrored her on the opposite wall. "You are dealing with some really big emotions, honey, and it's really hard, especially for a kid, to know how to handle them. What if I found someone who could help you?"

"What do you mean?" His face was still red and blotchy. He wiped his nose with his sleeve, and she let it pass.

"Someone like a coach who could coach you through all this. Give you things to do or things to think about that could help."

"I dunno." He started explaining, "It might feel weird if I don't know them."

"How about this? I will go in with you and be right next to you the entire time, and if you try it once and you think it's a bad idea, then we'll never go back. You get to decide, but you have to try it at least once."

"Okay," he said, and his breath caught a final time before he sighed and let it all out.

"Want to watch a movie with your mom?"

"Can I pick it?" His eyes lit up.

"Of course. I'll even make some pan popcorn if you want."

He smiled at her. It was the last thing in the world she felt like doing, but she knew it was one of his favorite things. She couldn't resist making it right now, wanting to do something that would make him feel better.

What happens when pan popcorn doesn't do it for him anymore?

She stood and pulled him to a standing position.

"Promise me something?"

"What?"

"If you feel like that again, you'll tell me?"

"'I guess," he said sheepishly.

"The closet is for clothing, not crying, mister." She ruffled his hair, teasing him. "Let's go start the popcorn."

She walked down the stairs, relieved that the yelling had stopped. Apparently, even Chance had a limit when it came to screaming. Part of her wanted to knock on the door and ask if he wanted to join them, but she ignored the urge. She knew she was on shaky ground with Dillon and thought maybe it wouldn't be the worst thing to have some one-on-one time with him. If she was honest with herself, she wanted space from Chance and his rollercoaster of emotions and disrespect.

She turned on the movie and snuggled up on the couch with Dillon, who laid his head in her lap, something he hadn't done since he was a toddler.

Being in the middle of this is forcing him to regress. I need to keep an eye on this guy.

She knew he needed therapy, but it was one more thing packed into a schedule that was already bursting at the seams, and she was overwhelmed.

How much more can I be asked to give to fix a problem I never created in the first place?

She sifted her fingers through Dillon's thick blond hair as she stared at the screen lost in her own thoughts. She craved a break from the chaos to calm her own overtaxed heart, but she didn't dare take one now. She had to stay on high alert. Letting her guard down now might be disastrous.

Dillon's breath slowed and he was calm, breathing rhythmically, his tiny chest rising and falling. Holly gently untangled him from her lap and lifted him up into her arms like she did when he was a baby. Her back twinged, and she fought it off, staggering up the steps one at a time under the weight.

When did he get so heavy?

She tucked him in and pulled the comforter to his chin. Watching him sleep, wishing he could stay that way while they fixed Chance. Tucked away safe in his bed where nothing would hurt him.

She closed the door quietly behind him and walked to Chance's room. She turned the knob with the handle and found the door was locked. Initially irritated, she brushed it off.

Pick your battles. This one isn't worth fighting.

She was still weary from the last one, so instead, she knocked on the door gently.

"Yeah?" she heard him say through the door.

"I love you, goodnight," she said and waited for his automatic response. But there was none.

"I said I love you," she said louder.

She heard him mumble, barely audible, "I love you, too." Then she rested her palm on the door one more time and closed her eyes before resting her head on the door and wishing she could hold him and hug him like she did when he was little. Back when his eyes danced with mischief and love. When things were easier and he was a happy boy.

THIRTEEN

There were only three school days left until the summer. The kids were bouncing off the walls talking about elaborate Disneyland vacations, and one of her students had to leave early to get a passport photo taken for their family's summer trip to Italy. There would be no vacation for her family, Holly was just looking forward to sleeping in and having a second to catch her breath. She hadn't had a chance to fully decompress from that night in the park, and she desperately needed a break. While the students were getting settled in the morning, she dialed into her voicemail while she doodled, making small connected circles on a scrap of construction paper left over from the art lesson she had just taught. The first message made her heart drop to the floor.

"Holly, this is Matt, Chance's counselor. I need to speak with you right away. It's important."

Her stomach soured, making her instantly sick. That one sentence had the power to destroy her day. The next few hours dragged by as she constantly checked the clock eager for her lunch break to begin so she could return the phone call.

Holly got her students settled in the cafeteria and then went out to her car to return the phone call. At school, you never knew who was listening, and the tone of Matt's voice was terrifying.

She sat on hold, waiting for the call to connect, and finally, Matt's deep booming voice came on the line.

"Thanks for calling me back, Holly. I have some bad news. Last night after treatment, two girls came to me to tell me that Chance offered them oxy after the meeting."

Holly was confounded. The wind knocked completely out of her. She was speechless. She felt the *thump, thump, thump* of her heart pounding deep in her chest. The air was sucked out of the van, and she scrambled to inhale.

Oxycontin? No way? He couldn't have. Where in the hell did a fifteen-year-old even get something like that?

Matt continued, "I've interviewed them both individually and together, and their stories line up."

"I'm sorry, I need a second. I'm in shock," Holly said when she was finally able to speak.

"I can imagine," he offered soothingly. "These are very serious allegations, and I wanted to be sure the girls were telling the truth. As you know, addicts lie."

"Yes," she agreed.

"I can say after questioning them both at length, their stories hold up. I believe them." Matt paused.

"Were the police called?"

"No," he admitted, "And it is not likely they would be in this situation."

"It would almost be easier if he had some charges. He's so smart and so slippery. Somehow, he always knows how to keep his nose clean." She sighed. "So, what do we do now?"

"We are forced to discharge Chance from the program."

The panic rose up in Holly's throat, making it hard to

swallow. "Please don't do that. He needs help." Her voice cracked.

"He does, but he can't stay in outpatient treatment behaving like this. He is putting himself at risk, but more importantly, he is making the environment unsafe for the rest of the people who are taking treatment seriously."

"I understand." Holly breathed out finally, having held her breath for nearly the entire phone call. "So, what's next?"

"Well, I think we should refer him to Sienna Recovery Center." Matt continued, "It's a residential treatment center. They are better equipped to work with a kid making these kinds of decisions."

"I don't even know..." Holly felt lost, swallowed up again in the storm.

"I will fill out the paperwork and see if he can get approved to go to SRC."

"I don't know if my insurance will cover something like that."

"Let me do some initial calling on your behalf. I will contact them and see if they have an open bed. A lot of times in this situation, the child is put into a child in need of assistance status with the state. The kid basically goes on Medicaid, and most residential treatment is covered. Obviously, I can't tell you this for sure, or if he would even qualify. You can start making a few calls on your own and see if Sienna can give you any answers. They can run over the application with you, and you can ask any questions you might have. I'll fax them Chance's discharge papers after I get off the phone with you."

"I'm so sorry, Matt."

"Hey, I know addicts, used to be one, so nothing surprises me anymore."

"I bet."

"He's a smart kid, Holly, and to be honest, the smart ones are the hardest ones to turn around. They know how to bend the rules and screw the system better than anyone. But at fifteen, he's not smarter than me. I know how addicts think, so it's easy to see what he's doing."

"Does Chance know he's getting kicked out of rehab?"

"No. You'll need to tell him. It's effective immediately. We can't have him here again. We have to protect the other kids who are in treatment, who are trying to make real changes."

"Of course, I totally understand. I honestly don't know what to say. We didn't raise him to be like this. I don't know who he is anymore."

"You know, Holly, I did a lot of shit when I was using, and some of the things that I most regret are the things I said and did to my mother. It took me a long time, until I was over thirty, to finally come clean and get to a good place with my mom again. All I can say is that life is long. He will come back, eventually, but it can take a really long time. With males especially, their brain doesn't fully develop until twenty-seven."

Twenty-seven? Holy shit, that's twelve years from now. That's like a jail sentence.

"I'll send the referral over to Sienna and get the ball rolling for you."

"Thank you," she said quietly. "And Matt, thank you for trying to help my son."

"Of course," Matt said. "Treatment can be a revolving door until an addict is ready to do the work. Don't give up. This was only round one."

She ended the call and sat in her car, wiping the tears away from her cheeks. Then she walked back into her school, washed her face, and focused on the little brains she was trying to shape. Holly was a compartmentalizing genius.

———

Hours later, she picked Dillon up from school and drove him home silently running over the phone call in her head again. Bracing for another showdown with Chance.

"Dilly, I need you to go to your room for a little while please," Holly asked when they walked through the door. Chance was sitting at the bar eating cereal and watching videos on his phone, ignoring her completely while shoveling spoonfuls of Cocoa Krispies into his mouth.

"Why?" he asked.

"Just go," she said too harshly. "You can grab a granola bar and a juice box."

"You never let me eat in my room," Dillon said.

"Just this once." She waited until Dillon darted up the stairs and she heard his door shut to reach in and grab Chance's phone, putting it swiftly in her pocket.

"Hey!" Chance pulled the earbuds out of his ears and looked at her angrily.

"Go sit down on the sofa. We need to talk." Holly ordered.

"Okay." Chance stalked into the living room and slouched down on the sofa, hugging his arms to his chest defensively. His white diamond supply hoodie hung on his thin frame. Black ripped skinny jeans traced down the length of his legs.

"Matt called me at school today."

"Yeah," he tossed back, unaffected. "So?"

"So? Is there anything you need to tell me?"

"No."

"Really?" she said sarcastically. "Because he seemed to

think there was. Think really hard, Chance. Because what you choose to say next will determine the actions I take."

"I don't know what you're talking about," he said evenly, meeting his mother's eyes.

"Let me enlighten you." She stared him down, looking for any sign of deception. He stared back unwavering. "Matt said you offered two people oxy at treatment after a meeting."

"They're lying."

"Two different girls?" she shot back. "Two *different* girls Matt interviewed that had the *exact same* story?"

"Yeah."

"It's impossible to believe that."

"It's the truth," he countered.

Is it?

Holly doubted herself for a second then. Hesitating. She thought about the likelihood of Matt getting it wrong.

"They are just trying to get me in trouble. They have it out for me," he started in. "Who was it?"

"I don't know," Holly answered. "It doesn't matter."

"It does matter, Mom. I should have the right to confront my accusers."

She felt sick watching him scramble to defend his despicable behavior. It was sad. Who was this boy who had an excuse for everything? The boy who once loved going to Sunday school and wrote little notes to his classmates? How had he ended up so far away from the values and life skills she thought she had taught him? Who was this defiant man-child that was smart enough about legal mumbo jumbo that he demanded to know who accused him? Convincingly lying like it was second nature, as easy as breathing or telling you what he ate today. It was difficult to stomach and made her nauseous.

"So, you're just going to believe them?" he demanded.

"They have it out for me. I can't believe you don't believe me. Oh my *God*!" He kicked the coffee table out of the way, dropped to the floor, and pounded his hands violently on the wood in a dramatic display of false persecution.

It was like watching the Oscar-worthy performance of a lifetime from an A-list actor. Holly was shocked at the lengths he went to make his outrage believable.

"You have to believe me," he begged. "Mom, seriously, I didn't do it."

"I *don't* believe you," Holly said coldly. "You can't go back. You got discharged from treatment."

"Good." He sat back against the sofa as a small flicker of glee crossed his face.

"No," she corrected. "Not good. Matt is now recommending residential treatment."

"What?" Chance jumped up then, his hands flew to his head and his elbows spread wide. "You're sending me to Sienna?"

"So, you already know about it?"

"Yeah, some of the kids in treatment came from there. That place is a prison."

"I honestly don't know what's next. We have to look at all the options."

"I'm not going to Sienna."

"It's not up to you."

"I want to call Dad." He snapped his fingers at her rudely, demanding the phone.

"The phone is mine. I'll call him and see if he can come to pick you up."

"Seriously?" Chance huffed and then collapsed back on the sofa dramatically, tapping his feet aggressively on the floor. Holly pulled the phone from her pocket and made the call to Mick from Chance's phone. Miraculously, he picked up on the first ring.

"Hey, Buddy!" his cheery voice said.

"It's me," Holly corrected. "Come get your son."

"Now?"

"Yes, now. He'll be spending the night."

Mick hesitated, then finally agreed. "Give me fifteen." Holly snapped the phone shut and turned to Chance. "He'll be here in fifteen minutes. Pack a bag. You're spending the night."

"Fine with me." Chance went to his room, slamming the door behind him.

Holly turned on her heel and walked away to her bedroom, and when the door closed, she let the first angry tears fall. Relief flooded in. To have a one night reprieve from the angry inferno that Chance had become was a gift.

FOURTEEN

The next morning, after making a cup of coffee, Holly threw her hair up in a messy bun with a pencil tucked inside and sat at her overflowing desk. New turquoise and leopard reading glasses sat perched on her upturned nose, and she had to admit, they *did* help. They were the first ones that didn't make her feel ancient, and she was glad she had grabbed them at the dollar store.

Buried in a thick stack of paperwork, it felt more like a churning sea of medical forms and tax return requests to see if Chance qualified for Medicaid. Her phone rang from a number she didn't recognize, and she answered on the third ring.

"Holly, this is Amanda from Sienna Treatment Center. Do you have a minute?"

"Yes, thank you so much for calling me back."

"We have a spot for Chance, but we need to see if he can qualify as a child in need of assistance."

"What happens if he doesn't?"

"You can choose to self-pay."

"And how much is that?"

"Full-time residential treatment with medication can run about three hundred and forty dollars per day."

Holly gulped. The information instantly choked her and shut down her brain. "Um.." She stammered trying to regroup, "And how long is a recommended stay?"

"Most patients are with us for about ninety days."

Holly mentally calculated the cost. "That's over $30,000!"

"Yes, it is, but I will do my best to get him to qualify for Medicaid," Amanda stated calmly. "Look, I know your world has been turned upside down lately. If you can fill out the paperwork and have it to me today, I will work as hard as I can to see if we can get it approved. We are in a tricky window because benefits always start on the first of the month. If we don't get him here on the first, you will have to wait another month."

"Oh, God," Holly said.

In a month, we might kill each other.

"He can't wait that long," she cried and was embarrassed as her voice broke. "He needs help now. He's out of control. I'm afraid he is going to do something."

"I understand." Amanda's warm voice was filled with compassion. "Take a breath. If you can get me the paperwork, I will put a rush on it to get an answer from Medicaid by the first."

"I will."

Holly hung up the phone and shuffled through the paperwork. "Focus. You need to focus." She took a long swig of her now room-temperature coffee.

She was powering through the forms one after another. She had located all the tax returns and w-2 forms and had scanned them all into a file on the computer. Four hours later, she submitted them and the finished application to Amanda. She called and left a voicemail on Amanda's line to let her know that the paperwork had been submitted. Holly didn't want anything to fall through the cracks. The urgency to get him to treatment superseded everything; nothing else mattered. Chance was spiraling further and further down, and she was terrified of what his bottom might be. The way he was acting, she knew he wasn't quite there yet. The consequences had not stung enough to get his attention and force him to understand he needed change. She was scared to death with the risks he was taking.

That night, she laid in her bed, tossing and turning restlessly. The litany of thoughts stoked a fire of anxiety deep in her belly that made it hard to relax. Sleep was so elusive now. Since the night at the park, she had only slept a few hours at a time. Flat on her back, she stared at the crack in the ceiling, while thoughts spun in her brain and the clock ticked on the nightstand.

What if they don't take him? There is no way we can afford to send him. What if he gets arrested or gets a record? This could stain his life forever. What if he overdoses and dies? What if he hurts someone else?

She laid there frustrated, her foot outside the sheet in the cool air. She glanced at the clock from time to time, counting how many hours of sleep she would get if she could just fall asleep right now, then twenty minutes later revising her estimate. The hours passed deep into the early morning. Finally, at three am, her eyes closed, and then the next sound was her blasting alarm. It jarred her rudely out of slumber where she had finally escaped from her insomnia to the dreamy place where the kids were okay and everything was peachy. Dazed and exhausted, it took a few breaths for her to get her bearings. Seconds after her eyes opened, the reality hit her hard again, forming a bigger knot in her already knotted stomach. The kids weren't okay, and everything definitely wasn't peachy.

FIFTEEN

Holly drove to Mick's and knocked on the front door. She never went inside his house anymore. It was just too weird to be in his personal space. After the divorce, she craved physical separation.

She noticed the chipped paint peeling around the front door and that the garden beds were overgrown. While she waited, she pulled a few weeds, unable to help herself. Weeding and gardening were activities she normally enjoyed. It was like meditation for her with a side of instant gratification. There were so many, though, she barely put a dent in them before the door opened.

"You can come over anytime you want to pull weeds, Hol." Mick laughed and lit up a cigarette, sitting down in an ash-covered chair right outside the door. It was his smoking chair, a good habit leftover from their marriage, the only one. Holly stopped yanking weeds and dragged her chair further away from him. The smell of cigarette smoke was something she couldn't stomach anymore. She had always said that smoking was a deal-breaker, but when she met Mick, all her deal-breakers went out the window. She was so enamored and clueless that she was willing to accept anything to have this man in her life. Now that she was no longer under his spell, the toxic stench of it irritated her. When she was in public, she could detect the faintest whiff of a cigarette from fifty feet away.

Mick coughed and coughed then laughed at himself. "Gotta get my lungs started this morning."

"Yeah, sucking down on that cancer stick is the right way to start the engine." Holly smiled grimly, looking away. "Where is the boy?"

"Sleeping, I'm guessing. I heard him gaming last night really late. Did you know he screams at the TV like that?"

"I can't believe you're letting him game after what he's done. This isn't a vacation."

"I guess I didn't think about it like that."

"That's a shocker," she said, infusing the words deep with sarcasm. "Thinking was never your strong point."

"You don't have to take your anger out on me."

"Why is it so hard for you to step up and just be a parent?" Holly asked. "He isn't going to like you all the time. You need to get over that. You aren't his friend. You're his father, and right now, he is screwing up and needs his *father* to set him straight. You can be his friend when he's an adult. Right now, the way he is acting, I'm not a hundred percent he's going to make it to adulthood."

"We should have spanked him when he was little," Mick mused, breathing the smoke out through his nostrils. "You never got on board with that, but a good ass whooping is what he needs. My daddy cold-cocked me more than once for making shitty decisions."

"It's too late for that now," Holly dismissed while wondering if he was right. She was finding herself overanalyzing all their past parenting choices lately. It was a waste of time, but she couldn't help herself. Desperate to find the starting point, the place where things went off the tracks. The source of origin.

"Chance said you slapped him."

Holly flushed with shame. "It's true. I did, and I regret that. But he was being an asshole."

"He probably deserved it then," Mick admitted and looked at his ex-wife. "You're not going to get any arguments from me, Hols. I haven't been in the trenches with you day after day with them."

"You're right, you haven't," Holly agreed smugly. "But thank you for at least acknowledging that." She changed her tone and stated plainly, "If we get approval, you are going to have to drive him up there. It's a four-hour drive."

"Wow. Are you sure we have to go this hardcore? It seems pretty extreme."

"He was accused of dealing *oxy*, Mick, and he was kicked out of treatment." Holly pinched at the tension at the top of her nose. It was always hard to get Mick to do the right things. "I don't think it is over-reacting at all."

"We don't know for sure if he did that. He denied it again last night."

"Those are serious allegations. Matt checked out their stories. He had two different people telling him the same exact thing. It's time to face it," Holly urged. "Our son is incredibly comfortable lying to us and other authorities."

Mick took a long drag on his cigarette and then exhaled.

"I don't know what we're going to do if they deny his Medicaid application," Holly confided. "I don't have an extra thirty grand lying around, and I know you don't either."

He sighed. "That's true."

"Well," Holly sighed and stood, "that's all I wanted to talk about." She paused for a moment, her voice getting more somber. "I wanted to keep you in the loop. Do not talk to Chance about any of this. He could decide to do something rash, maybe run away, and then he'd lose his spot."

"I'm not going to lie to my son," Mick responded, making Holly frustrated.

"You lied to me our entire marriage," Holly said. "Trust me, you're good at it."

Tree, meet apple. Cut from the same cloth. Birds of a feather. Like father, like son. She hated that all the cliches were true.

"Touché," Mick said and looked down, avoiding eye contact.

"I'm serious, Mick, not a word. If he gets accepted, we need to take him immediately. This is a life or death situation."

"Okay," he agreed and crushed his cigarette with the bottom of his worn shoe. Everything at Mick's house felt neglected—his front door, his shoes, the garden. She looked around, seeing the physical manifestation of a life spent avoiding any real work.

"There is a whole list of items he needs to bring to treatment. I'll get them together, and as soon as I hear anything, I'll let you know."

The next forty-eight hours passed in a blur, endless rounds of texts and emails with no definitive answer. Holly prepared like they were going to accept him because she had no other choice. Her stomach was on edge the whole time. Every phone call sent her rushing to answer, something she usually avoided at all costs.

Amanda's number popped up on caller ID, and Holly stubbed her toe chasing down the cell phone.

"Hello?" she said breathlessly.

"Hi, Holly, I wish I had better news, but the truth is that the application is taking longer than usual. It's going to be a buzzer-beater. Considering you are four hours away, and tomorrow is the end of the month, you might have to make plans to drive down here without knowing if he was accepted or denied."

Her heart sank. She twirled her hair at the base of her neck, a self-soothing ritual she'd developed as a child.

"He has to be in the system before five pm tomorrow night, or he will need to wait until next month," Amanda continued. "I know it's a gamble, considering you might just have to turn right around and go home."

Holly hesitated. She hoped the trip wouldn't be made in vain. "We don't really have a choice. If he gets approved, it'll be worth it." Holly sighed. "Thank you, Amanda, for all your work trying to get him admitted at Sienna. I appreciate it so much."

"You're welcome."

"I just don't know what else we can do," Holly said, tearing up. "I'm so scared."

"I understand that, too, Holly. I promise you I will do everything I can to get him approved tomorrow. We will be in touch."

Holly opened a bottle of wine and poured herself a glass. She drank it quickly, letting the merlot warm her from the inside. She poured another and then looked in the empty refrigerator. Trying to concoct meals from what was inside was becoming a daily episode of *Chopped*.

I need to get groceries. I need a clone.

One really black banana sat abandoned on the kitchen

countertop, and there were mostly condiments in the refrigerator.

Mother of the year over here.

"What's for dinner?" Dillon asked, walking into the kitchen.

"Mickey D's?" she asked, internally groaning. Cheap and fast, it hit at least a couple of the requirements.

"Yeah!" Dillon fist-pumped. McDonald's was his favorite place to go. He ran to get his shoes on in record time, not needing her to find them this time, and they drove there quietly.

"Where's Chance?"

"At your Dad's."

"Spending the night?" he asked incredulously.

"Just for a couple of days, honey. He's been acting out and needs a time out."

"Lucky," he said under his breath.

Great. This one barely tolerates me, too.

They walked into the restaurant and sat down. Dillon always picked the table with the Ronald McDonald statue. Holly watched him dip his fries in his chocolate shake and shovel them into his mouth happily, completely engrossed in enjoying that oddly delicious combination.

Glancing up at the clown statue, another merry fragment surfaced. Chance was barely two years old. They stopped to get a quick meal, a shake, and to just get out of the house. Those early days were a blur; getting out of bed, bathing, and chasing after an active toddler consumed nearly every useful minute of every day.

That day, Ronald McDonald himself made an appearance. Actually, it was an underpaid employee wearing a faded yellow clown costume and giant red shoes for some special promotion. He waved his white-gloved hand at Chance, who ran along the bench seat toward him, trying to get closer to the figure with the horrible red wig. Chance pointed at him excitedly, saying "Lown! Lown! Lown!" He rocked back and forth, his body dancing to music only he could hear, and the entire restaurant laughed at him. Drool ran down his chin, as a huge smile sprawled across his open mouth with only six teeth. Chance bounced up and down with excitement as the clown got closer. Then Ronald clapped his hands, and Chance laughed and clapped back. Finally, Ronald handed him a cookie, gave him a high five, and then moved onto the next table. But Chance never took his eyes off the clown and cried when they left, saying, "Lown. Lown!"

She bit into a fish filet half-heartedly and then put it down. The fake cheese sat like a brick deep in her belly.

"Chance might be going away for a while."

Dillon's eyes got big. "Where?"

"We're trying to arrange for him to go to a place that can help him."

"What's wrong with him?"

"Well, buddy, a lot of things. He isn't happy, and he's not healthy. He might need to get help that I can't give him right now."

Dillon dragged another fry through his melting chocolate shake. "But you're a teacher, and you're so smart. You know how to take care of everything."

"Not this, buddy. I can't fix this."

"Okay," Simple and easy as pie. Okay. Like she asked him if he wanted more eggs.

Why is it so easy for a ten-year-old to understand, but so impossible for me to accept?

SIXTEEN

The next day, Holly watched the clock tick by, minute by minute. She was thankful it was summertime and that she wasn't forced to put up appearances anymore for Dr. Remington, or force a smile on her face and pretend that everything was fine when she just wanted to crawl into bed and shut the entire world out. She checked her email nearly every second, hitting refresh again and again and nothing. As the hours passed, she grew more jittery and restless, her thoughts spiraling in her mind making it hard to breathe. Finally, it was time for Chance and Mick to depart, and she still had no answers. She had no idea if they were going to admit him or not.

She drove over to Mick's with a laundry basket full of essentials he would need during his stay there. Tucked into towels, she hid a note to him.

Chance,

I know you don't agree right now, or think that treatment is even necessary, but it is. The behavior you have been engaging in is very risky. You could have died, and if you did, I would never forgive myself. Seeing you on that stretcher in the park that night almost killed me. I don't want to live in a world without you in it. I don't want to miss your laugh or your smart-alecky commentary about my life decisions.

I want my boy back. I want you to get healthy again and to find a way to be happy in your own skin. Being a mom is the hardest thing in the world because sometimes you have to make choices to save your children from themselves. Someday, I think you will understand why we decided to send you to a place like Sienna. You are getting the gift of a fresh start and a clean slate. You can go on to do whatever you set your mind to. You can get right back on track, try out for the baseball team like you talked about. Your whole life is waiting. Right now, focus on yourself and on what is being asked of you and learn what you have been sent there to learn. Focus on getting better and learning about yourself. You are so loved. I love you. Dillon loves you. Your dad loves you. We all are waiting for you to come back to us.

Work hard, dig deep, and you will be amazed at what you learn about yourself.

Mom

At Mick's house, she rang the doorbell and was surprised when Chance answered the door.

"I have your stuff here that you'll need for treatment," she offered, forcing a sunniness into her words that missed the mark completely.

"Just set it down," Chance said dully.

"I love you," Holly said, her arms opened wide. He folded his hands across his chest. He was closed off and saying nothing, then bent down to rifle through the basket. Finding her note, he asked, "What's this?" He started to read it and then abruptly stopped and crumpled it into a ball. "I don't want this." He rudely handed it back to her. "There is nothing you could write in this letter to make what you are doing okay. You are tearing me out of my school, away from my friends and all the people who know and love me. I am losing my entire summer, and for what? Dad doesn't even know why you are taking it to this extreme."

Mick appeared, finally hearing his name. "Go get the rest of your stuff and I'll say goodbye to your mother."

Chance disappeared as Mick walked out onto the porch.

Holly wiped away the tears. "In the future, if you can keep our private conversations to yourself, I would appreciate it."

"Sorry," he said weakly. "Did they confirm his funding?"

"No, Amanda said it might happen this way." She glanced at her watch. "You need to leave now to get him to the treatment center before five pm." She handed him the address written neatly on a piece of paper. "Do you understand? He cannot be late."

"Yes. I know that, Holly. You've told me twenty times."

"Will you tell him I love him when you drop him off?"

"Yes. I can do that." He then opened the door and shouted inside. "Chancey! We gotta jet, brother!"

Chance came out of the house, grabbed his basket of things Holly had lovingly packed, and walked to the car without even a glance at his mother.

"Hey, can I drive?" he asked.

"Sure. Just try not to kill us." Mick laughed and tossed the keys to him.

Holly watched them pull away, waving at him and getting nothing in return. It hurt, little fresh jabs at her every day, the callous way he disregarded her attempts to connect. She drove home to make dinner for Dillon, knowing that she wouldn't be able to fully relax until she knew he had a bed at Sienna.

Holly sat at her computer desk in her bedroom, hitting refresh over and over. Willing an email from Amanda to appear in her inbox. Three hours and four thousand agonizing email checks later, the news she had been waiting for finally came through. Chance was approved for ninety days of treatment, and it wasn't going to cost them anything.

Holly burst into tears. Her hands flew to her face, and she sobbed and sobbed until she felt empty. Locked in her bedroom so Dillon couldn't hear, she let the news wash over her. The relief was palpable, shifting the weight on her chest to an almost manageable position.

Chance is going to be okay.

That night when Holly fell into bed, she slept like a rock. It was the first time since the park that she didn't have to be hyper-vigilant and on high alert. She could take a breather knowing Chance was in a facility that could heal him. He was safe in the care of well-trained professionals that help teenagers work on their mental health issues and substance abuse problems. For the first time in a long time, Holly let herself hope. She let herself relax, knowing that he was in the very best place he could possibly be and that her boy would finally come back to her—the sweet little cherub-faced boy with the curly hair and enormous brown eyes.

That little boy who loved his mother was still in there somewhere, hidden under the pain and pressure of being a hormonal teenager during a time that was already crazy with school demands and social media. She just knew that Sienna Treatment center was the answer she had prayed for, and this time away would give them all a chance to heal. Away from walking on eggshells with Chance, Dillon could get some counseling and she could bring some normalcy to his life. Holly had the next ninety days to focus on getting herself and Dillon as healthy as possible.

Maybe she would even have some time to explore counseling for herself. Find a healthy way to process the fear and unease that being the mother of an at-risk teenager brought into her life. She knew they had a long way to go, but this time she knew without a doubt that things were going to be okay because the experts were handling it. Holly was naïve like that.

SEVENTEEN

After all the tension and stress leading up to getting Chance admitted to Sienna, she was shocked at how tranquil it became immediately after. Without the swirling chaos and outbursts, her home was peaceful and quiet. Holly anxiously waited by the phone for any news, checking it constantly, not wanting to be a helicopter parent and get in the way of treatment, but the silence was difficult. Her trauma brain had become incredibly adept at filling in the blanks with frightening stories. Holly was desperate for a phone call from Sienna, from Chance, to know that things were progressing. After days of no word, she reached out to Mick.

She was shocked when he picked up on the first ring. "When did you start answering the phone?"

"Funny." He exhaled, and she pictured him on the porch, thankful she didn't have to inhale his secondhand smoke.

"Have you heard anything?" she asked.

"What do you mean?"

"About Chance?"

"The first forty-eight hours, he wasn't allowed phone calls. But now he calls every night."

Every night? Another fresh puncture to her heart. Holly swallowed, saying nothing. Hot tears welled up in her eyes.

"You haven't heard from him at all?" Mick asked.

"Nothing," she stated.

"He's got a pretty big chip on his shoulder where you're concerned," Mick answered.

"That's not fair. We made the decision together," Holly interrupted.

"He's not stupid, Holly. He knows the big decisions come from you."

"Are you doing anything to help convince him otherwise? You have to make him understand we did what we had to do to keep him safe."

"I don't want to get in the middle of what is going on with you two," Mick objected. "Isn't it better that one of us maintains contact with him?"

"Yes, but it can't always be a good cop, bad cop situation. I need you to help shoulder this decision in his mind so he doesn't only blame me."

"I'll talk to him, but I doubt it will make much difference."

Getting nowhere, Holly changed subjects, "How is he doing?"

"He hates it, but he is getting into a routine."

"Has he started therapy yet?"

"Yes, and we are required to go to family therapy every Sunday. They prefer it to take place in person."

"In person? But it's four hours away!"

"I know, and you can phone it in if you want, but I am going to show up for my son."

"Do you think that I won't?"

"It isn't a competition, Holly. Everyone knows you love him."

"But does he know that?"

"He's just mad. Let things settle and he will call you. I'll do what I can from my side to help smooth things over."

"I appreciate that."

"We're on the same team."

When did that start? We haven't been on the same team for years.

"Let me know what happens," she said and pressed the button to end the call. She had given up being on the same team with Mick. How could she when her teammate constantly found new and interesting ways to completely undermine her? Holly was angry that he got all the calls and got to always slide through life. It was impossible to be on the same team with someone who only did the bare minimum, who constantly found ways to place more of the burden on her shoulders.

He was her only source of communication with Chance. Once again, she was scrambling for a place in her son's life. Chance was shutting her out. Using the only power play he had left—completely cutting off contact. She knew it was just his immature mind, but it hurt just the same.

EIGHTEEN

"Why can't I come with you?" Dillon begged. "I miss Chancey, too."

"You will get to see him soon, buddy, but this first visit is just for parents," Holly answered as she pulled up into Stacey's driveway and parked the van. Her friend stood, waving, wearing gardening gloves and a floppy sun hat.

"Dilly, my man!" Stacey sang out at him. "Sarah is inside playing Xbox. Tell her I said she has to take turns." He opened the door and ran inside, forgetting his desire to see his brother, seduced by the lure of Xbox.

"Love you!" Holly shouted after him and shut the car off before walking over to where Stacey was weeding. "I can't thank you enough for this."

"Hush, woman, you don't even need to say that. I'm just glad there is finally something you're letting me do for you," Stacey said as she bent back down and continued to weed.

"I really suck at asking for help," Holly admitted as she leaned down to pull a few weeds, happy to have something to do to curb the edgy energy welling inside her.

"True story." Stacey began to deadhead daisies in her garden bed. "Are you nervous?"

"A little," Holly confided. "Chance hasn't spoken to me since he was admitted, but he's been calling Mick every day. All of a sudden now, they are besties."

"That has to be incredibly frustrating."

"It hurts." Holly admitted. "He sees me as the enemy since I'm the only one who has ever punished the kid. He's been angry before, but he's never frozen me out like this." She paused and then confessed softly, "Actually, he's doing a lot of things lately he's never done before."

"You're doing all the right stuff, and I know it has to be hard, but stay strong."

"Honestly, the hardest part was sitting on the fence, waiting to see if he would be approved for funding. We could never afford to send him to a ninety-day residential treatment program otherwise. I'm so grateful that Amanda was able to get him in Sienna. It's a miracle." She paused, considering. "Now that he's there, I've slept better than I have since this nightmare started. I feel like I can breathe again. We aren't having to walk on eggshells anymore, with Chance blowing up at the drop of a hat. Even Dillon is calmer," Holly acknowledged. "But to be honest, I feel guilty that it feels better not having him around." She looked down, dragging a toe in the mulch. "What does that say about me, that I'd rather have my kid living hours away locked up at a residential facility?"

"I'm going to have to stop you right there," Stacey cautioned, holding up one gloved hand in a stop signal gesture for emphasis. "The mom guilt, you need to let it go. You are dealing with the substances and the anger, not your child. His brain is so cloudy and foggy right now that everything sets him off. Add in the typical teenager rage and hormones that are coursing through his body at fifteen, and it's no surprise you feel that way." Stacey studied her friend. "You're holding up better than I ever would under these circumstances."

Holly felt tears prickle at the corners of her eyes. She didn't feel like she was holding up at all; she felt like she was white-knuckling it the entire time, holding on in terror, afraid of the next step she would be forced to take. She looked at her watch. "Shoot! I gotta run. We have family therapy at two, and I don't want to be late for the very first one. You sure this is okay?"

"Of course, silly, go! I think I can handle warming up some chicken nuggets later and refereeing the Xbox access until you get back."

"You're the best."

"I know," Stacey deadpanned and then turned back to the weeds. The garden was thriving under her efforts and now looked even better.

Holly walked back to her minivan and pulled the seatbelt across her body. She backed up carefully and set the GPS to the address for Sienna Treatment Center. Then she opened up a self-help book on audible and got lost in it and her thoughts as mile after mile sped by on the marker.

———

"Your destination is on the left. Sienna Treatment Center," the robotic voice stated plainly, but the location tied her stomach up in knots. Pulling into the parking lot, she felt her muscles begin to clench in anticipation.

This is silly. He is my son. Why am I so anxious to see him?

The treatment center was a new facility with bursting

petunia-filled flower boxes and copper sculptures out front. Warm and welcoming, with a warm brick façade and lots of windows, it didn't look like the 1970s institutional building she expected to see. She opened the door to the van and looked around for Mick's car. Not seeing it in the parking lot, she stretched and then walked to the door. There she was buzzed in quickly and registered as a visitor with the kind lady behind the welcome desk. A wall fountain gurgled soothing water down the stone front. The effect meant to have a calming effect, but Holly's jittery anxiety was overpowering its effects.

"You can have a seat in the lobby, and Adam will be with you momentarily."

Holly nodded and chose a comfortable looking chair and sank down into it. A loud buzzer sounded, the door opened, and a teenage boy shuffled out of it, his forearms covered in tattoos, looking bored and tired. Then a huge smile broke out across his face, and he started running when he saw his mom. He picked her up off the ground, laughing and swinging her around in a circle with glee.

The door opened again, and her heart jumped up into her chest, desperate to see Chance walk through it, but instead it was a youngish man with hair thinning on top.

"Holly Simon?" he asked.

Holly stood and shook his outstretched hand.

"I'm Adam, Chance's counselor. It's nice to meet you."

"Am I going to get to see Chance?"

"Of course, in a moment, we will bring him in and have the family session, but I'd like us to get acquainted first."

He led her through a door, first waving his security badge in front of it.

"How is he doing?"

"Pretty well. Obviously, he's frustrated, which is

completely normal, but he's settling into the routine here." He continued walking down the carpeted hall with cheery yellow walls that were covered in inspirational art. "He hasn't called you?"

"No," Holly admitted with a twinge of longing as she kept pace behind him.

"Is Mick planning on joining us?" Adam asked.

"I honestly have no idea," Holly answered. "I can try to text him."

"Now that you say that, I might have gotten an email that he's going to try to phone in during the session," Adam mentioned.

So much for showing up for his son.

The thought was self-righteous and petty, but she couldn't help it. Her anger had turned her into a scorekeeper, ruthlessly tallying points in her desperation to prove she was a good mother.

He unlocked one more door with his badge and settled her into a chair in his bright office. Light streamed in from the windows, and a group of orchids and plants were thriving in the corner of his desk, projecting a cultivated growth vibe, the perfect nurturing touch for a treatment center.

"Before we bring Chance in, I wanted to chat with you a bit."

"Okay," Holly said warily.

"He is pretty closed off right now. Anger is the dominant emotion we get from him." Adam's eyes met hers. He was small-statured, like his entire body had been scaled down by twenty percent. "I don't need to tell you this." He smiled. "Chance is very smart."

"He is," Holly agreed, prickling with pride.

"He's decidedly angry at you. Can you tell me why? Help me fill in some of the background information?"

"I wish I knew. It's like he turned into a different person the second he turned fifteen."

"How about his dad?"

"His dad is an alcoholic and an addict."

"Chance said his father is going to AA meetings."

"He knows more about what Mick is doing than I do then. But I honestly wouldn't believe a word either of them says. They both struggle with the truth."

"Addicts lie."

"Mick lies even when it is unnecessary. It's almost like he is incapable of telling the truth," Holly accused, then immediately felt guilty that she was using Mick's shortcomings to make herself look better to Adam. "Sorry, let's bring this back to Chance."

"It's important to understand the family dynamic," Adam offered. "When we think about the end of treatment and Chance going home and being integrated back into his life, how will that look?"

"I hadn't really thought about it much, to tell you the truth. All my energy was consumed by putting out the current fires."

Adam nodded his head in understanding.

"I mean, he can't go back to his dad's. It's not a safe environment there, but at my home, his behavior is destructive to my other son, Dillon. All of this is affecting Dillon profoundly. It is changing who he is, and he has done nothing wrong. I'm walking the tightrope of trying to do what is best for both of them, and it's exhausting. I always feel like I'm failing."

"You are in a very rough spot," Adam acknowledged. "For now, let's focus on today. Do you have any questions for me before I call Chance down?"

"I don't think so," Holly answered, feeling a flutter in her belly at the idea of seeing Chance again.

Adam turned to his phone and called for Chance. Holly picked at the fingernail polish that was chipping off of her thumb, looking down at her hands.

When had they gotten so old with bluish veins and sunspots?

She scraped at a hangnail repeatedly, her leg bouncing up and down to dispel nervous energy.

She heard the metallic click of an industrial door as it opened, and there he was, in ripped skater boy jean shorts and a t-shirt. His eyes were bright and focused. Nervously smiling, Holly jumped up quickly with open arms, and he surprisingly walked into them. He was stiff, but in her arms for a moment, and that was good enough for now. He patted her back dismissively like he was trying to say, *okay, that is enough* and pulled away more quickly than she wanted him to.

Adam pointed at the chairs and offered Chance a seat. Holly drank him in with her eyes. Inspecting him from head to toe. Observing the way he sat on the edge of his chair and identically bounced his leg in tune with hers, a nervous trait they obviously shared.

"You look good, honey. I've missed you so much." He ignored her, so she pointed at her leg and then at his and winked at him, desperate to connect with him. He ignored her lighthearted attempt again, leaning onto Adam's desk, propping his head up with his hand and looking bored.

Adam dialed the phone on his desk, and Holly heard it ringing. "Mick, you are on speakerphone. I'm here with Chance and Holly."

"Hey, Chancey. How are you, son?"

"Good, Dad," he said, smiling. "As good as you can be stuck in here."

It was wonderful to see him smile.

"Let's get started. Obviously, we are united with the same goal, to see Chance walk out of here and go on to continue a healthy life."

"Yes," Holly agreed, nodding fast.

"Addiction is a family disease. I know you have heard that to death, but it is true." Adam paused and then said, "After treatment, Chance is going to need a healthy environment if he has a shot at making a sustainable change."

"Yes," Holly agreed. "That would be at my house."

Chance bristled, then leaned back into the chair. "I'm not going back there with *her*."

Her? He spit it out like a dirty word. Holly felt her face redden.

"You know that's true, buddy," Mick said into the speaker. "I am fighting my own battles right now."

Chance folded his arms across his chest defiantly. "I am not going back there," he repeated woodenly.

Holly looked at Adam, begging silently for the therapist to weigh in. Adam said nothing, observing the dynamic.

"It's your only healthy option," Holly said. "It's me or it's nothing."

"Nothing it is then." Chance stood up. "Are we done?"

Holly was shocked, her mouth dropped open. "What? We just got started." She reached out a hand to calm him down, and Chance shook it off, making her more embarrassed.

"Honey, please. You have to be reasonable," Holly begged. The visit was going downhill quickly. The sensation was eerily similar to being forced to ride a terrifying roller coaster over and over again, unable to get off. The insane free-falling stomach drops and exhilarating heights when he walked through the door. It was a ride she wanted to end with every fiber of her being. He was pacing the small room like a caged animal, ratcheting up Holly's uneasiness. She sat silently, waiting for Adam to intervene, desperately searching her brain for common ground to diffuse the anger radiating from him.

"I can see that this is doing more harm than good right now," Adam offered. "Why don't you go grab lunch?" he asked Chance.

"Wait." Holly stood, trying to get the visit back on track, wanting to start over. "Can I see him after lunch during the family free time?"

"Not interested, Holly," Chance said and walked out of the room, letting the door slam behind him.

It was a dagger to the heart. Holly sat on the edge of her seat in stunned silence. Mick coughed loudly over speakerphone. During the exchange, she had completely forgotten he was there listening.

"He's going to have to accept that he can't live with you," Holly muttered, sliding to the back of the seat in defeat.

"I know. I'll talk to him."

"Can you try to take some of the responsibility of him being here off my shoulders? The raw hostility coming from him seems to only be directed at me."

"I'll try."

The dial tone filled the room as Mick disconnected.

"So that's it?" Holly asked, shellshocked at the events of the last several minutes. Astonished at how fast things could go sideways.

"Yeah, I think we are done for today. He is not in a good place to continue. At this point, it would do him more harm than good." Adam's voice was empathic.

"I agree, but I drove four hours to sit in a tension-filled session for fifteen minutes. It's a slap in the face."

"I understand." Adam stood up and started walking Holly to the reception room. "He's a tough one, but he'll come around. It's only been a few days. I appreciate you making the effort, and even though he is saying otherwise, he does too."

"Seems like this was a huge waste of time to me."

"It will make a difference later. He's angry, but anger is just a socially acceptable way for boys to process their hurt. He'll figure it out."

"I hope so."

Holly walked dejectedly back to her car and pulled away as hot tears filled her eyes. She felt angry and hurt herself.

Seems like the only emotions I get to feel anymore are fear, anger, and sadness.

She drove through the tears for an hour and then found herself in an Arby's drive-thru ordering a chocolate shake and two orders of mozzarella sticks, trying to fill the gnawing hole in her heart with fried cheese and sugar.

NINETEEN

She would never admit it publicly because the guilt would eat her alive, but it was calming to have the quiet. The swirling chaos that always seemed to escalate when Chance was around had dissipated, so all was finally peaceful and still. Over the last couple of weeks, Holly felt herself relaxing for the first time since that night in the hospital. She was tying her shoes, getting ready to take a walk to clear her head when Dillon appeared, dressed in shorts and an old basketball camp t-shirt.

"You know what would make you the best mom ever?" he asked, a hopeful smile making his brown eyes twinkle.

"But I don't want to be the best mom ever," Holly joked. "I want to be the mom that always disappoints, but occasionally comes in clutch just to keep you guessing." She sat up on the stairs, waiting expectantly for the rest of the request she knew was coming next.

Dillon shook his head and rolled his eyes at her. "Can we make cookies?"

"What kind?"

"Duh, Mom, chocolate chip," he groaned. "It's the only good kind."

Holly laughed and ruffled his hair and then pulled him in for a hug. She was hugging Dillon more now that they were alone, but the boy seemed to need it more, or at least understood on some level that his mom needed to be a mom and allowed her to hug him more frequently.

"Go get the brown sugar out of the cabinet and the mixing bowl," she told him. "I'll be right behind you." She slipped off her shoes and put them back in the hall closet.

Sugar beats exercise any day. I can get my steps in later.

She walked into the powder room and looked at her reflection in the mirror. The dark circles under her eyes were getting lighter every day; the tossing and turning and constant worrying were on pause. For now, he was at Sienna. For now, he was in a safe, controlled environment, surrounded by doctors and restricted by drug tests that confirmed he was sober. It was easier to let her guard down and sleep. She washed her face and swiped some sunscreen over her cheeks, noting that her split ends were getting ridiculous.

Need to get a haircut. Self-care is not exactly something I excel at.

She hadn't thought to do a single thing to take care of herself since things went off the rails with Chance, and whatever energy remained was consumed by trying to get help for Dillon. She was endlessly laboring to cover their basic bases, leaving little energy for her own needs. On some level, it felt selfish to worry about trivial things like haircuts when there were bigger issues at the forefront. Pushing away her thoughts, she walked into the kitchen where Dillon was pulling the required items from the pantry.

"Did you find everything, buddy?"

"Almost." He struggled on tiptoes to pull down the five pounds of flour just over his head.

She pulled out the plastic measuring cups and handed them to him, one by one, calling out each ingredient. He carefully measured out the packed brown sugar that still held the cup's form when he dumped it into the bowl like the sandcastles they'd made during their final family vacation to Florida when he was four. She handed him an egg, secretly smiling because she knew it was his favorite part. He banged it on the countertop before cracking it open and adding it to the bowl, but a huge chunk of shell fell down into the cream-colored dough.

Instantly panicked, "I ruined it!" he cried. "I knew I should have let you do it. I tried to do it perfectly."

"Hey there, stud," Holly said soothingly. "It's not the end of the world. No one died. You just need to find it and pick it out of the batter." She pushed the beater up and out of the way to enable him to see better.

He looked into the bowl for a few minutes, finally seeing the white of the shell, and fished it out with his fingers. He picked it out carefully and washed it off his hand and down the disposal.

"Good job. See? That wasn't so bad, was it?" She turned toward him. "Look at me." He met her eyes with his identical brown ones. "No one expects you to be perfect. When you learn how to do new things, sometimes you won't do it perfectly the first time. In fact, most times you won't."

"But I want to be the good boy."

"You are, honey, but you will also make mistakes, and since I don't plan on cracking eggs for you when you're thirty, you're going to have to learn how to fix it yourself when problems happen." Concerned, she brushed his hair from his eyes. "What is this really about, Dilly?"

"If I do everything right, then you won't be sad anymore."

Her heart dropped, and the dull ache surfaced again. Holly scooped him into her arms for a tight hug. "It's not your job to make me happy, honey. It's my job to make me happy." She kissed the top of his sweaty head and then pulled back to look him square in the eyes. "You can't fix all this, and neither can I. That's the hardest part. Chance has to fix it. We can cheer him on and encourage him from the sidelines, but he has to run the race." Dillon was quiet, absorbing the information. "Do you understand what I'm saying?" Dillon nodded solemnly. "Your only job is to be a kid, that is all. Oh, and to get me the vanilla." He rushed to put the vanilla in her hand. "Do you have any questions or want to talk about what's happening with Chance?"

"No."

"How are things going with Dr. Greg?"

"Good, we play and draw pictures and talk about things that are bothering me."

"Does it help to talk to him?"

"Sometimes."

That is good enough for now. I'll take that as a win.

She stirred up the batter. "Now we need the chocolate chips."

"That's my favorite part." He went to the pantry and pulled out the yellow bag. "Can we put in the whole thing?"

"But the recipe only says half," she corrected and then paused and considered his request. "But…" At her hesitation, a smile broke out over his face. "What could it hurt?"

"Really?" He looked up at her eagerly, waiting for permission. She nodded, and he gleefully dumped in the entire bag. The chunks of chocolate made the clumpy batter harder to mix.

"It will be an experiment. That's how all the most important discoveries are made. After all, someone once looked at a cow and said, I wonder what the white stuff coming out of those dangly bits tastes like."

Dillion giggled. "Yuck, Mom, so gross." Holly laughed.

"Not every experiment is going to yield good results. Every serious scientist knows that."

She stirred the chips into the batter. "Now we need an official taste tester. Go get me a spoon!"

He ran to the drawer and yanked it open, pulling out the huge stainless steel serving spoon she kept for special occasions to dish out casseroles.

"Kid, you are so literal. I can see what you're doing there."

"You said a spoon, so technically…" He smiled at her adorably as his words drifted off, and he rocked side to side waiting.

"You drive a really hard bargain." She grabbed the enormous spoon from his hand and scooped four cookies' worth of batter onto it, enjoying watching his eyes get bigger and bigger in delight. Handing over the spoon, she cautioned, "That argument is only going to work once with me, mister, so savor your victory."

Dillon shoved the raw dough into his mouth with the tip of the spoon, happy with himself.

"Love you, Dilly. I'll call you when the cookies are done."

"'Ove oo, too, Mo'," he said, his mouth full of batter.

It felt so good to hear those words. It was like a balm to her broken heart.

TWENTY

She decided it wasn't the worst idea to consider getting therapy for herself. Having never gone before, she wasn't sure what to expect.

What do I say? Do I just talk? Will I be expected to lie down on a couch?

At her first appointment, Holly sat in the plain, nondescript waiting room, hearing the soothing sounds of the white noise speaker and the ocean tide undertones. It felt like a cocoon—warm, quiet, calming. She inhaled the scent of lavender from the diffuser that sat next to her on a small table covered with last year's issues of People Magazine.

"Holly Simon?" An older woman with post-menopausal hip thickness and a straight grey bob called out her name from an open door down the short hallway.

Holly stood and walked over, then reached to shake her hand. "I'm Susan. Have a seat wherever you feel comfortable."

Holly looked around the homey room filled with soft pillows and an overstuffed sofa and sank down into it, feeling awkward when she nearly disappeared into the crack between the cushions. She chuckled, "Sorry," and then extracted herself from it and readjusted.

"Tell me what brings you in today," Susan asked after taking her own seat across from Holly and cranking up another white noise speaker in the room. She sat in a chair with a notepad in her lap and studied Holly intently.

Holly exhaled a long sigh and admitted, "I don't even know where to start. Everything is such a mess. My life is spiraling out of control."

Susan watched her gently over the rim of her purple reading glasses, waiting for Holly to share more. When she didn't, Susan encouraged, "Just pick any place you feel comfortable."

"My son is in a residential treatment center. My other son is like a sponge, soaking up all the chaos and drama around him, and it's affecting his life. My ex is an addict and an idiot and has never had to grow up." The first confessions spilled out of her mouth, messy and fast.

"Let's talk about these people one at a time."

"Okay, my fifteen-year-old, Chance, hates my guts. He overdosed in the park a few months ago and was just kicked out of outpatient treatment meetings for attempting to sell drugs—to people at his treatment center." Holly stopped abruptly as the vocal revelation rendered her speechless. "That's the first time I have ever had to say that out loud." Hot tears welled up in her eyes, and Susan pushed the box of tissues toward her gently. "What kind of kid tries to proposition addicted people in treatment? It's so sick. I am so ashamed. These are not the values I have spent my life trying to instill in him. It's like I don't even know who he is anymore."

"When our kids start to do things outside our family values, it comes with a lot of feelings of guilt and shame,"

Susan offered stoically, acknowledging her shame, and it gave Holly the smallest measure of peace to see her deepest failure exposed and met with empathy.

"So much guilt," Holly agreed, wiping at her face with a tissue. "And then I drove four hours to our first family therapy session last week, and he got so angry and shut down and sent me home. It was humiliating. He couldn't even stand to be around me for more than ten minutes."

"Tell me about Chance's dad. Are you on the same page?"

"Not at all. Mick is a mess, too, and really needs to be in treatment himself." Holly remarked, "He gets to be the Disneyland Dad, never having to discipline or do the hard things. He's never had to grow up."

"When did Mick start using?"

"At ten. His brother gave him his first drink at a party just to see what would happen, like it was some kind of game. How messed up is that?"

"Addicts stop maturing and stay at the level they were when they started using unless they get in treatment and start doing the work."

"Work has never been his strong suit," Holly said grimly, but it made a lot of sense. Mick was incredibly immature, stunted by alcohol, trapped in his ten-year-old mind. It was easy to slam Mick and blame him for his shortcomings. She counted them all on a scorecard she buried deep in her brain, black mark after black mark, and then used them as weapons.

"You seem to have a lot of anger," Susan said objectively. "Have you heard of the term codependent?"

"That's not me. I don't need other people to take care of me."

"That's not really what it means at all." Susan stopped for a moment; she set her pen down and began to explain. "Back in the eighties, a woman named Melody Beattie coined the term codependent. She is responsible for making the term mainstream. She wrote a book called "*Codependent No More.*"

Inwardly, Holly groaned. She wasn't weak and needy. She wasn't codependent.

Susan continued, "Researchers found a commonality, a dynamic that was found more often than not between alcoholics and people that were in close relationships with them."

"I think I'm more independent than codependent," Holly argued, unable to accept what Susan was trying to say.

"It's not what you think it is," Susan started softly. "Have you ever made excuses for your ex, or tried to keep his life together while softening the consequences of his decisions?"

Holly nodded silently.

"Have you spent more time worrying about your ex or your son's problems or finding solutions for them than they have?"

She nodded again.

"Are you a martyr? Do you give until it hurts and then resent it when no one gives back to you?"

Holly winced as that last statement hit a major nerve. Instantly, a tear fell from her eye, and she swiped at it with her tissue.

"The truth is you didn't create this, and you can't fix it. I am sure you have heard this mantra to death, but what happens with codependency is that you think you can. You fool yourself into thinking that with enough effort and enough love you can fix this. But you can't. The addict is the only one who can."

"I know," she said softly. "But how do I stop caring?" She wiped at the tears again. "It's like we are all on a bus that is going to crash into a ravine, and Chance and Mick are the ones who are driving while Dillon and I are screaming and pleading, begging them to stop."

"That is an accurate analogy," Susan confirmed. "The truth is you never stop caring," Susan answered. "You just put the power back on the addict to make the changes. Sometimes you have to get off the bus and let them crash and burn."

Holly gulped. She was willing to let Mick crash, but it was hard to swallow the idea of doing the same for Chance. "Sometimes I feel like I care more than they do," Holly admitted.

"This is completely normal," Susan continued. "They will pull you in to fix things as much as you allow it. You need to learn how to provide support but not weaken them by over-helping. Learn to keep your resources to yourself. Don't spin your wheels brainstorming solutions and fixes for them. When you do that, you weaken them, and it never forces them to grow up or take responsibility." Susan looked at her over her glasses again. "Stay in your own lane. Reconnect to yourself again. Is there something you can do for yourself to replenish all that has been taken?"

"That's been my last priority. It takes all my energy just to cover everyone else's bases."

"Did you hear what you just said?" Susan reprimanded gently.

Holly was instantly sheepish.

"That needs to change, even if you just take ten minutes alone. After work, go to your room, decompress, maybe do some breathing and mindfulness activities or a little yoga."

"I hate yoga."

"I did too," Susan confided, "but the more you do it, the easier it gets. I think if you really gave it a try, or maybe six," she smiled, "you might feel differently."

"I feel guilty taking time for myself when my life is blowing up."

"That is part of the disease of codependency. It takes you out of yourself and gets you over-involved in the life of another capable human being. But instead of doing the hard stuff, they get to rely on you. It chains them to you, and you deplete yourself to fill their bottomless holes of need. They will take as much as you are willing to give. All your resources, all your energy."

"It feels selfish to focus on myself when my kid just overdosed."

"I am sure you have heard the phrase 'you can't give from an empty cup,' right?"

"Yes."

"It's true on so many levels." She glanced at the clock. "Here's your homework: Give yourself a bit of time where you can do something for yourself, something that you like or even love. Start small. And I would highly recommend you read *Codependent No More*."

"I'll think about it," Holly conceded.

Great, more things to do. I need that like I need a hole in my head.

"Would you like to set up another appointment?" Susan asked, and to her surprise, Holly heard herself answer, "Yes."

TWENTY-ONE

The next day, after a long day of shuffling Dillon to baseball practice and his therapy appointment, she put on her flannel pajamas and padded into the kitchen barefoot. Holly poured a nice big glass of red wine and then scrolled through Amazon to order the book.

I wonder if drinking wine counts as doing something I really love?

She sat at the dining room table with its years of abuse evidenced by the chipped finish and scratches and sipped the room temperature merlot slowly, letting it warm up her tongue. She savored it slowly while swiping through the dedication and table of contents and started reading the first chapter, and then there was this sensation of being pulled into a tunnel as the rest of the world slowly disappeared that consumed her senses. Her hearing was muffled and distant, but the words jumped out of the screen. Screaming truths she wasn't ready to hear.

"Passive-aggressive."

"Anger."

"Martyr complex."

"Putting on a pretty face."

"Obsessive care-taking"

"Keeping Score."

Each statement was like a slap. A confirmation of her behaviors and her compulsion to take care of everything, to be the one who everyone could count on. Two hours later, blurry-eyed, she picked up her gaze from the tablet. She rubbed her fatigued eyes, exhausted from the sea of words that began to swim together under the focus of her reading glasses.

She rinsed out the glass and placed it on the drying rack and then set out the brioche bread for French toast in the morning, knowing it would bring a sleepy smile to Dillion's face in a few hours. Holly climbed the stairs to her bedroom and fell into bed, exhausted in every way— emotionally, physically, mentally. Bone weary from the never-ending supply of anxiety and tension and a deep new sense of knowing. Trying to settle her mind, she fluffed the pillows.

I love you, Chance.

Those words were how she ended every day, looking forward to the day when she could say them to him again. When Chance would be ready to hear them. Seconds later, she fell asleep, snoring slightly and tossing fitfully. Two hours later, her eyes popped open in the darkness. With her heart hammering and her breath caught in her throat, Holly panicked, feeling flushed and hot.

She reached out instinctively for her phone, scrolling through notifications that were completely unimportant. Seeing nothing troubling, she exhaled deeply.

You are okay.

Chance is okay.

Dillon is okay.

You are safe.

In the darkness, she squinted at the large red numbers on the alarm clock. 3:02 a.m.

Maybe it's time for an eye exam. Later. I'll call later.

Wide awake, she yawned. Frustrated with conflicting signals from her body that were equally as exhausted as they were keyed up, she lay there another thirty minutes, frustrated at her inability to relax, staring at the ceiling and wondering what Chance was doing right now. Surely, he was sleeping and safe in his bed at treatment. Or maybe he was awake staring at the ceiling like she was.

I guess I might as well start my day.

She turned on the little lavender lamp by her bed and gathered her hair into a messy bun on top of her head, then pulled her laptop from the charger on the table beside her bed. Opening it up, she tapped into google.

How to stop being codependent.

Shit, if I'm going to be reading the hard stuff this early, I need coffee.

Holly tiptoed past Dillon's room and down the stairs, sinking into the soft pile of carpet that was installed when she first moved in. Her toes nearly disappeared into the fibers it was so plush. She caught a glimpse of the crack in the wall by the door when Chance had punched the wall in a fit of rage.

Wish I could just cover that up and it would disappear from the wall and from my memories like it never happened.

She absentmindedly ran her finger down the crack, cursing its existence, yet gaining a perverse form of comfort knowing it was one of the last things Chance had physically touched. Padding across the cool wood floors into the kitchen, Holly turned on the Keurig that roared to life, surging and gurgling to heat up the water. She pulled a coffee pod out of the cabinet. The Keurig had also been a splurge. It was the one thing that she looked forward to, to start her day on a high note.

See, Susan? I do occasionally take care of myself.

Patting herself on the back, she put the pod into the chamber and pulled down the handle. It made a soft popping sound as the needle pierced the coffee pod and started to brew, then made two loud spewing sounds and abruptly stopped. The message "Sorry brew interrupted" flashed on the LED Screen.

Holly sighed in frustration.

She restarted the process and was hit with another warning. "Oops, this pod wasn't designed for this brewer."

Sweet Jesus. These are the recommended cups.

Three more tries, three more rejections, each one making Holly hotter under the collar. The anger was rising, and her remaining patience was microscopic. She flung the offensive cup across the room in frustration, somewhat toward the trash can, but it hit the wall and left a long brown stain across the wall where it connected.

I just want some coffee. Why does everything have to be so hard?

She sank down on the stool, weighing her options at nearly 3:30 am. Starbucks was closed. Gas station? Twenty-four-hour diner? Get in the car and drive as far away as she could on the tank of gas that was in it?

She pulled her shoes on and grabbed the keys, heading toward the gas station that was only a block away. The idea of driving past the gas station to the highway and flipping a coin to see which way to go was incredibly alluring. It took all her reserves to pull the van into the dirty gas station parking lot and shuffle into the store to the overworked coffee pot.

Please, God, at least let it be fresh.

She pulled the largest cup from the dispenser and filled it

to the top, paid the attendant, and then cruised back home, ignoring the magnetic pull of the van to the interstate.

It would be so easy to just run away and let Mick deal with the fallout for a change.

Then Dillon's face popped into her mind, and she made the responsible decision and pulled back into her garage.

Holly carried the coffee back to the bedside table and opened the laptop, trying to find comfort in the blogs of parents who were dealing with addicted children. Their vivid descriptions of the life she was currently living were hauntingly accurate. Different people stuck in the same hell. Their stories were nearly identical to hers, just with different names. It made her feel a little less alone but killed any hope that only one round of treatment would fix the mess they'd been dragged into. The odds were stacked incredibly high against that ever happening. Addiction is a relapsing disease. They might be dealing with it forever. More information wasn't more power. More information was more anxiety, more despair, and more terror in an already terrifying new reality.

Two hours later, after shutting the laptop, with the coffee finally cold, she laid back on her pillows once again. The tears appeared, leaking down her laugh lines, tracing down her temples to the pillow. A track that had been all too familiar lately. Her bed was where she cried her tears, hidden away from the anxious eyes of her vulnerable younger son. Dillon was the son she could save. Hiding them was a necessity. He wasn't able to handle his own emotions, let alone witness his mother falling apart in front of him. She didn't want to be the reason another one of her precious babies turned to something dark to make himself feel better.

TWENTY-TWO

Sitting on Stacey's deck in the sun was a relaxing treat. Holly pulled her feet out of her flip flops and wiggled her toes, looking down at the tiny red dots of polish remnants from the last pedicure she had indulged in at the beginning of May. Another before marker that made her heart ache for her past life.

"How is therapy going?" Stacey asked, setting a tray of lemonades and gingersnap cookies on the patio table.

"Good, I guess." Holly picked up a napkin and caramel-colored cookie. "Truthfully, I feel like my life is just one big therapy appointment."

"I can see why you'd say that." Stacey pulled a flask of vodka out of her pocket and looked around to make sure Dillon and Sarah weren't around before sliding it secretly to Holly.

"You're so sneaky, but I have never loved you more." Holly quickly unscrewed the cap and tipped a conservative amount of it into her lemonade. "With Mick's history and Chance's stuff, I feel like I can't even have a drink like a normal adult around Dillon."

"You haven't done anything wrong. You've always been responsible, usually the *only* responsible one."

"He's so high strung, Stace." Holly stirred her drink with a chopstick that Stacey laid on the tray for that purpose. She swirled and swirled it around, watching the yellow liquid twirl with her mind spinning. "The kid can't relax. We made cookies the other day, and he lost his shit when a piece of egg shell got into the batter." Looking up, she set the chopstick back on the tray. "I hate this so much. I feel like I can't protect him, that I've failed Chance." She paused and then uttered sadly, "I am a terrible mother."

"You stop it," Stacey said abruptly. "Stop beating yourself up right now. I won't allow it."

"I can't get my head to slow down. Sleeping is impossible."

"Maybe you should ask your doctor for some prescription help for the time being. Just to get you through."

"I worry about having something like that lying around. Eventually, Chance will be coming home, and I'll have to have a plan to lock all those things up."

"Let's cross that bridge when you get there. Right now, you need to take care of yourself so you can have the energy to handle all that is being asked of you."

Holly exhaled a deep sigh.

"Whoa, woman, I felt that deep."

"It's exhausting. Keeping all the balls in the air, juggling my ass off, while Mick just prances through life having everyone take care of him as usual." She took another long sip. Can I tell you something terrible, that you can never, ever repeat?"

"Of course."

She whispered, "Sometimes, I wish I had never had kids. I think that my life would have been so much easier without them." The words crushed her to admit, and her hand reflexively clamped down on her mouth to prevent more awful confessions from escaping. "How horrible of a mother do you have to be to think like that?" She cried as her voice cracked.

"Honey, that's the guilt talking." Stacey put a hand on Holly's forearm and squeezed. "Who can fault you for feeling like that? You've been deep in the trenches being both mom *and dad* for those kids since birth. I'm your only support system, and my life is so busy I can't help out like I should."

"No, no, no." Holly shook her head quickly. "That is not true at all. You've been the only one there for me. I truly appreciate you being able to help with Dillon so I can get to meetings and therapy. It is such a relief to know he is in a normal, healthy environment."

"Honey, ain't no one normal and healthy."

"It's hilarious how your proper English disappears when you add a little vodka."

"I like to think I embrace all the dialects." Stacey smirked at her and then continued. "You never told me how therapy went with Chance."

"Brutal," Holly confided. "It's like having your heart ripped out of your chest and then savagely stomped on." She sipped from her drink. "And then stomped on again." She laughed to hide the pain.

"Aww, woman." Stacy reached out and squeezed her shoulder. "It's gonna take time."

"I don't know if there is enough time in the world for that," Holly admitted. "He's so angry, and for the life of me, I can't understand why it is only directed at me."

"That's got to be so hard."

"I just don't know how we got here. He was a momma's boy his whole life, and then it was like, one day a switch flipped and here we are, and I have no idea how we got here.

All those values and morals I tried to instill in him for years, they are all gone. I barely recognize him. And as usual, Mick has come out smelling like a rose. Chance is falling all over himself to make his dad happy."

"Wow, that's a lot to deal with." She sipped thoughtfully. "They are still there, honey. All those things you taught him. All those lessons on right and wrong, they are all there. Someday, he will be in a place where he can remember."

"I don't know if I'll ever live to see that day." Holly laughed mirthlessly. "He was angling to go live with his dad after treatment. Can you even believe that?" Holly stated, shocked.

"That man can't take care of himself. What makes him think he can take care of a high-risk teenager?"

"Exactly," Holly agreed. "The funny thing is that Chance doesn't know it, but Mick would never agree to that. It would require him to grow up finally, and he is not interested in doing that at all."

Sarah and Dillon came running out of the house with a frisbee followed by a labradoodle, a floppy curly black mass of hair and sweetness. Holly watched the children laughing and playing with the dog, soaking up the sun.

"It's so nice to see him smiling and laughing again." Holly noticed. "Thank you for listening to this everlasting line of bullshit that is my life."

"Of course, love, that's what friends are for."

"This is the first time in weeks I've been able to decompress for a little bit."

"You need to find little pockets of you-time throughout this, or you're going to burn out."

"You're right," Holly agreed and drained the last bit of lemonade from her glass, the condensation running down her fingers. "I love your face."

"Ditto."

"Thanks for always having my back. You're the only one I can count on."

"You'd do the same for me."

It was a nice afternoon in the middle of her nightmare. It felt normal and good, but strange at the same time. Her life had gotten so far off track and into the ditch that indulging in normal everyday pleasures felt strange and selfish. She watched the kids play and closed her eyes, feeling the warm sun on her face. Grateful for one moment of perfect normalcy, hoping that her life would get back on track and days like this would become an average Tuesday again, having no idea that the worst was yet to come.

TWENTY-THREE

Holly was driving to Sienna Treatment Center again, this time not as fearful. Knowing what to expect was a little better. She was listening to *Codependent No More* on audiobook. Committing the words to heart by listening to them repeatedly, she used the long day of driving to work on herself. She was ready to take control over the part she played, now fully understanding it was the only element of the entire explosive dynamic she could change.

Looking down, she rolled her eyes and then answered the phone.

"Yes, Mick?"

"Hey, Holls. Just giving you the heads up, I'll be in the room for therapy. Didn't want you to feel ambushed."

"Okay," she said dully. "Have you heard from Chance?"

"Every night."

The barbed wire around her heart constricted tighter. She was frustrated and bitter for the oversight. It wasn't supposed to be a competition, but it was in a way. Growing up, Chance had always been closest to her, and now that he obviously preferred Mick, it was a sour truth to swallow. It hurt so much, a pinprick of pain every time she let herself be vulnerable and opened her heart. Every night, she spent waiting by the phone for a call that never came.

"Haven't you?" he asked.

"No," she answered truthfully. "I thought you were going to work on it."

"I'm trying to grease the wheels, but you know teenage boys. They're stubborn," Mick answered. "I did tell him again that his dream of moving in with me is never gonna happen."

"And how did he take that?"

"He acted like he didn't hear me say it."

"The kid hears what he wants to hear," Holly answered. "Anything new to report?"

"The psychologist evaluated him and put him on medication. Anti-anxiety, anti-psychotics, and something to help him sleep."

"Wow, that's a lot of prescriptions."

"It is. But the way they explain it, it's all necessary."

"Okay. Anything else?" Staying on the phone with him was exhausting, and she needed to conserve her resources for therapy.

"Nah, see you there." He paused then offered, "You know, we could have ridden together."

"Nah," she mimicked him. "There's a reason we're divorced." Then she punched the end call button on the phone.

Needing a break, she pulled up a Tony Robbins podcast. His excitement and passion for living a healthy life always recentered and inspired her. She needed to go into therapy with her A-game. She listened thoughtfully to his words, spiraling her mood up and up, and vaguely wondered if she would have the cojones to do a fire walk like he talked about on his podcast. Would she sit at the edge and wait in fear, or could she suck it up and be fearless and run across those coals if given the chance? She added fire walking to her mental bucket list. It was a long list of someday items that resurfaced every January. Not many things were crossed off yet, and it was filled with hopeful longing to own a tiny home in the mountains, to take a hot air balloon ride, and to grow her own food hydroponically.

An hour later, she pulled into the parking lot at the treatment center and took a few deep breaths, trying to center herself and mentally prepare for battle.

This is so messed up. I'm not going to war. I am just having a conversation with my son. When did every interaction become so confrontational?

She closed her eyes, took in one more deep breath, and then jumped when someone rapped on the driver's side window.

Mick's wide easy smile splayed across his face and was one of his most dangerous attributes. It made him naughty and dangerous back when those things were irresistible character attributes to her. When she was young and stupid and being in love meant an adrenaline-filled, love-you-so-much-it-kills-me type of energy. The kind that burned hot and fast and usually exploded in your face like one of the defective fireworks the YouTube idiots blow their fingers off lighting every fourth of July. She didn't crave that anymore. Her time in the high heat spotlight of loving Mick Simon was over, and she was never going back there. She had been burnt so badly, but dammit if occasionally the sun hit him just the right way and she still melted a little. Even after everything that happened. Even after all that water under the bridge, he still had the occasional effect on her and she hated herself for it.

She shook her head to clear it and got out of her van, then

followed him into the center. As usual, Mick let her take care of the mundane tasks and made himself comfortable on a sofa in the waiting room, putting his feet up on the pretty coffee table in an act of aged ex-rocker defiance. She gave their names to the receptionist and was just turning around when she heard the door open.

"Dad!" Chance ran through the door and into his arms, and she watched them embrace from across the room. Chance's smile lit up his face. The planes of it were slimming down, and time was carving him from the slab of marble every day, transforming him into the man he would become.

I used to think he changed so much week to week when he was a baby, but it's even more pronounced when he's not around to numb my observations by seeing him every day. He is morphing into a man, and I am not even here to see it.

"Your mom is over there." Mick waved to her across the room, and Chance's eyes swept over to meet hers. Holly walked quickly over to him, eager to hold him in her arms. It was harder now as the daily hugs had become a thing of the past. It wasn't affection on her terms anymore; it was whatever morsel he decided to fling at her when the mood struck. Like a tiger in captivity, starving and ignored, she paced around aimlessly and waited for feeding time, which was becoming less and less frequent.

"Hey, honey." She pulled him in for a hug anyway, and he reciprocated stiffly. "I missed you so much. Dilly sends his love. He'd really like to talk to you sometime soon. If you could call him, I know it would make his day."

"How is he?" Chance asked. "I never thought I would miss that annoying little pecker head, but I do."

Holly rolled her eyes but let the insult slide. "He is great. Staying busy with baseball and therapy."

Adam was next through the door. He smiled hello and got right down to business. "Are you ready?"

"As ready as we'll ever be," Mick said, ruffling Chance's hair and following Adam down the hall. Chance walked like he was headed to the gas chamber. Holly frittered around trying to make small talk, accepting one-word answers and grunts from Chance.

Adam waved at the chairs. "Thank you for coming. To be successful, Chance is going to need both of you in his corner after treatment. The more support, the better."

Holly nodded. "Yes, we know that, and we are ready."

"I always tell my clients that this is the easiest part. Being in a controlled environment. Working the steps, getting clean, and developing new foundations. While you are in here, your addiction is out there doing pushups, getting stronger, ready to pick right back up where it left off."

Holly listened to him quietly. Chance looked bored, his ankle resting on his knee absentmindedly as he jiggled his knee up and down.

"He's got to change his people and places. Relapsing is a reality. I'd love to tell you that it is one and done, but the statistics prove otherwise. He needs to form new friendships and a support system with people who are sober. Find new activities to keep him busy, new hobbies, new places to go. Being exposed to the old places where he used to use will just increase the rate of relapse. Do you understand?"

Mick nodded his head like it was his job. Putting on the dutiful parent cloak that disguised his own addictions and transgressions. It was an act that was a little difficult for Holly to swallow.

He's such a phony. There I go again, keeping score.

She caught herself falling into familiar patterns that she now knew needed to change.

"Don't you think it would be beneficial for Mick to seek out some treatment as well?" Holly asked saccharine-sweetly, hiding the passive-aggressive tones expertly.

Mick balked at her like he had been burned, shooting daggers at her with his eyes.

I don't know why it is so important for me to destroy the façade he's constructed. But it is.

There was a modicum of slight triumph at unveiling the truth.

I am a terrible person.

"What do you think, Mick? Do you need treatment?" Adam asked.

"I like to drink, but I wouldn't necessarily say I have a problem."

"Correct me if I'm wrong, but isn't that what all addicts say, Adam?" Holly interjected.

Chance was taking in the exchange and getting more anxious. There was a definite energy shift. Like when a severe thunderstorm is coming, and old ladies can feel it in their arthritic joints and stay at home moms take to their beds with migraines. Holly knew she was walking a really fine line, but she just couldn't sit there and listen to any more of Mick's bullshit.

"Yes. That is true."

"Isn't there a men's program at this facility as well?" She pushed harder, not able to help herself.

"Holly," Mick grumbled. She could tell from his tone he was at the end of his rope, and she wasn't going to be allowed much farther.

"We can't provide a safe environment for our son if one of us is an active addict."

Chance jumped up, "All you do is nag, Mom. You always drive people away. Can't you just stop?"

Holly bit back the words on her tongue, flustered at Chance's outburst. Although she was embarrassed that she was the target again, a part of her shamefully agreed with what he said.

"No. I won't stop," Holly declared when she found her voice. "If you are going to spend any amount of time at your dad's when you get released, it's time we deal with the elephant in the room. We stop dancing around the real problem. We must address the obvious active alcoholism that is part of your life." She turned to Adam to plead her case. "You said he needs to be around sober people. Doesn't that start at home?"

"Yes," Adam agreed. "But we are not here to force anyone into treatment."

"Why the fuck not? I was!" Chance shouted.

"Language."

"You're a broken record," Chance's annoyance at the basic rules surfaced again.

"No, Chance, there is a minimum expectation of respect. I do not like it when you swear. It is not allowed in my home. I would save that kind of language for use around your friends. And to be clear, we are not your friends."

"No shit."

"Again, I will caution you to stop the swearing. It is not acceptable."

She turned the conversation back to Mick. "We are off topic. You know you need help to be able to support Chance when he is released," Holly explained slowly and carefully, speaking the way she did to her six-year-old students. Mick rolled his eyes. Her teacher's tone was like nails on a chalkboard to him.

"You are like a dog with a bone, Holly," he said, exasperated. "I am not an addict, and I am not at a place in my life where I want to seek treatment."

"Then the kids can't stay with you anymore. It's not safe."

"You would keep my kids away from me?" Mick's voice got louder.

"Mom! Can you just stop? Jesus Christ. You never know when to stop."

"Chance, this is between me and your father."

"No, addiction is a *family* disease, right, Adam?" Chance said the words infused with sarcasm.

"He's right," Adam responded.

"He's an *addict*!" Holly cried, emphasizing the last word. "I feel like I am the only person in this room with any common sense." She groaned an irritated sigh, shaking her head in frustration. "There is no way I will risk the safety of my children by putting them in the care of an active addict."

"They are my sons, too, Holly."

"Exactly!" she yelled louder. "Then do the right thing. Give them a healthy father. Give them a chance at a healthy life!" She was aggravated, the words falling fast, tumbling out of her mouth rapidly, out of her control. "Your whole life, I have had to take care of you. Can't you, just for once, suck it up and put their health and happiness above your own?"

Mick recoiled but said nothing.

"Just once, could you grow the fuck up and do what needs to be done?"

"Language!" Chance said, mocking her.

"You know what, Chance, you're right. I shouldn't use profanity. But when you've wasted the last seventeen years of your life taking care of a grown man, sometimes that's the only appropriate response."

"I think you've given Mick a lot to think about, right,

Mick?" Adam interjected diplomatically, and Mick grunted in agreement. "I think this is a good place to stop for today. You have two free hours to hang out with Chance since it's family day."

Chance sat back in the chair sullenly, his arms folded over his chest, his brow creased in anger.

Great, this should be fun.

"Can we take him for ice cream?" Holly offered, trying to smooth the ruffled feelings in the best way she knew how, with sugar.

"He needs to earn that privilege. He's not quite there yet, but there are snacks and a bunch of board games in the Rec Room. If you want to use any of those, you are welcome."

Chance got up and walked out of the room, and Mick followed him close behind.

Two peas in a pod.

"Thank you for navigating that," Holly said to Adam, trying to smooth things over.

"There's definitely some work to do there," Adam acknowledged. "But you're right; his dad needs to provide a safe environment for both of the kids, especially for Chance."

Then why didn't you have the balls to say that during the session when it might have made a difference?

She didn't have the balls either. She swallowed the rest of the words she wanted to say and walked out of his office as frustrated as she was when she walked in.

TWENTY-FOUR

Running late to her next therapy session, Holly whipped into the parking lot at the last second and then ran into the building and sat down quickly. Susan's grey and white bob appeared from behind the door, her reading glasses perched on her nose. "Holly?" She smiled. "I'm ready for you."

Holly jumped to her feet and settled on one of Susan's sofas, still a little breathless from rushing around.

"How about you start with a deep breath?" Susan asked. "You seem a little stressed."

"Sorry, traffic was crazy, and it's been hard to keep all the balls in the air." She followed Susan's directions and breathed in deeply, closed her eyes, and let it out slowly. It was the first full breath she had taken all day.

"I bet. How have you been?"

"About the same," Holly answered. "But I did read that book you suggested."

"And what did you discover?"

"It was very eye-opening." Holly looked around the office at the cheery aqua and yellow chevron patterns printed on almost every surface. Nice and neat. "The word dependence always threw me off. I thought codependence meant I was dependent on someone else, and I did not identify with that at all."

Susan scribbled a note and listened thoughtfully.

"The book was definitely an education. It was bizarre, actually. I felt that I had been given an owner's manual for my life. I highlighted my way through it, and now it's covered in ink. I've been listening to it in the car on audiobook, too, so I can let it sink in."

"Nothing wrong with that. Being able to identify these kinds of behaviors is the first step to make lasting changes. Growth is constant, so when you read it the next time, different passages will stand out for you because you are better prepared to receive the information."

Holly nodded in agreement.

"What are you doing to take care of yourself?" Susan asked.

"I was supposed to be doing that?" she joked. Humor was always her favorite means of deflection.

Susan smiled a sage smile. "We talked last time about trying to give from an empty cup. Do you recall?"

"Yes. I guess I just keep thinking I'll get around to that later, once things get more settled."

"You're a mom, Holly. Things will never get settled." Susan smiled and then continued, "What about fitting in a few moments here and there? Nothing crazy, just a small little distraction for yourself."

"I used to love to work in my garden."

"Perfect!" Susan said. "Two birds with one stone, you can get some exercise and do something you enjoy."

Holly added that to the to-do list reluctantly and confessed, "I'm struggling with Chance. He blames me for everything. He doesn't call. The only time we speak is at the mandatory family therapy sessions."

"That has to be hard."

"It is. I don't know why he blames me, but I hate it."

"It may seem counterintuitive, but many times, when a child is acting out their anger is directed at the healthy parent, the one they know they can always rely on. They will push all your buttons to see if you mean what you say. Chance is seeing if your love has limits. He has seen you cut off Mick for his addictions, and he is wondering if you will do the same to him. He is afraid and unable to articulate it, so he tests you instead. Oftentimes, a child will go out of their way to maintain the relationship and get approval from the addicted parent. They feel a oneness with them since they share the addiction. It's a sick dynamic, but it plays out a lot in these circumstances."

Holly felt the tears well up and pulled a soft tissue from the box on the table, then she sighed and sunk back into the couch again. "This disconnect just hurts so much." The tears rolled fast and heavy. "I have never felt pain like this. It is soul-crushing, and I feel so powerless. All I can do is react to the next wave of misery and focus on damage control. It is killing me, I don't know how much more I can take." She sobbed into her hands and pulled a wad of fresh Kleenex out and pressed it to her face. The intensity of the emotion as it wracked through her body made her body vibrate with shame. Once started, she couldn't stop the flood of tears and the tidal wave of pain that felt like it was consuming her. It was the source of the long, guttural, agonized cries that ripped through the white noise in the office. Susan sat with her in silence, waiting, softly murmuring occasional affirmations and words of understanding. Eventually, Holly quieted and exhaled big breaths before inhaling deeply through her congested nose. The release wore her out.

Susan gently spoke, "It is good to process the hurt. These are incredibly heavy emotions that need to come out in order for you to heal."

"I used to just stuff them down," Holly admitted, her voice nasally as she fought through the congestion.

"I am happy to see you choose not to do that anymore. It is very instrumental to your healing process."

"When things get tough with Chance, he needs you to reassure him. He needs to know that you love him no matter what."

"I love you no matter what," Holly repeated, considering the words. They were true, even though they were painful and scary to say. The "no matter what" part left the door open in a frightening way.

"I would suggest that when Chance is integrated back into your lives, you take time to do things with him that aren't so heavy. Do an activity together where you can simply enjoy each other, not have another long conversation about what he is doing wrong. If the tension comes up, or the desire to lecture, just redirect and say something like, 'Today, we are going to put that on hold so we can have some fun.' Talk about silly things. Get to know who he is now and what he thinks about. Ask him frivolous 'would you rather' questions if you are drawing a blank. You can find tons of examples of those on the internet."

"That's a good idea." Holly bit the inside of her cheek, nodding and taking in the advice. "He tunes me out after the first few words of a lecture anyway."

"Have simple interactions at first, ones that aren't heated or about anything over the top. Just get used to communicating again."

Susan stopped talking, and there was a long pause. Holly looked around the room uncomfortably.

"I hate Mick," Holly admitted abruptly and then covered her mouth. The words had popped out of her accidentally and felt like a confession.

Susan sat patiently waiting.

"He's a mess. I could never count on him when we were married, and I now feel him edging me out of Chance's life. They have this unspoken bond lately, this sick attachment because of the drugs. I think Chance feels this weird connection to his dad because they have both indulged and I never would. So now I feel like I am on the outside looking in, watching them get closer than ever. And then I feel like an asshole for feeling left out. Isn't that sick?"

Holly swiped at the tears on her cheeks and then looked down, pulling the wet Kleenex into long, thin strips in her lap.

"I hate that he is the father of my kids, and I blame him for his diseased DNA," she confessed. "The biggest mistake I ever made in my entire life was marrying him."

Susan penned a note on her notepad and continued to study her quietly.

"Am I going to have to pay for that terrible decision for the rest of my life?" She sniffed; it was hard to breathe with her nose so congested. "I loathe him. I hate that my bar was set so low that a semi-talented musician with an addiction was able to glide easily over it. Why did I accept that? That one thought is on repeat in my brain constantly. I wish I could go back in a time machine and slap myself for being so stupid. Ninety percent of the bullshit in my life stems from him. We're divorced and he is still messing up my life royally. Even from a distance."

"That's a form of self-abuse," Susan interjected. "Going

over and over the past in your mind and beating yourself up for the mistakes you made."

Holly hugged her arms to her chest. The air conditioning kicked on and sent shivers down her arms.

"You have to forgive yourself for not knowing." Susan looked at the clock. "Before you go, I want you to focus on today. You are spending so much time in the past, and there is nothing you can do about it. When you find yourself there and beating yourself up for what has happened, just re-center yourself. Take a breath and say, 'Today is all there is. I am okay today.'"

"Today is all there is. I am okay today," Holly parroted back. The words felt weak and powerless on her tongue. She made another appointment and started her drive home, feeling slightly relieved at saying the words out loud, but knowing they weren't going to be enough to calm her broken heart.

TWENTY-FIVE

A week later, before bed, dressed in loose shorts and a tank top, Holly laid on her floor on her back, grabbing the arches of her feet and pulling them down. The pose was called Happy Baby.

This actually feels pretty good. Maybe there is something to this after all. Susan would be proud of me.

She rolled on her back, side to side, deepening the stretch. Closing her eyes, she enjoyed the rocking sensation on her spine.

Murph wandered in, happy to see his owner sprawled out on the ground within licking distance, and took the opportunity to plant many sloppy kisses on her face. She laughed at him and pushed his nose playfully away when Dillon appeared.

"What are you doing?" he asked.

"Yoga, this pose is called Happy Baby." She looked up at him. "Come try it. You used to do it all the time when you were a tiny guy."

He landed on the floor next to her and pulled his legs into position easily. Children had incredible flexibility.

"You're a natural. Nice job," She praised. "Now rock slowly side to side."

Her phone rang, and she jumped to her feet and strained to listen for it, finally finding it buried on her bed. The Caller ID said unknown. Cautiously, she pressed the button and gave a wary, "Hello?"

"Hey, Momma," Chance said into the phone, and her heart lifted, a smile blooming on her face.

"Hey, Chancey." She felt her eyes moisten. He finally called her on his own, and she didn't realize how much she had missed the sound of his voice and how much she needed to hear it until that moment.

"What have you been doing?" she asked.

"Lots of homework. I'm pushing hard because there is nothing else to do here. My teacher says if I keep this up, I'll get a whole year of credits done here so I can graduate early."

"I didn't know you even wanted to do that."

"I'm considering it." He was quiet. "School really isn't my thing."

"There are other paths you can take, honey," Holly offered. "An apprenticeship. Or job shadowing in something you're interested in."

"That's a little too far in the future right now, Mom. Gotta go day by day."

"Right. Day by day," Holly agreed. "Well, you sound good."

"I do?"

"Yeah, you sound clear and focused."

"Thanks," he said. "Dad says I'm going to need to stay at your house when I am released."

"Yeah. That is for the best."

"Do I have a say in it at all?" he asked, his tone neutral.

"I'm afraid not. Your dad needs to fight his own battles. You need to focus on yourself and staying out of trouble."

"Okay," he conceded. Holly was relieved to hear his acceptance. It had been a battle for control since the beginning. "Can I talk to Dilly?"

"Sure. I love you, honey, and I am proud of the work you are doing on yourself."

"Thanks, Ma."

Holly handed the phone over to Dillon, who lit up when he was told his brother wanted to talk to him. He walked around the room and hallway as they chattered on and on and Murph ran alongside him jumping in excitement. Dillon must have saved up all his words over the last few weeks and was planning on using every single one of them now that he had his brother's full attention. Holly was struck by how normal the one-sided phone call sounded. It was sweet to hear them talk about video games.

He called.

Holly hugged herself. It was the first bit of good news she had gotten in months. He had a long way to go, but she felt hopeful that her boy was coming back.

TWENTY-SIX

A few days later, it was family therapy day at Sienna. Family therapy was getting easier, as Chance was beginning to accept that he was going to be returning to Holly's home. Chance was in a great mood, ecstatic that he had earned a pass and got to leave the facility grounds. After taking him out for ice cream, they had two more hours of time together and were sitting at a table chatting.

Holly was the odd man out, trying not to feel like a third wheel sitting at the table, quietly listening. Mick sat closely next to Chance, talking animatedly about guitars for a few minutes, a conversation she couldn't join because she knew nothing about instruments. Chance and Mick had played together since he could hold a guitar.

"Remember when you played at the farmer's market and made a hundred dollars in an hour?" Holly asked, trying to add something that didn't sound forced to the conversation. It was an old memory, from four years ago when he first learned to play a few real songs on the guitar.

Chance smiled. "Guess that is one of the perks of being tiny for your age." He turned toward his mother. "You made me make that sign saying I was playing for college money, and then I had to put half of it in my savings account. Once again, Mom is a total buzzkill."

"You probably could have made enough for college if you had stuck with it," Holly mused. "You were so excited, all those single dollar bills. You made it rain all over your brother."

"It didn't take much to make me happy back then," Chance admitted. "Life was easier when we were all together."

A fresh pang of sorrow laced guilt jabbed her chest. She still felt fully responsible for the destruction of her family.

Holly looked around the room at the small groups of parents visiting their kids. A stab to her heart, each one of these families was trapped inside the same nightmare.

Chance focused on a particularly pretty dark-haired girl next to them for a second.

"Who's that?" Mick asked, raising his eyebrows and squeezing Chance's shoulder in the familiar bro hold.

"Mackenzie," Chance answered. "She's super hot."

"I can see that," Mick agreed.

"Really, Mick? That's totally inappropriate," Holly chastised him.

"Relax, Mom, they keep us separated at all times. It's not like I can sneak out and bang her in the bathroom."

"Wow." Holly was floored.

Chance laughed at the rise he was getting in his mom. "You can't blame me. It's unnatural being locked up like this. I am having to take matters into my own hands on the daily."

Mick laughed and high-fived him, making Holly's blood pressure shoot up ten points.

"Dude," she said, trying to insert a playful tone into her

voice, "I don't want to hear about that. That's the kind of talk you save for your friends."

Mick looked away.

"Let's play some Uno," Holly suggested, trying to change the subject. She walked to the pile of games and pulled the cards from the stack.

"I have to go to the bathroom." Chance said and stood then leaned down conspiratorially and whispered, "I have to clear it with Anthony first. They don't let you take a shit here without permission."

"Come on, buddy," Holly said again. "You know I don't like it when you talk like that."

"Try not to say that stuff in front of your mother," Mick tried.

"Fine." He straightened up and walked to Anthony, leaving Holly and Mick at the table alone.

They both sat quietly for a minute. Holly took the chance to say something that had been on her mind since their last family therapy appointment. "You need treatment. You have for a long time, but now you need to be an example for Chance."

"You don't get to tell me what to do anymore. We aren't married."

"When it comes to keeping our kids safe, I will do whatever it takes to protect them."

"Is that a threat?" He sat up taller, and she could feel the shift in his disposition.

"If it has to be. I'll take you back to court if necessary."

"Can't you let go of your urge to control people for one second?"

"I will when you finally grow up."

"You never let up. You repeat the same things over and over. No wonder Chance is starting to tune you out."

"One of us has to be an adult. We have to be a team if we are going to be able to keep Chance on the right path. He will need two *healthy* parents supporting him when he gets out of here. We have to have a united front."

"I know that."

"But part of that means you need to get control over your own addictions. You need to admit you have a problem and address it, or how can we expect Chance to stay clean?" Holly continued. "Teenagers love to expose hypocrisy, and Chance seems to take more glee in it than most."

"Not now," Mick hissed as Chance sauntered back into the Rec Room. He stopped at a table, doing some kind of weird handshake with the tattooed boy sitting alone at it before heading back.

"Who is that?"

"That's Diego. He's hardcore. Dude is legit in a gang. He gave me this." He untucked his shirt and flashed an obnoxious gold Gucci belt buckle at them.

"And why did he do that?"

"Because we're homies."

Homies?

"It's like a family, Mom. We have each other's backs."

"You *have* a family."

Chance rolled his eyes at her again. "You'll never understand it."

"A gang isn't a family," Holly confirmed and started to deal the cards out one by one. When did his thinking get so messed up? Did she let him watch too many prison documentaries on YouTube? Where did this fascination with prison culture come from? Chance wasn't a gang banger; he was just a kid from the suburbs who listened to too much hip hop. Was it the music? Was it that stupid phone that was glued to his hand that he begged for and promised to pay for?

She scanned and scanned her memories, looking for the point of origin. The action, the day, the root cause of this behavior. When had all of this started? When did he stop being her sweet boy and turn into this wannabe thug? At first, she chalked it up to typical shock and awe teenage antics. A normal coming of age desire all teenagers succumbed to in order to separate from their parents. It was something that she had gone through herself ages ago.

I listened to Two Live Crew *and lived to be a decent human being. I thought my parents were idiots and out of touch, too. I snuck out at night to kiss boys.*

But Chance had taken it to a whole new level. He was barely recognizable anymore, and his thought process scared the hell out of Holly.

TWENTY-SEVEN

This is the summer from hell.

Holly was stuck at a red light with her windows rolled down. The van had become like an oven in the sustained upper ninety-degree temperatures. The gray vinyl cracked from heat exposure.

Perfect time for the AC to go out. I wonder if I can hold off on the repair until next summer. In another month, it will start cooling down.

Sweat prickled in her hairline and pooled behind her legs, making them stick to the seat. There was a line of wetness gathering at the bottom of her bra line. She lifted her hair up from the bottom of her neck and used an old brochure she found stuffed next to the console to fan herself. When they started moving again, Dillon was waving his hand out the window, swooping it down and like his fingers were surfing the winds. The gush of scorching air ruffled his hair.

"So, buddy, I wanted to talk to you. Chance is coming home in a few weeks, and we need to set some ground rules for everyone. I want to make sure you're ready."

"What kind of ground rules?"

"Nothing for you to worry about, silly, mostly things like treating each other with respect and the basics like no vaping, no smoking, no drinking, and no drugs."

"I know, I know."

"Life definitely is going to have to change."

"Again?" Dillon asked, slightly panicked.

"Not much for you, sweetness, but I just want to make sure you know that I am trying to do everything I can to provide a healthy place for all of us. I'm going to need you to speak up for yourself. I won't be able to see everything, so if you start to get worried or anxious, you need to come to me right away. Don't wait and worry and hope things will get better. Use your words and come to me right away. If you're feeling bad at all, I want to know about it. Understand?"

"Yeah," he said, no longer dancing his hand through the sweltering air. It sat stiffly in his lap.

She looked over at the boy. "You know we can talk about anything, right?"

"Yeah, Mom. I know."

"You're going to get your brother back."

Dillon sat back in the seat, silent.

"It's a good thing, Dilly. I promise."

A few days later, she answered a phone call. "Hey, Mom," Chance said into the phone. His voice was changing, getting deeper. It took on a more manly quality that pulled at her heartstrings. This was officially the longest amount of time he had ever been away from her.

"Hey, honey. You sound good."

"I do?" He laughed. "I'm actually having a good day today. We got to go to this park and climb this trail, and at the top, there was the most beautiful view. We had to write letters about the things we had done that we weren't proud of, and we could share them with the group or just keep them to ourselves, and then we burned them."

"That sounds very therapeutic. Did you want to share anything with me?"

"I'm an open book, Ma. I mean, I always get caught. The park, the car, the credit cards." He laughed at himself wryly. "It's like you have a sixth sense."

"You must have been sleeping in science class, but when the umbilical cord forms, it's like a superhighway of information from mother to baby. Even when it's physically severed at birth, the connection remains."

"You're such a science nerd."

"Are you excited to graduate your program?"

"Yeah, Diego graduated two days ago. It's been weird not having him around."

"I bet."

But I am glad.

She kept the last part to herself, knowing nothing good would come from saying it out loud.

"I'm ready to get back to my life again. It feels good to get back on track."

"We'll have to find you a sponsor and some local meetings."

"I know, Mom." He sighed. "They have been drilling it into us for weeks."

"I'll sign you up for driver's ed too."

"Hell yeah!" he said. "Everyone else probably finished already."

"It's not that big of a deal, honey. In a month, you'll be caught up."

"I always feel like I am falling behind." He paused. "Like I am always struggling to keep up."

"In what way?"

"All my friends' parents give them everything on a silver platter. One of the kids at my school got a brand new Camaro for his sixteenth birthday, and two days later, totaled it. And do you know what his dad did?"

"What?"

"Went right out and bought him another."

"Well, that's just ridiculous," Holly insisted. "That kid won't value anything. Even if I was so wealthy that I could do that for you, I wouldn't."

"I know," Chance answered and continued in a higher pitch, mocking her voice with a phrase she had repeated to him over and over. "These are the kids that peak in high school and will never survive in the real world."

"It's true!" Holly said. "But that doesn't sound like me at all." Smiling, she added, "I guess I *am* a little predictable." Her voice softened. "I miss you, honey, and I am looking forward to having you home."

"I know I've been a jerk lately. And I am sorry."

"What? An apology from a teenager?" Holly said, shocked. "I didn't think such a thing existed in the wild."

"I'm sorry, Mama, and I love you."

"I know, and I love you, too."

He had come a long way. They all had. Everyone had evolved from the situation except Mick, who remained stuck in his own addiction and was unwilling to face it. Holly was proud of Chance. He had come so far, but she knew the hardest battles were still ahead.

TWENTY-EIGHT

Release day was a sunny yet thankfully cool day in late August, the week before school began. Holly got up early, unable to sleep more than four hours. Having Chance gone left such a void, and she ached to have both her boys under the same roof again. She drove the now-familiar four-hour long route the final time and waited in the lobby. Holly chose a seat and picked at a stain on her t-shirt while she waited, tapping her sandaled toes against the chair leg nervously. Adam opened the door and beckoned her down the hallway all smiles. "Today is a good day."

"It is." She let out a breath. "But I have to be honest, I'm all over the place."

"That's completely normal. Chance is, too. Let's talk a bit before we bring him in." Adam waved her to a seat next to his desk.

"We are going to be writing a sober living contract together that Chance will sign as part of his treatment plan." He handed her a sheet of paper. "Read through this generic one and then, if there is anything to add, we can amend it."

Holly glanced through it, noting the required meetings

and random clean drug tests. "I'd like to add that he treats all family members with respect. No swearing, follow the household rules. No vaping."

"These are all good additions. But I have to tell you that nicotine use is a tough one to completely eliminate. It is a crutch that is heavily leaned on in the recovery community."

In shock, Holly's brow wrinkled in frustration as she tried to accept what he was saying. "But it's still wrong. He's only fifteen. It's against the law."

"Absolutely, it is. But the reality is that Chance will be participating in meetings where adults will be present. An overwhelming majority of the people at these meetings use nicotine in one form or another."

"What, so I'm just supposed to overlook illegal behavior?"

"No. You can try to fight it, but I am telling you from experience it will be an uphill battle. And of all the battles you are going to be asked to fight, you might want to save your energy for the ones that really matter."

Holly's mouth dropped open; she stammered and then was silent, sitting in shock. Stunned that Adam was asking her to look the other way. "But it's terrible for his lungs and his developing body, not to mention studies show it is incredibly addictive as well."

"I wholeheartedly agree. It is a bad habit for anyone, whether you are fifteen or not. But I'm telling you from experience that you will need to be constantly vigilant and that will get exhausting. You want to set yourself up for success, and if you lose some of the smaller battles you have a better chance of winning the war."

"I just cannot accept that."

"And you don't have to, but it is likely he will do it anyway."

Holly swallowed her urge to fight for what was right. Adam had done this song and dance hundreds of times before, so she knew she had to defer to his wisdom, but everything inside of her hated it. Despised the fact she had to change her normal expectations and rules for her children in order to be more successful in supporting Chance's sobriety.

"He's been in a tightly controlled environment here at Sienna. Now that he will be released, it is important that he still has a very structured day, that he has responsibilities to take care of himself and his surroundings. He needs to contribute around the house, maybe get a part-time job when he's sixteen or play a sport. To be successful, Chance needs a purpose and a daily schedule that will keep him busy. The worst thing you can do is give him too much unrestricted free time at this stage. He's been told what to do and when to do it for the last few months. To go from that to total freedom is a recipe for disaster. If he finds himself bored or with too much time on his hands, he will find an excuse to use."

Holly nodded. "I understand."

"I cannot stress enough that putting him back into the same environment that created this problem is what you need to avoid at all costs. He's going to need new people, places, and things in his life to replace the old ones. He will likely fight you on this and try to give you excuses or just outright lie about his old group of friends and his hookups. Saying things like, they used to do drugs and are now completely clean. Always remember that addicts are incredibly adept at getting what they want. Master manipulators, you could call them."

"It's like you're giving me a newborn baby again that I have to take care of twenty-four-seven, but instead of being sweet and cuddly, he's a teenager with raging mood swings that hates my guts."

Adam laughed. "There is some truth to that. Don't be a friend. He can be your friend when he's an adult. Right now, he needs a parent. Remember, boundaries. Tough love."

"That's never been my problem. His dad is the one who insists on being his friend."

"Mick is going to have to change as well. Has he thought any more about treatment for himself?"

"He'll never go because then he'd have to accept the party is over, and that is not something he is ready to admit."

"Then it is important that Chance stays with you. You have the only healthy household in this situation, so until Mick addresses his own issues with addiction, it is not safe for Chance or Dillon to have overnight visits with him."

"Can you say that to Mick because I swear, the minute my mouth opens, he tunes me out completely."

"Yes, I will call him today and speak to him about it."

"What about the music? Is it dangerous for him to be listening to all that gangster rap, lyrics about popping pills and smoking dope? Seems like it would just put bad ideas in his head, and the kid has enough bad ideas for three people already. He doesn't need any help."

"I wouldn't worry about that. The studies don't support that as being a problem or contributing to drug use. It's just part of pop culture."

"Okay," Holly relented.

"Are you ready to see him?"

"Yes." Holly was apprehensive yet eager to take him home. It had been a long summer without him, a piece of her heart had been missing and now she was going to get it back.

Adam turned to the phone and made a call, and two minutes later, Chance burst through the door.

"Mommy!" he said ironically and then swept her into his thin arms. Holly hugged him so tight, closing her eyes and breathing in his scent of cinnamon and pine. It had been a really long time since he had been genuinely happy to see her, and she was starved for his affection.

He pulled back and sat down on the chair chomping on gum. Holly studied him, his clear eyes and quick smile. He was keyed up, but in an excited night before Christmas kind of way. He was calm and sober and buzzing with happiness. The flat, angry, aggressive boy that he had been was replaced with this fresh new one. A slate wiped clean by his hard work and perseverance. Like he had shed a toxic, diseased skin and now was regenerated and brand-new again.

"We have a sober living contract to go through together, and then we are ready to release you and send you on your way."

Chance clapped his hands together. "Can't wait. No offense, Adam, but I am never coming back here."

"No offense, but we don't ever *want* to see you again." Adam smiled. He turned toward the paperwork and explained the contract line by line. Chance scribbled his initials hastily at each spot, as fast as possible, knowing that each little line he filled was a step closer to his freedom.

"You've done a lot of good work here, Chance. You have all the resources you need to go home and be successful. Now, the hard part starts, and it is up to you."

Adam separated the papers and handed the carbon copy to Chance, who folded it and promptly shoved it into a box of his belongings that sat on top of this crumpled laundry.

"Are we good now?"

"We're good." Adam stood and opened the door.

Holly held out a hand awkwardly and then hugged Adam instead and said, "Thank you for giving me my boy back."

"You're welcome. Remember, structure is key. Good luck, Holly."

Walking out into the sunny summer day felt incredible. With his basket of clothing and books in his arms, Chance stepped out into the sun and ran to the van, eager to put physical distance between himself and the treatment center.

"Did you want to drive us home?" Holly asked with a smile, dangling the keys in front of him.

"Really?" He beamed at her.

"You need the practice if you're going to start driver's ed soon."

She tossed the keys at him, and he caught them with his left hand and then jumped into the driver's seat, wrapped the seatbelt around himself, and adjusted the mirrors. "I feel so good, Mom."

"You look so good, honey." And he did. He was her sweet boy again, smiling and content. Morphing the past few months closer into the man he would become, giving Holly flickers of what he would look like as an adult. "Treatment was hard, but you did it. You did the work, and I am so proud of you." It felt incredible to say those words. It had been so long since he had done something that would warrant her pride. His smile was as wide as hers as he sat up straighter in his seat, puffing up from her praise.

"Feels like I've been gone forever," Chance admitted.

"Feels like we are all getting released from jail," Holly agreed. "Now, we just need to work the plan and do the things you are required to do. Get you set up for outpatient services. Fulfill your end of the sober living contract."

"Why do I still gotta go to outpatient? I am so sick of treatment." Chance was irritated.

"It's part of your discharge plan," Holly answered. "It's non-negotiable. Besides, it won't be half as hard as what you've just gone through, and if you work the plan and complete your steps, you'll be able to phase it out pretty quickly."

"I know." She could tell he was frustrated, but he wiped his face clean of it. Putting the van in drive and pressing the gas pedal, he said, "Today is a good day, Mom. I can't wait to get home and see some of my friends."

TWENTY-NINE

"Surprise!" Dillon shouted the loudest, happy to see his big brother walk through the door of their home. Her heart squeezed when she saw the boys embrace. Her small house was crammed full of kids and parents for a surprise party that Stacey dreamed up and fully executed on her own to welcome Chance home.

"Careful there, guys. It almost looks like you might love each other," Holly teased.

"I missed you, Chance." Dillion idolized his brother, looking up at him like he was Captain America with stars in his eyes.

"I missed you too, nerd." Chance ruffled his hair and then pushed him playfully away, and then dissolved into his group of friends, giving Blake a bro-hug as the group rushed him and thrust him up on their shoulders. He narrowly missed hitting the dining room chandelier, laughing the entire time.

Shaking her head at their antics, Holly walked over to Stacey. "Thanks for setting all this up, girl."

"Of course," Stacey said, "this is a huge day! Your summer sucked, but we finally have something to celebrate."

The room was filled with Chance's friends and a few of their parents, Stacey and Sarah, Dillon's best friend was over, and Mick was in the corner. Chance's playlist was on, and everyone pretended to tolerate it and ignore the lyrics.

Holly busied herself with setting out silverware and getting plates set up on the tables, and then she started pouring soda into glasses. It was the first time at any social gathering that there was no alcohol for the adults, and it felt strange.

"What can I get you?" Holly smiled at Blake's mom. "We're creating a safe environment for Chance, so we don't have any wine, but just about everything else you could ever want in terms of sugary soda is an option."

It felt good to celebrate her son's success instead of hiding. To show the parents of Chance's friends that he was healthy and doing well and his head was screwed back on straight. She had heard through the grapevine that, collectively, many of the parents were leery of him. She didn't blame them, if the tables were turned, she would feel the exact same way. The summer had forced Chance to lose so much, and she didn't want him to have to lose his friends too. She was relieved to see that he hadn't burned any bridges yet. Starting over again without any friends would have been even harder.

After serving all the drinks, she finally sat down on the sofa, exhausted from the eight-hour drive, and bit into a slice of pepperoni pizza. As she wiped the dribble of grease from her chin with her hand, Mick crossed the room and sat next to her, folding into the group of parents.

"He looks good, Holly," Mick said.

"He is good. For now," Holly said between bites. "But we need to keep a close eye on him. Major structure and boundaries are what he needs to be successful."

The parents in the group nodded their heads. "Structure is so important for teenagers. They fight us on it, but it is truly something they need and crave," Anna said, taking it upon herself to become the unauthorized spokesman of the group.

"I want to thank all of you for giving Chance the ability to prove that he has changed. I know as a parent it is terrifying that something like this could happen, and your natural tendency is to cut him out of your kids' lives, but the fact that you are giving him a chance to redeem himself means so much to me—to us." She awkwardly adjusted to include Mick.

Most of the adults nodded and met her eyes, letting Anna speak for them again. "You know we absolutely adore Chance. And we all hope this gets him back on track and living a normal, healthy life again. We just want to see him healthy and whole." Her voice was dripping with fake concern. It was a little much to swallow, but for now, Holly let it slide.

"Me too," she agreed, raising her glass of Pepsi. She was glad to host the welcome home party, but what she really craved was quiet. She felt judged for what had happened, like she was always under a microscope with the parents in her neighborhood. It was hard to fully relax under their suspicious eyes that calculated and recorded every little thing she said and did. Mick assumed his regular post as the mayor of bean town, and Chance put a guitar in Mick's hands, and he played requests. He lapped up their applause and attention like a kitten with a dish of cream while Chance sat next to him, starry-eyed and his biggest fan.

Mick always has to make everything about him. Even today.

She was annoyed, finally seeing a lot of his behaviors as they truly were. Her therapy and her books were shining a light on bad behavior that she had ignored for far too long. Her eyes were open now, and there was a shift happening. She was no longer numb and oblivious to what Mick was doing. She saw him for what he was. A man who needed help, but who needed to save himself. It had taken her so long to see that one simple truth; that no matter how much she begged and pleaded and tried to keep things together, it was impossible. Divorcing him had been the right decision, but now she needed to free herself from the guilt and work through her own issues of self-worth. She needed to return the responsibility for Mick's life back into his own hands.

An hour into the impromptu concert, and likely when the shakes probably started in, Mick excused himself, hugging the boys before he left, and then slipped quickly out of the house without so much as a goodbye to Holly.

As the party started to dwindle and Holly made promises to parents to drive their boys home, she was happy to see the parents relax enough to leave and trust their children's safety in her home. At first, Anna narrowed her eyes at the suggestion, but to save face in front of the other parents, smiled and nodded when Zach asked to stay because saying no would have exposed her as a hypocrite, something she couldn't allow.

Zach pushed Chance playfully into the wall as the boys ran up the stairs two at a time.

That's interesting. When did they become such good friends?

"Go! Sit." Stacey pointed at the sofa. "You have to be exhausted. Let me get this." She picked up random dirty plates and glasses and filled the dishwasher and emptied the trash.

"We can leave it until tomorrow." Holly offered before collapsing into a pile on the purple sofa. She yawned and put her feet up on the rustic coffee table, a table that was worn and scratched the day she got it. Every piece of furniture she owned was aged and weathered on purpose. It was a trick she had learned when the boys were babies; the inevitable scratches and damage that came with raising teenage boys just made her simple furnishings that much more beautiful.

"Don't start that now," Stacey chastised. "It's catching." She stifled her own yawn. "You did good, Mama. He's home."

"Yeah. I'm a little concerned about him acclimating to life again. Putting him right back into the same system that broke him. Same school, same friends." She yawned again. "He's got so many restrictions on his time and hoops to jump through that I'm expecting his anger to eventually rear its ugly head." Hearing the boys whooping and laughing upstairs, she explained, "Sure, he's happy today. Just getting to leave treatment was one of the best days of his life, but I'd be lying if I didn't say that my anxiety is ratcheting up and I'm bracing for blowback."

"I can understand that." Stacey's warm eyes met hers. "But you can't stay hyper-vigilant. It's not sustainable."

"I know." Holly exhaled. "It was nice to have the parents here, but honestly, I'm glad they have cleared out. The scrutiny is painful."

"You have nothing to prove to them."

"I feel like I do," Holly corrected her. "I mean, I *am* teaching some of their kids. They are going to want me to lead by example."

"You did that," Stacey pointed out. "Immediately. When you saw there was a problem, you addressed it in a significant way. I know for a fact, Bob's son got busted, high as a kite sleeping in his car a few weeks ago, and he was never sent away to treatment. They just swept it under the rug."

"Well, in Chance's case it was a bit more than being passed out in a car. But yes, parents in this school district are more at ease covering things up and protecting their kids' futures at all costs. It just teaches them to lie and manipulate. I will never do that for my kids. If they can make the choices, they can live with the consequences."

"Good for you."

"That's the only way they will ever learn. God, I wish I had a glass of wine," Holly lamented.

"I bet. You're living in a dry county now?"

"Yes, that was the recommendation, until I have an effective way to lock it up, and honestly, I don't have the energy to even think about it."

"That will give you the perfect excuse to visit me then," Stacey said. "I'll keep some rose in the chiller at all times for you."

"That's how I know you love me." Holly loved how easy things were with Stacey. She never had to put up any defenses with her or explain anything. Stacey just loved and accepted her as she was. A friend like that was one of life's greatest gifts.

THIRTY

The happy homecoming was short-lived. Less than a week later, Chance was pitching a fit at the idea of going to more meetings. Holly was finishing up the dishes after grilling hamburgers and the last of the summer's sweet corn. The last thing she wanted to do was get back in the car and take him to an AA meeting, but she had made a commitment and was determined to see it through.

"I don't want to go."

"Come on, buddy, you have to go. You have to find an AA group that you want to attend regularly. Maybe this one will be better."

"It's such a waste of time. A bunch of old dudes sitting around complaining about their lives and begging for sympathy."

"It's part of your sober living contract. That is what the center recommended, and that is what we are doing."

"Fine," he mumbled, accepting his fate.

"You can drive to it," Holly offered as she typed the address into the GPS. Chance drove slowly, focusing on the task ahead of him, following the directions of the navigation system. Holly gripped the handle on the door and pressed the lock button when he turned a corner on the roughest side of town and the destination was a church parking lot. There on the lawn, a horde of nearly fifty significantly older teens and young adults stood in groups, smoking and vaping in such a frenzy that there was a cloud of smoke that permanently hovered above them held in place by the low tree branches. Congregating in loud groups, it was a mass of young adult energy that instantly spooked Holly, and she was surprised by the intensity of the fear gripping her belly.

This is part of his sober living contract?

It felt sick and wrong, and she was so internally conflicted, she began to chew on her thumbnail.

Chance pulled in and shut off the car.

"We can stay here until the meeting starts," Holly offered weakly, pressing the lock button on the door again to be sure.

"No, Mom, I will be fine." He unlocked the door and walked out into the group, finding someone he knew from treatment right away. Chance pulled him in by the elbow for a fist bump that turned into an elaborate handshake. Holly kept her eyes locked on Chance, watching his interactions and scanning the crowd. She felt uneasy leaving him in the center of a throng of 'kids' that felt so much older. 'Kids' that had face tattoos and grew up on the wrong side of the tracks. Kids that weren't really kids anymore at all.

Her son was one of them now, lumped in with the other addicts. She struggled to accept he was no better than they were. Until this summer, she had always been able to draw a thick black line, separating her son and the good kids from the bad apples. Now, the line was blurred and indistinct. Now, she knew the reality was that addiction crossed every line— economic, social, the barriers of wealth and privilege. No one was safe. No one was exempt. Addiction didn't discriminate.

As much as the parents at her school wanted to believe they were safe and sound in their upper-class neighborhood, she knew the truth.

Chance waved a small wave back at her, and then the crowd of smoke swallowed him up. Holly scanned the group feverishly for a glimpse of him, panic crawling like a spider up her spine. The total loss of control made her feel like she was in free-fall and tightened her chest. Her eyes scanned and scanned, searching for that familiar wave of brown hair, his thin frame, but found nothing.

How is this a safe place for Chance? How is this a good environment?

She didn't want to leave. She wanted to walk into that church and pull him into her arms and to safety. It took everything in her to finally put the van in reverse and pull out of the parking lot. Every minute of the next sixty ticked by painfully slowly.

He's so young. Why did all of this have to happen with him so young? This is terrifying.

The slippery slope of things she never wanted her kids to be exposed to was now part of her normal. The bad kids she had screened against, the troublemakers and the thrill-seekers. She had carefully curated his list of friends since birth, and now all that work was for nothing. All those lectures and all that effort was for naught. He was now surrounded by kids who experimented, whose lives had been touched by addiction and trauma and suffering. They had welcomed her son with open arms, and it was a group she had wanted nothing to do with. This group was filled with the castoffs and the accidents, the kids who were born into homes with parents that weren't involved, that had no business being parents in the first place.

I have become the judgmental twat that I always hated.

And now these throw-away kids have become the treatment approved support system for my son. Chance's new healthy habits require him to be surrounded by recovering addicts and alcoholics.

Holly discovered the word recovering did nothing to soften the blow. She drove the streets aimlessly chewing on her lip, glancing nervously at the clock as the minutes slowly ticked by, and then pulled into the parking lot ten minutes before the end of the meeting. At precisely eight pm, droves of teenagers and young adults poured out onto the lawn and sidewalks again, immediately lighting up a cigarette or sucking hard on a vape. A sight that filled Holly with dread. Finally, Chance emerged from the cloud of people and smoke with a big smile on his face. Holly pasted one on her own to match his as he opened the door and climbed into the van. The sharp scent of cigarette smoke hit her nostrils and made her see red. She swallowed back the words she wanted to say, hearing Adam's advice in her head, and instead asked, "How was it?"

"Pretty cool," Chance said. "Some of those kids have really been through it."

"Anything you want to share?"

"Nah." He settled into the car quietly, and she drove them home, lost in her own thoughts. She was scared to admit that the fear in the pit of her stomach seemed to be permanently lodged there. It was her new normal, one she was forced to accept, but one that she loathed.

THIRTY-ONE

Chance was cagey, drumming his fingers on the countertop while he fidgeted on the stool. His energy was off the charts. "Today's the day, Mom." He had finished the classroom portion of driver's ed in record time, completely focused on the freedom that was on the other side of the test he was taking that day. It was the final hurdle he had to clear to get his license. He chewed at his fingernails, which were bit down to the quick already.

"It's a big one. Try not to be nervous." Holly forced a hug on him.

"Have you met me?" Chance joked. "If I don't pass this test, I'm going to want to end it all."

"It's just driver's ed. You can take it again. There's no need to be so melodramatic."

She dropped him off at the school for the final test. He swiped his hand through his hair and gave her a little wave and then rushed into the building.

Dear God, let him pass this test. This taxi driver is exhausted.

She passed the time grocery shopping and picking up the

ingredients for her homemade mac and cheese, hoping they would have something to celebrate. Two hours later, she sat in the parent pick up line, waiting for him to come back out of the building. He finally emerged heading toward the car, head bowed, walking fast. She studied him, trying to decipher if it was a jubilant walk or one of defeat.

Shit. He doesn't look happy.

He pulled open the door and sat quietly, revealing nothing.

"So?" Holly asked, unable to wait any longer.

"I missed it by one."

Holly was silent. Visions of him picking up Dillon after school and swinging by the grocery store for a gallon of milk disappeared in a puff of smoke.

Then the corners of his mouth started to curve into a small smile as he pressed his lips together. Confused, Holly looked over at him, her lips pursed and her forehead crinkled as the grin broke out even bigger. "I mean, I only could *miss* one more." He waved the freshly earned driving certificate in Holly's face.

"Uhh!" He grunted, gloating loud and proud, dancing in his seat. Uhh!" He rolled his shoulder toward her and laughed. "I did it. No more feeling behind the other kids. This guy is back on track." He punched one fist in the air. "Uhh!" She chuckled at his weird triumphant grunting noises.

"You little turd." Holly shook her head in disbelief. "You got it? No lie? For real?

"For real, for real," Chance said. "We have to go to the DOT, but it's a done deal."

"I am so proud of you, honey."

Holly reached forward and lovingly stroked the dashboard of the rusting van. "Looks like we are going to be sharing this sweet ride together."

"I hate this thing. It's so embarrassing."

"It's freedom," Holly corrected. "And it didn't cost you anything. My dad made me buy my own car and get my own insurance. I'm not asking you to do either of those things."

"I know."

"Maybe you should get a job, and then you'll be able to get your own car that you're not so embarrassed to drive around town." Remembering Adam's advice to keep him busy, but not wanting to push him, she was planting the seed.

"Maybe I will." He crossed his arms across his chest. "I forgot to tell you I got a sponsor."

"You did?"

"His name is Cody."

"How old is Cody?"

"Twenty-three."

Shit. He's an adult.

"I'd like to meet him."

"I knew you'd say that." Chance tapped his hand on his leg. "He's coming to pick me up for the meeting, and then we are going to a house party after."

"House party?" Holly's voice registered up an octave.

"Don't worry, Mom. It's people from AA and NA. It's a sober party."

But they are still five to seven years older than you, buddy. There is a massive difference between the maturity levels of boys between fifteen and twenty-three. A night and day difference.

Holly kept her mouth shut, biting back her own fears and worries about her son hanging out with people so much older. People who were in recovery.

This is just another thing I will need to get used to. Another reality I will need to accept. He is growing up faster than I ever wanted. I hate this so much.

THIRTY-TWO

Holly changed into her pajamas after work and put a frozen pizza into the oven. After successfully surviving another week of school and appointments, she pulled out a beer from her secret closet fridge and cracked it open. It was the only place to secure her drinks that made any sense. She had installed a combination lock on the door, and for the time being, she had to lock up her booze.

It's like being a prisoner in my own home.

Pizza and beer was a Friday night treat she always loved, left over from her college days. She took a long sip, the hoppy notes bitter on her tongue, and then heard the doorbell. Walking toward it slowly while looking at her phone, Chance came running down the stairs, jumped onto the landing, and then whipped open the door. Standing there was a tall, dark-haired man dressed in jeans and a gray Affliction shirt. "Mom, you said you wanted to meet my sponsor. This is Cody."

Holly tucked a loose curl behind her ear and pasted a smile on her face as she adjusted her flannel pajama top.

"Well, I would have loved a little more warning, Chance."

She stepped forward and shook his hand. He looked clear-eyed and clean-cut. Sporting a military high and tight haircut, he smelled like cedar, a welcome change from the second-hand smoke she had anticipated. "Please, come in." Cody took a step into the house. "It's really nice to meet you," she replied, hoping the beer wasn't on her breath. "We're getting ready to have some pizza if you'd like a slice." She walked into the kitchen, pretending to check on the pizza, then she slid her beer can behind a cereal box that was left out on the counter.

Cody watched her effort to conceal the beer and laughed. "You don't have to do that, you know. You're not the one with the problem."

Holly flushed. "I try to lead by example, but at the end of a long week, pizza and a beer is my reward."

"Totally understandable," he answered and sat down on a stool at the counter.

"Can I get you anything to drink?" she asked without thinking. "I mean…" she stammered.

"It's okay." He laughed good-naturedly. "I'm sure this is rough for you."

Holly nodded in relieved agreement. "It definitely has not been easy." She smiled at him and relaxed a bit. "Can you tell me about yourself?"

"Well, I'm not sure what you want to know, but I have been sober for nine years. My DOC was alcohol."

She looked puzzled.

"Drug of choice," he answered. "I have a four-year-old daughter, and she's my why. I am focused on re-establishing a relationship with her." He stopped for a minute, and his voice took on a much more somber tone. "My alcoholism hurt her so much."

Holly studied him as the obvious pain and shame washed

across his face, and he wrung his hands after the confession, but then continued on, "I am a house painter. A Virgo. I like long walks on the beach," he teased, and Chance enjoyed watching his mom shift uncomfortably.

"You're also a joker, I see." Holly smiled.

"Only on the things that don't matter. I promise." He put his hand over his heart like a boy scout, and she laughed at his earnestness. "We're going to a meeting tonight and then the house party. Don't worry, it's 100% drug and alcohol-free. We will be pretty late, but I'll make sure to get him home safely." He looked at the phone in her hand. "You can add me as a contact. That way you can always get a hold of me when I take Chance to meetings."

Hearing that sent a burst of relief that decompressed her worry valve slightly. She unlocked her phone and handed it to him.

"How did you guys meet?"

"I run the young people's meetings once a month at Cornerstone."

"Ah."

"We have a really good group of kids and young adults there. It is easier for the younger ones to feel more comfortable among their peers. The other meetings are filled with angry grandpas, and it's hard for kids like Chance to relate."

"I can understand that," she admitted. Cody was clean-cut, looked directly in her eyes when he spoke, and had a calm purpose that made her feel safe enough to entrust her fifteen-year-old in his care. "It's just that he's so young. All of this is overwhelming."

"Jesus, Mom, what's with the third degree?" Chance was at the door, hand on the knob, itching to go.

"With Chance's history, it is the safest place for him to be right now. And he'll get to meet other people with a similar story. Developing relationships with other young people in recovery is incredibly important for his sobriety. Chance has had to start all over, so he needs new friends that are sober and working the program, or he will get swept back up into using all over again."

The words 'using again' cued up the panic in her heart. Sensing this, Cody reached out and squeezed her shoulder. "You can trust me. I've got him."

She paused and let go. Cody was right. He was sober and trustworthy and obviously had a lot more experience with the battle Chance was fighting than she did.

"Okay then, have fun," Holly said, wrapping up the conversation.

"Hey, knucklehead!" Cody razzed Chance. "Tell your mama you love her." He turned and started walking out the door and toward his truck.

"I love you, Mom," Chance repeated obediently and then left quickly, falling in line behind him like a baby duck.

I like this guy already.

———

She heard his familiar clichéd knock on the door. *Da-Da-Da-Da-Da. Pause. Da. Da.* "Guys, your dad is here!" Holly shouted up the stairs as she opened the door to Mick's lazy smile. She waved him inside to wait for the boys.

"I met Chance's sponsor yesterday," she offered.

And he's more solid and stable than you are.

"You did?" Mick asked. "What's he like?"

"An adult," Holly answered. "He's twenty-three, but he definitely has his shit together."

"That's good," Mick said.

"They've been going to meetings every day and talking

on the phone. Cody has been really good for Chance." Mick looked bored, so she changed the subject. "What are you guys up to today?"

"Well, I was thinking laser tag," Mick said excitedly, and Dillon whooped, scrambling to find his shoes with Chance right behind him.

"Anytime I get to shoot the old man is a good time," Chance teased him.

"Old man?" Mick asked, somewhat hurt. "I'm not that old. Last time we were there, the waitress thought I was your older brother."

"Dude she was lyin' to you." Chance punched his dad in the arm. "Those girls work for tips. She's gonna say what she needs to say to get you to part with your money."

"You're probably right," he said and then preened in the entry mirror while Holly rolled her eyes.

Jesus. He probably still thinks he can bag a twenty-something.

Dillon grabbed Mick's hand and dragged him from the mirror, impatiently chomping at the bit to go.

"Dad!" he whined, "Let's go—o," dragging out the syllables in protest.

"Ready to shoot something?" Mick asked, throwing the keys to Chance. "Wanna drive, Champ?"

They walked out of the house, ribbing each other loudly, and Holly sank down on the step, enjoying the silence. Boy energy was fierce and loud. Like having a herd of elephants running around, destroying and consuming everything that wasn't nailed down. Even to have a few hours of silence seemed like a gift.

It almost felt normal again. The boys were off playing with their dad. Mick was a terrible father, but a fun playmate. She probably should grade some papers, but the idea of having a little bit of time to herself to read a book or hit the garden center for a new plant was calling her name. Using the excuse of wanting to give Susan something to be proud of at the next session, she gathered her things and drove to a nursery and picked out two new plants, including a fussy orchid that she rescued from the nearly dead sale rack. She had learned enough from her elderly neighbor to keep it alive and to possibly coax out another bloom if she was lucky. Holly saw orchids as a beautiful challenge, and she loved being able to force beauty from what looked like dead twigs. She also chose a lime green pathos that would flourish anywhere. Her two plants were as different as her two boys.

After getting home, she put on an audiobook to listen to, then she put on her gloves and repotted them into pretty pots with proper drainage, and then found them the right light in her home. Just digging in the potting soil for an hour made her feel brand new.

Look at me! I am killing this self-care thing.

THIRTY-THREE

I t was late September, and the air was getting cooler and the days were getting shorter. In the school pick up line, Holly waited for Chance. Finally, he poured out of the school amongst the surge of hoodie encased teens talking to Zach while laughing and looking down at his phone. Chance walked toward her van with Zach in tow. Zach was the New Hope golden boy, somehow always looking like moneyed casual personified. Wearing designer jeans and thick hoodies from Supreme and other high-end skater brands, he followed behind Chance with his eyes hidden behind aviators. Pulling open the door, Chance leaned in with a big smile and asked sweetly, "Can Zach drive me home? He just got his license."

"I don't know." Holly was unsure.

"Come on, Mom. I'm doing everything I've been asked to do," he begged, and Holly was having a hard time disagreeing with that statement. It *was* true that he was doing everything. Daily meetings, clean drug tests. So far so good. "Please?" He laced his fingers together and pleaded, "Please?"

"Straight home," Holly finally agreed. "I'm not kidding."

"I promise, Ms. Simon." Zach smiled his winning smile with his perfect white teeth and crossed his fingers over his heart in a gesture that felt like he was mocking her.

She watched them walk away, recognizing a familiarity she had never seen between the two before. Zach was always in the group of boys that came around the house, but always on the outside fringes of it. As far as she knew, Zach was somebody that Chance barely tolerated. But the way it looked now as they walked away together cutting up, she had a feeling they were becoming closer than Chance had let on.

Awesome. Going to be forced to spend more time with Ahna. Can't wait.

She picked up Dillon and was happy to see Zach pulling away when she got to the driveway. Dillon and Chance were both in great moods, chattering away at her, asking every teenage boy's favorite question.

"What's for dinner?"

"How about the steakhouse tonight?"

"Really?" Dillon was immediately excited. "What are we celebrating?"

"That both my boys are doing well in school."

"Yeah! We haven't been there in so long."

Holly felt like letting loose a little. It was more than she liked to spend on a meal, but things were going so well, and she wanted to take Susan's advice and leave the rules behind. "There's one catch."

Chance groaned. "I knew it was too good to be true!"

"No talking about anything yucky. No treatment, no grades, no rules, no work."

"Really?" Chance asked, a big smile breaking out across his face.

"Yep. Just quality time."

Maybe Susan is on to something.

The hostess sat them at a booth, and the boys slid in across from her. It was obvious her boys were siblings; they shared so many of the same characteristics—the long, thick, skater boy hair; the square jawlines; the brown eyes. Dillon's hair was lighter, but otherwise, he was a carbon copy of his older brother. Chance was getting leaner, with elongated arms and legs, but he was short for his age and had always been the smallest kid in the class.

They pulled peanuts out of the galvanized bucket on the table and cracked their shells, dumping the empty shells onto the floor. A rebel act of defiance that no teenage boy could resist. Then a sweet waitress set a basket of warm, buttery rolls in front of them and handed out white containers of whipped cinnamon butter. They were already on their second basket when Holly asked, "Would you rather be able to fly or be invisible?"

"Fly," Chance said. "No, invisible. That way you could spy on people and know what they were saying about you when you weren't around."

"Fly," answered Dillon. "No doubt."

"Would you rather have three legs or three arms?" she asked.

"Legs!" Dillon responded. "Man, I could run so fast with three legs."

"Arms, totally," Chance answered. "Imagine how awesome you'd be at Call of Duty."

Both boys nodded in agreement and stuffed more bread in their mouths. The waitress came by again.

"Are you ready to order?"

"Yes, please. I'd like the New York strip, medium, with the loaded baked potato and a salad with ranch." She usually ordered for the boys. It was an efficient habit, but this time, she pointed at Chance while the waitress hovered, poised with her pad.

Shocked, he opened the menu nervously and then said, "I'll have the same. Medium well, please."

"Dillon, tell the lady what you'd like."

"A sirloin, right, Mom?" He looked up at her, so serious. Holly nodded back, encouraging him.

"And for your sides?"

"Steak fries and green beans, please!" he said proudly. Holly enjoyed watching him level up, understanding that ordering his own food at a restaurant was super manly. He sat up straighter in the booth. The waitress thanked them and walked away with their menus to put their order in.

"Good job, guys," Holly praised them.

"You've never let us order before," Chance said. "Are you sure you're my mom?"

She laughed. "Yes, honey. It's time I let you start doing things for yourselves that you should have been doing all along. You are both old enough to start doing more."

She took a sip from her water glass. She wanted to tell them they would be doing their own laundry now and that they would have to take out the garbage on garbage day, but she bit the instructions back. Tonight, she just wanted one day without worrying or controlling them. She wanted one day where she could relax and enjoy the men they were growing up to be. To let her guard down and enjoy being with them fully in the moment.

"Next question. You got one?" she asked Dillon.

He smiled wide and said, "Would you rather eat rotten eggs or drink rotten milk?"

Holly made a gagging face. "Disgusting. Man, this one is hard. I think the milk. Although I might puke."

"Eggs all the way," Chance said. "Sheer volume, one bite and you're done."

"Smart," Holly said, laughing at him.

It felt good. Eating dinner like a normal family, discussing silly things. It felt so normal, and she didn't realize how much her life had changed over the last summer. The constant pit of worry in her stomach and the brain spinning, mind-occupying stress she had been under. Playing a simple game and listening to them laugh and eat their weight in cinnamon buns was so wonderfully simple and good. She had missed it so much.

THIRTY-FOUR

Holly sat in the sun on the patio at Stacey's house on an unseasonably warm fall day, the kind that was rare in October as they sipped on chardonnay and nibbled on olive tapenade on French bread and green grapes. Huge ceramic pots of orange mums and cheery white pumpkins decorated Stacey's deck.

"How are things going, love?" Stacey asked with a warm smile.

"Actually, they are looking up. Therapy is helping. Even though I needed another appointment in my life like I needed a hole in my head."

"Finding the right therapist is so hard, but when you do, they can change your life."

Holly nodded in agreement as she sipped the wine slowly. "She's been more like a guide helping me shift my thinking. Susan's pointed out some things about myself that were hard to hear, and she suggested I give the boys more responsibilities and treat them more like the men I want them to become, instead of babies I need to care for."

"That's really good advice."

"She also said I was abusing myself."

"Wow," Stacey commiserated. "That's pretty harsh."

"At first, I was offended, but then I thought about it, and honestly, if it isn't abuse, I don't know what else you could call it. I mean, look at my decisions about men for instance." Stacey nodded in agreement and listened, popping a few grapes into her mouth.

"The last priority on my list is always me," Holly recounted. "It's hard to argue with the facts." She took another sip of her wine. "She suggested some mindfulness activities."

"Not yoga!" Stacey laughed.

"You know how much I despise that!" Holly laughed. "I spend most of the class hating myself for doing it wrong."

"You need to come with me to the eight am at Lifetime with Brendan," she suggested wistfully. "His Downward Facing Dog is the thing dreams are made of." She made squeezing motions with her hands. "That ass. I fumble around with my form on purpose so he has to come and correct me." She made air quotes with her fingers when she got to the word correct.

"You're terrible." Holly giggled to herself. "I was thinking more along the lines of taking a Zumba class. I used to love to do that." She pulled her pant legs up to get some sun on her legs. "This feels so good. Gotta soak up the Vitamin D while I can."

"Yeah, you definitely could use more D in your life." Stacey snickered.

"That too." Holly tipped her face back to the sun. "God, I miss sex. It was the only thing that Mick got right."

"Don't tell me you are thinking about taking another ride on that crazy train."

"Hell to the no," Holly said and shuddered. "Never know where he's been warming his wiener lately."

"Warming his wiener." Stacey snorted. "Good one."

"My battery-operated boyfriend comes with zero baggage, and afterward, I can eat as much chocolate as I want with no judgment. The only thing missing for me is snuggling. I used to love being the little spoon."

"I just like having somewhere to warm my feet when it's cold."

"I have a dog for that," Holly answered.

"Ever think you'd get married again?"

"Gosh, girl! What's with the big questions today!" Holly took a sip and considered it. "I'd never say never, but he'd have to be a saint. After everything I've gone through with Mick, he'd have a hell of a wall to scale."

"That's not really fair to ask a good man to do that," Stacey stated.

"I'm pretty sure all the good ones are gone." Holly focused on her glass. "Dating in your forties is like finding the least smelly thing at the thrift store."

"I would think it would be much more scientific with apps and everything."

"You'd be wrong. There's a lot of crazy out there. Married men on dating apps, couples together looking for a third."

"No way!"

"Way! I dipped a toe in the dating pool last year, but with everything else happening, there just isn't any time. And, to be honest, I'm not really ready."

"Just promise me you won't shut down that part of yourself forever. Someone might come along when you aren't even looking." She changed gears. "How are the boys?"

"Actually, pretty good for the first time in a long time,"

Holly admitted. "Susan suggested we take a break from rehashing the past and just have silly, normal fun with each other. So, a few days ago, I took them to dinner and we played would you rather. I never thought Chance would participate, but he actually enjoyed it, as much as a teenager can enjoy forced bonding moments with their family."

"You should count that as a win, woman."

"Honestly, he has settled down. The only thing that I'm iffy about is his new friendship with Zach. They seem to be a lot tighter than I ever remember them being."

"Friends change quite a bit when you're a teenager. It's a fickle time."

"Well, I hope it's short-lived. The idea of having to socialize with Anna regularly gives me the hives." Holly ate another grape. "I shouldn't be like this. It's judgmental and petty, but it's hard to relate to a woman whose most difficult daily decision is if she wants two pumps of hazelnut syrup or three in her latte. She's so fake and condescending. I always feel like I'm something she scraped off her shoe."

"What do the boys have in common?"

"I have no idea. They used to play on the same basketball team in seventh grade, but that was ages ago. They have always had the same group of friends, but until recently, Chance didn't like to hang around him because he was always bragging about his Apple watch or newest iPhone. Now, all of a sudden, they are besties."

"It will get old again. Just give it time. Guys like Zach Leighton-Blackwell are hard to be around."

"I hope so. High school sucks," She commiserated. "Remember feeling like everything was a life or death decision? It was all so superficial and stupid. Turns out none of that really mattered at all."

"True," Stacey topped off their glasses with the rest of the wine. "It's natural for teenagers to pull away from their parents to find their own identity."

"I know. It just doesn't make it any easier."

THIRTY-FIVE

Sixteen. Her firstborn was sixteen. Finally old enough to do things like drive alone and get a job. There was a splintering away that happened with teenagers, the deep-seated desire to cut themselves free from the family tree. A natural shift toward their own independence and living their own lives. Sixteen was the first major break away from the parent-child unit and the first real taste of freedom, and it scared the hell out of Holly. In her mind, when it came to Chance, freedom and recklessness went hand in hand.

Holly laid in bed and tried to control the panic that rose up in her throat. She inhaled deeply while chanting to herself.

You are okay. Chance is okay. Dillon is okay.

A few minutes later, her heartbeat slowed down. He was getting his license today, and the used car she wasn't sure he was ready for, but that Mick was driving over that afternoon anyway.

A few days earlier, she had been talked into just looking at the car dealership by her house with Mick

"He's doing everything we're asking him to do, right?"

"Yeah."

"Then what is the big deal?" he asked.

"It feels too soon. I don't know if he's ready for that kind of freedom yet. They warned us about giving him too long of a leash at Sienna."

"You need to relax. You've been rubbing your anxiety everywhere like you always do. Give him a chance."

And that was what did it, the stab of guilt making her go against her own better judgment.

"He's going to have to agree to be monitored by a driving app."

"I'm sure that won't be a problem."

So, she chipped in with Mick and bought a used car for Chance, a transaction that was in her name only because Mick couldn't sit still long enough to fill out all the paperwork. Fidgety and needing nicotine, he ran outside to pollute the entrance with secondhand smoke while she walked through tax, title, and licensing options with a slick salesman. An hour later, she left with all the paperwork in her purse, and they decided to hide it at Mick's house until the party.

She got out of bed and stumbled to the coffee pot, sleepy and reaching for a dark roast. Then she pulled four sticks of butter from the refrigerator. She loved making homemade birthday cakes for the kids, teaching herself how to make buttercream that rivaled the bakery down the street. Her frosting was so good you could eat it right out of the bowl.

He had chosen a peanut butter chocolate combo that she was going to cover with crushed Reese's peanut butter cups after liberal amounts of both peanut butter and chocolate buttercream coated the top layer of the cake. It was a time-consuming labor of love that she enjoyed. Today was a day to celebrate.

If things had gone the other way last May, I wouldn't be making a cake today.

The brutal truth of that thought took her breath away, and she thanked God that he was here and safe and alive. That she got to hug him and see him and even argue with him instead of sitting in front of a headstone today.

Chance slept until nearly noon while she finished up his cake. She piped the buttercream, mixing the two flavors in large loopy lines until it filled the entire top layer and trickled down the edges. Seeing it, his eyes got big.

"That's slaps, Mom."

"Slaps?" Holly asked. "Is that a good thing?"

He smiled and shook his head at her question. "Yeah. It's a good thing."

"Want to lick the beater?" She held it out to him, and he grabbed it eagerly and licked the long metal lines. He was a kid again, transported back to the hundreds of other times in his life when he enjoyed the simple pleasure of buttercream, and when nothing more than diabetes was a threat. Seeing him lick the beaters like a little kid, she felt her heart fill. A mother's mind is a time machine, careening forward and back through time with a single look. One second, you see your teenager as the almost man he is, and the next second, you see his four-year-old self begging for a turn to lick the beaters with his huge brown eyes and grubby fingers.

Maybe things would be okay, after all. Maybe fifteen was the end of the nightmare. She couldn't wait to shut the door forever to fifteen, padlock it up, and throw away the key.

"Happy Birthday," she sang out and then walked behind him and pulled him into her arms while he sat on the stool, continuing to lick the beater. "Mommy loves you." She delivered loud kisses to his cheek, and for once he didn't shrug her off. "Want to get your license today? Be official?"

"Can we?"

"Of course. Your sixteenth birthday is the only day I will

willingly sit in line at the DOT without complaining." She offered, "Why don't you take a quick shower, that way your hair isn't ridiculous for the photo."

"You worry about the dumbest things," he said, then agreed and put the beater in the sink and then walked back upstairs to get ready.

———

An hour and a half later, he was standing in front of the DMV with his paper license in his hand and posing with it wearing a cheesy smile on his face while Holly snapped a photo of him. He drove her home with quiet self-assurance while she observed his larger hands grip the wheel. They hovered obediently at ten and two, an act she was pretty sure he did only for her benefit. She texted Mick and told him to drive over with the car and to back it up in the driveway so it would be there when they got home.

Twenty minutes later as Chance pulled into the driveway with his brow wrinkled, he asked. "Who's that?" Still not understanding what was happening, he looked at her, and then saw Mick get out of the car with a big smile on his face. "Did dad get a new car?"

"I don't know, honey. Let's go see." The giddiness was building in her own belly.

Mick looked like the cat who ate the canary, dangling the keys in front of him while he leaned back onto the car in the sun.

"Happy Birthday, Stud!" Mick said and hugged him, clapping him on the back. "What do you think of your new ride?"

"Mine?" he shrieked and looked at Holly, who nodded.

"Yep, yours." It was a four-door silver Buick, nothing special, but also *not* a minivan.

He grabbed the keys from Mick, yanked open the door, and sat down in the driver's seat. "This is awesome. Thanks, Dad." Holly's heart sank.

"Your mom and I chipped in together," Mick corrected him.

"Thanks, Mom!"

"Do you want to go pick up your friends and bring them home for the party?" Holly asked.

"Can I?"

"I don't know. Can you?" Mick joked. "You have a license now, silly. Nothing is stopping you."

Chance smiled big and turned over the ignition.

"Come right back, okay, buddy?" Holly asked.

"I will." He pulled out and gave them both a wave before sailing down the street as Mick and Holly watched him go. Although she was slightly alarmed that he was solo now. She wouldn't be there to warn him about his lead foot and to put on his seatbelt. He was growing up, and she was going to have to let him.

———

An hour later, he came home and parked the car carefully in the driveway with Zach and Blake in tow. She called in an order for pizzas, and at ten pm, she called the boys up from the basement and lit the candles on the cake. Dillon sang loud and off-key, and she gave up trying to harmonize with him as she recorded the video of Chance red-faced and embarrassed in front of his friends at their vocal spectacle. The candlelight flickered in his dark eyes as she stood in the sweetness of that one milestone moment, holding her phone shakily in her hand while her mind walked through the last few months she had endured getting here.

We made it.

Finally, after the last chorus, he inhaled a big breath and blew the candles out with a single breath, then swept his dark hair away from his face and rewarded his mom with one real smile. Happiness. Finally. Seeing an authentic smile on his face, she let her guard down and let herself believe they had turned the corner. She could relax. Chance was sixteen and safe and healthy. They had survived. She had no idea why she let herself believe this as an absolute. Holly obviously was living in denial, not knowing that instead of the game being over, it was only halftime.

Chance's unexplained good moods were a double-edged sword for Holly. She wanted to relax, but the responsible part of her knew she couldn't dare. She pulled on her shoes and got her keys in her hand. Looking in the mirror, she finger-combed her hair, made a mental note to schedule a visit to the salon, and then checked her watch again. Her colorful maxi dress was a recent self-care inspired splurge, and she had to admit it felt good to look in the mirror and like what she saw.

"Guys!" she yelled up the stairwell. "We gotta go!"

Finally, both boys came running down the stairs with their backpacks, grumpy and pushing each other out of the way, scrambling to cram their shoes on their feet.

"Knock it off," she chastised and handed them each an Oreo pop tart.

There are a few vitamins and minerals in there. Who am I kidding? It's the nutritional equivalent of a candy bar.

"Why can't I drive my car?"

"I'm not totally sure you're awake enough to drive in the mornings," Holly reasoned.

"That's bull," he said, and she was pretty sure he mumbled 'shit' at the end, but she wasn't sure enough to call him out on it and didn't want to start her day in an argument so she let it go.

"And I still have to get you a parking permit at school. I'll get it settled today, and you can probably start driving tomorrow."

Chance rolled his eyes and bit into the pop tart. Something told her to ask for his phone; it had been several weeks since the last random check. She put her hand out. "Chance, let me see your phone."

"Why?" he asked suspiciously between bites.

"Just a random check." She tried to keep her voice even. She hated this part. He grunted and then slapped the phone into her hand. She swiped it to unlock it and typed in the password that was rejected. "Did you change the password?"

"It's all sixes," he answered. "It's black. Like my soul."

"Nice," she muttered and punched them in quickly, making sure it opened, and then tucked it into her purse.

"I need it for school. We use it every day in class."

"Too bad. I'll call the principal and tell him to tell your teachers you will need to borrow a real calculator today."

He gave up, groaned, and then walked to the garage. Dillon said nothing, munching his pop tart quietly and then walking to the car.

She drove them to school silently, the air thick with tension. Her stomach knotted up again, wondering what she would find on his phone. She pulled into the drop off lane.

"Have a great day. I love…" Chance slammed the door shut before she could finish, striding away sullenly.

Dillon piped up in the back. "I love you, Mom."

Always the peacekeeper, that one.

"I love you, too, buddy, but it's not your job to fix us, you know."

"I know, I just wanted to say it."

"It's nice to hear, sweetheart." She glanced at him in the rearview mirror. "How have you been, buddy, since Chance got home."

"Good, I guess."

"You guess?"

"I'm good," he repeated.

"You know, if you are upset about something, you can tell me, right?"

He was uncharacteristically quiet, and she knew there was something on his mind. So, she pushed him a little harder. "Right, honey?"

"It's just that everything for you is so hard right now. I don't want to add to it."

She pulled into the parking lot instead of the drop-off line. This was a conversation they needed to have where she could look in his eyes, not through a rearview mirror. She patted the front seat. "Come up here for a minute. Let's talk."

He unfastened his seatbelt and slid into the passenger seat.

"You only have to worry about you," Holly started in. "I am strong, like Captain America strong." She flexed a bicep at him to prove it. "You are my top priority, too, sweetheart. All of my effort and love isn't focused on Chance, as much as it might feel like it is." She squeezed his knee playfully. "I have a spot right back here that no one knows about." She pointed to the bottom corner of her heart. "This spot is reserved just for you, okay? So, tell me what is on your mind."

He took a deep breath and blew the hair out of his eyes by

puckering his bottom lip and exhaling up. "He's different, Mom."

"Chance?"

"Yeah," he continued carefully. "He's not the same. He gets angry all the time, locks his door."

"Sometimes, that is what teenagers do, honey. Someday, you will, too."

"I never will."

"Never say never."

"I think he's been sneaking out at night."

Holly's radar peaked, and her heart started to race. "What makes you say that?" She forced her voice to sound easy and light, a feat that had proven to be nearly impossible.

"Once in the middle of the night, I went to his room when I couldn't sleep, like I used to do when I was little." He stopped and she smiled at his use of the word little. "He was gone, but his window was open and the curtain was blowing in the breeze."

"So, what did you do?'

"I crawled into his bed and fell asleep, and when he came back, he was angry and smelled bad."

"When was this, honey?"

"About a week ago."

"Why didn't you tell me earlier?"

"Chance made me promise never to tell you, but he's been being such a jerk to you that I don't think it's fair to keep any promises like that."

"Thank you for telling me, sweetheart."

He looked scared for a minute. His eyes were huge, already understanding the weight of what he'd said.

"Don't worry. I won't tell him you told me."

Hearing that, he brightened immediately.

"Is that all you wanted to talk about?"

"Yes." He exhaled in relief. "I thought you were going to be so mad."

Not at you.

"Of course not, sweetie, but in the future, please come to me right away when things like this happen." She hugged him tightly, her mind racing. "Have a good day at school, sweetheart." He smiled and then opened the door and ran out to meet his friends, but glanced back at her one more time and waved before he disappeared into the enormous throng of backpacked kids at the entrance.

———

Later that night, after a particularly punishing school day made harder by the distraction of Dillon's confession and a feeling of fear she couldn't shake, she dropped Chance at another young people's meeting and pulled a canned margarita from the little refrigerator she had installed in her walk-in closet.

She popped open the tab and punched the code into Chance's phone. As the dread formed a tiny ball in the pit of her stomach, a prickle of foreboding made the hairs on her neck stand up. It felt like an intrusion, combing through his phone, looking for something, anything that would give her an eye into what he was thinking and doing. She remembered Tim's words, *"Trust but verify,"* and pushed the doubts about invading his privacy away completely.

Holly opened up his camera roll and scrolled through the photos. There were two sets of friends. The kids she recognized from neighborhood playdates and birthday parties and then the new ones, puffing huge clouds of vape, with so many tattoos and facial hair. She studied the photos one by one, scrolling through them. They were another painful before and after. She wished she could delete those new friends from Chance's life by dragging them to the trash icon.

Jesus, will you listen to yourself? These are someone's children. Kids that have been broken by life, too. They are not trash.

The guilt hit her hard, and she pushed it away, hating herself for thinking like that. She took another long sip of her margarita, and the tequila on an empty stomach hit her bloodstream quickly. Then she touched on Snapchat, a social media platform that never made any sense to her. On it, all the memories and photos disappeared after you saw them when all she wanted to do was to hold on. She tapped on chat and opened every chat log and she continued to tap on random buttons on random screens, not having any idea how it worked, until she got to a long string of an old conversation between Chance and Zach. At first, it was typical stupid banter between teenage boys. But as Holly scrolled deeper, certain words jumped out at her:

Molly
    Bud
    Hookup
    An ounce is
    I have the money
    Set up a snap account make bank
    They don't know the difference
    Bars, 4 bars
    Xannies
    Dank bud
    Dabs
    Rolling
    Need Xan

Get rid of it

Mom's a nosy bitch

My mom doesn't know shit

Zach? Ah-nah's Zach? Mr. Perfect with the wavy blond hair, bright blue eyes, perfect teeth, and amazing ability to kiss ass? She had never been a raving fan, but the other parents ate him up with a spoon, calling him a remarkable young gentleman. He was able to walk through their world undetected, using Chance as a scapegoat, knowing the heat would never fall on him. Zach was the golden boy of the neighborhood, cherry-picked to be the quarterback since his first seventh-grade season and groomed accordingly. Anna was so proud of all of his accomplishments, racking up their photo evidence in post after post on Facebook. His perfect smile shined on and on in social media. There were so many photos, it was the most painstakingly documented childhood there ever was.

The panic thickened her tongue and made it hard to swallow. She scrolled deeper. More code, more drug references, more words she had never heard before from a kid who was becoming a stranger to her message by message. From what she was gathering, Zach was more deeply entrenched in this than Chance was.

She read and re-read all of the messages. There were no tears this time, just the hollow knowing and the brutal truth that he had managed to do it again under the radar. He'd completely blindsided her when she thought everything was back on track. Holly pinched the bridge of her nose to quell the tension. Turning the messages over and over in her mind. They melted together and then back again. She needed to tell the truth to Anna, and she needed evidence to prove her accusations. She took a screenshot and immediately saw the words in gray appear on the screen, CHANCE TOOK A SCREENSHOT OF THIS CHAT.

Shit.

Holly jumped to her feet, found her iPad, and scrolled through to the beginning of the messages. She took photos of the phone with her iPad. Scroll and click, Scroll and click. Ten photos later, the login screen appeared, locking her out of the account. She tried and tried to log in but was locked out. Instantly shaky, she bit on her fingernail.

Someone knows.

Feeling sheepish at first, like she got caught doing something naughty, she shook off the guilt.

I have nothing to feel guilty about.

She sat on her bed. These were the times she wished she had someone special in her life. To talk through the challenges of parenting teenagers. Someone to lean on when things got heavy.

I have to tell Anna what I've found. I could lose my job if I know something and don't report it. Technically, it's a gray area, but if something happened to him or anyone else, I'd never forgive myself.

"Ugh!" Holly vocalized her frustration and fell back down on her pillows, looking up at the crack on the ceiling that was getting bigger by the day.

That's the perfect metaphor for this shit show.

A few hours later, she picked up Chance and Dillon and ran through the drive-thru grabbing fries and burgers again. Another supper from a greasy sack, it was becoming a bad habit.

"Sorry, guys. It got late, and I didn't get a chance to cook dinner."

She handed the bag back to Chance and unwrapped the tissue paper around her double cheeseburger with extra pickles. Stopped at a red light, she looked over at Chance, who was shoving handfuls of fries into his open mouth.

"When can I have my phone back?" he asked brusquely between bites.

"I need to talk to you about that when we get home."

Instantly worried, he looked at her. "About what?"

"We will talk at home," Holly said firmly. "Not now." She tipped her head back, indicating Dillon.

"Whatever," Chance mumbled and continued to cram fries into his mouth and then sucked down long drags of Coke. Holly ate her burger silently, going over what she wanted to say in her mind. The burger sat in her stomach like a brick. She pulled into the garage and then reached out and squeezed Chance's forearm. "Stay here." He shook her off and it hurt.

She pushed the button to open the sliding door on the minivan. "Go inside, Dilly. Let Murph out and unload the dishwasher. We'll be inside in a few minutes."

Dillon unclicked his seatbelt and walked in. After the door shut, she turned to Chance. "Do you need to tell me anything?" Holly started, hoping that by giving him a chance to confess, he might do the right thing.

"Nope." He grunted at her, avoiding eye contact and looking out the windshield. His eyes fixed on the Christmas decoration tubs on shelves by the ceiling.

"I went through your phone."

"I know."

"Want to tell me what you and Zach have been up to?"

"Nope."

"I'm not stupid, Chance. I can see that you guys are dabbling in some scary things."

"Those are old messages. From before treatment." He rolled his eyes and continued sarcastically. "Way to go, detective. You cracked the case. Are we done?"

"No, we aren't done. I am going to have to go to Anna with this."

"With what?"

"With the fact that you guys seem to be the hook-up at school."

"You sound ridiculous when you say stuff like that."

"Stop lying. Just stop," she begged, exasperated. "If you keep making stupid decisions like this, you are going to end up in jail. You know that?"

"Calm down, Holly."

"Don't call me that." Holly felt her voice raise and get louder. "You are not getting the phone back now. Maybe ever."

"Whatever." He sat in the seat, waiting to be excused.

"Go do your homework. I'm going to set up a sit down with Anna and Zach, and we are going to get to the bottom of this."

He said nothing, and when she stopped talking, he got out of the van and slammed the door hard enough it made her teeth rattle.

THIRTY-SEVEN

"Come on." She prodded Chance up the sidewalk to the front door and then rang the doorbell. A flurry of chimes played as Holly looked down and tugged on her fleece jacket to keep the cold out. Pumpkins and hay bales decorated the elaborate porch, and fake cobwebs crept up the pillars. Anna's front porch was already Pinterest perfect Trick or Treat ready. An intercom buzzed, and she heard Anna's voice from far away.

"Come on in. We're in the kitchen."

Holly took a deep breath and turned the knob of the massive oak door that led into the immaculate French Country home. Light-filled, it had perfectly aged plaster walls that looked like they had been commissioned in the 1800s, even though they were barely a year old. It was impeccably furnished with rustic crystal chandeliers that gleamed.

Anna appeared and waved them down the long hall into the kitchen. As always, she was flawless and perfectly pressed in Prada. Holly sized up the woman standing in a black pants suit with strappy Jimmie Choos, and then looked down and smoothed her skirt that had become wrinkled that day sitting on the carpet with the kids during reading circle time. She loved getting down on their level and seeing life from their perspective. It helped her connect in a way that towering over her students never did.

"Cappuccino?" Anna asked, and Holly nodded and watched her turn to the built-in maker, pulling an antique mug from the drawer and setting it underneath the spout. The massive island was impressive, nearly twenty feet long. Sitting on a stool at it was Zach, who didn't look up from his phone to acknowledge her at all. Chance sat down on an empty stool next to him.

Anna smiled a tight smile and brought the tiny cup to her on a saucer. "Thank you," Holly mumbled. Accepting fancy coffee from her in this circumstance was so bizarre. Anna stood at the island across from Holly, tugging on the bottom of her jacket and fingering her necklace. "You said there was something we needed to discuss in person regarding the boys?"

Holly cleared her throat apprehensively and swallowed, trying to find the perfect words to begin an explanation that pained her. "Can we have the boys set the phones down for a minute?" By boys, it was obvious she meant Zach since she had not given Chance's phone back. It was a stupid little game to say it like that but seemed less confrontational.

"Of course." Anna nodded and held out her hand a full minute before an irritated Zach finally plopped the phone down into it.

Wow. Entitled much?

She decided the best way to deliver the information was to just get right to it, so she started in. "I did a random check on Chance's phone last night."

"Wow!" That is such an invasion of privacy," Anna

exclaimed, and Zach nodded. "I would never violate Zach's trust like that."

"Well, I guess that is where we can respectfully agree to disagree. I pay for the phone, so technically, the phone is mine. It is a *privilege* that I allow Chance to enjoy, but it comes with limits."

"I can see why you would do that with Chance's history, but we don't have that issue with our Zach."

Chance bristled and bubbled with anger at her words. Suddenly, his energy jolted from utterly bored straight into hostile territory as only the energy of teenage boys can.

Holly dismissed her comment, waving it away. "I found some communication on there between Zach and Chance that was troubling."

"What kind of communication?" Anna asked.

"There were Snapchat threads that were saved between them. References to drugs and sex. Buying drugs. Selling drugs. Finding a hook-up." She pulled out her phone and scrolled to the screenshots she was able to take before being locked out of the account. "There were many more messages. I read them all and started taking screenshots to show you, but the boys figured it out and locked me out of the account."

Holly saw Zach kick Chance's foot out of the corner of her eye.

Anna pulled out her zebra-patterned reading glasses and slid them on her face, scrolling up to read through all of the screenshots. The room was heavy and silent, and the sun went behind a cloud, fading the light down and darkening the room.

Anna returned the phone to Holly and said, "I just don't see what the big deal is."

Zach stifled an entitled smile and then covered it with his hand.

"The big deal is that the boys are engaging in very risky behavior." Holly was bowled over by her non-reaction. "Did you even read the chats?"

"Yes, I did." She paused. "I think that for now maybe it's best if the boys don't hang out together anymore."

Chance stood up fast, and the stool clattered down behind him, hitting the tile with a crash. Holly rushed to set it upright. "He's the one who's looking to be a hook-up. He's the one who wanted to start selling it, not me!" Chance's face was red, the veins in his neck throbbing and tight. "Mom, you have to believe me." He begged with his eyes, and Holly could tell instantly he was being truthful.

"Now, where would he get an idea like that?" Anna said icily. "Maybe from his juvenile delinquent acquaintance who just got released from rehab?"

"You will not speak to my son like that." Holly stood up. "You've only read a fraction of the messages, but I read them all. It's crystal clear the motivation came from Zach. There is some very damning proof that Zach is running a thriving business at New Hope Academy."

"I don't believe you."

"Why would I lie?" Holly asked.

"To keep your job and the heat off you, perhaps," Anna stated cooly. "A single mother with a mortgage to pay can be properly motivated to do all sorts of shady things, I imagine."

Holly wanted to slap that look of sly condescension right off her face. Her palm itched at her side for contact, but thankfully, her cooler head prevailed and she spoke in a low, emotionless tone. "I have done what I came here to do. You've been informed, so I am not responsible for what happens now. Chance, we're leaving."

Holly walked out of the light-filled kitchen in Anna's two-million-dollar home, and for once felt like she had won the prize. She didn't have all the material trappings of Anna, but at least when presented with a crisis, she didn't stick her head in the sand and ignore it.

She drove them home quietly.

"You stood up for me," Chance said quietly.

"Of course, I did. You've made your mistakes and apparently still continue to choose the wrong kinds of people to associate yourself with, but you've done your time, and I will only hold you responsible for the things you have done. Anna is delusional."

"You're the only parent who cares about this stuff, Mom. Every single one of my friends has tried pot. Some of them smoke more than I do, but I am the only one who got sent away."

"We didn't send you away," Holly answered. "You were making alarming decisions, and so we followed the advice of the professionals."

"Nothing is going to happen to him. Zach's dad will fix it all. Sweep it under the rug and pretend nothing happened."

"I don't care if they do. I can't control them or their household. I am only worried about you. You and Dillon are my responsibilities. If they want to let Zach grow up to be a total douchebag, then that is on them."

Chance snickered at her word choice. "He *is* a douchebag."

"Hopefully, someday, he'll recognize that and decide he doesn't want to be one anymore."

"Doubtful," Chance muttered and then rolled down the window and hung his head outside, feeling the wind rush across his face and fluttering through his longish bangs as she drove them home.

THIRTY-EIGHT

A few days later, her shipment from Amazon arrived. Holly picked up the box on the front porch and walked into the house. Tucked under her arm were the at-home drug test kits she had ordered. She walked upstairs and slipped off her dress shoes, then took off her dress and hung it up in the closet to wear one more time before it had to be dry cleaned. In shorts and a ragged college t-shirt, she sat on her bed, staring at the box, not ready to open it yet. Because seeing them with her eyes would confirm a reality she still struggled to accept. She was the kind of mom that had to perform random drug tests on her children.

She finally pulled out a box cutter and sliced the tape open, pulling out the cups and test strips. She opened one and read the directions.

The last time I did something like this, it was a pregnancy test.

She pulled out the instructions, noting the time required to get the most accurate results. Reading through all the instructions thoroughly, Holly made sure she was going to be ready to follow them to the letter.

She heard the door slam and jumped. Pulling out one test cup, she hid the box in her closet and walked out to see Chance rifling through the refrigerator, looking for a snack to eat after school.

"How was your day?" She forced a smile on her face and looked at him. He was closed off and apathetic again, two emotions she was getting used to seeing on his face. His guard was always up and he had constructed high walls that were impossible to scale. Holly was drained riding this roller coaster with him. A few days ago, she had an amazing day with him celebrating his birthday, then two days later, the shock of the messages on his phone sent her reeling. It was always one extreme or the other; it seemed almost like parenting two different kids.

"There's some leftover pizza in the back," she offered, and he grunted and pulled it out, putting a couple of slices on a plate into the microwave.

"Use a paper towel please."

He was annoyed but did it anyway, and leaned up against the cabinets while the slice circled endlessly in the microwave as the clock counted down. There were two more minutes, so she held up the cup and said, "I'm going to need you to pee in this."

"You're drug testing me?" His voice raised high on the last syllable, unable to believe what she was saying.

"Yes." Holly decided to use as few words as possible to diffuse the situation, but it wasn't working. "I can't believe this surprises you after what I saw on your phone."

"I just left rehab and now this?" He played on her sympathies. "Jesus, you never give me a chance to breathe."

"I need to be sure you are clean and not using, especially after seeing all those messages between you and Zach. How is this any different than complying at treatment?"

"It's not. I just thought that at home I was actually going to get a break, but you seem to be hellbent on proving I'm still screwing up." The microwave beeped, but he didn't move.

Holly set the cup on the countertop and slid it toward him.

"Now?" His voice was steeped in disgust. "Of course, fine." He yanked the cup off the table and walked to the bathroom. A few minutes later, he returned it completely full to the top, and as he walked it toward her, a little spilled onto the floor, and he snickered at the mess.

"You better clean that up," Holly said, instantly incensed that he was being such an asshole.

"Screw that, do it yourself. I am not cleaning it up."

Holly wanted to scream at him, wanted to shake him, wanted to slap him. To get his attention in any way she possibly could.

She forced herself to remain silent and dipped the plastic container holding the six test strips into the glass of urine and set her watch.

"Yes, this needs to be precise, Holly. Get out your stopwatch." Chance sneered.

The heat of anger roiled in her belly. She wanted to punish him for his disrespect, but she knew it wouldn't do any good. So, she sat and watched the second-hand tick by agonizingly slowly on her watch. Finally done, she pulled it out and looked at the pamphlet for the results.

"You're positive for THC."

"It's just pot, Mom."

"That's unacceptable, Chance. We said no drugs as long as you are living under my roof. You sat there at Sienna in front of Adam and signed the sober living contract."

"I would have signed anything to leave that fucking place."

"You don't get to swear either. You are not following the rules and standards that I set for you."

"Everything is a rule and a standard. It's practically legal anyway, Mom. It's only a matter of time."

"True, but it is *illegal* now, and it would never be legal for a sixteen-year-old." Holly's voice was straining tighter and getting more constricted. Her hands were in balls at her sides, and her heart beat erratically in her chest.

"This is bogus." Chance ate his pizza, not making eye contact with her and refusing to acknowledge his own mistakes.

"You're grounded. There are consequences for breaking your sobriety."

"There always are."

"You're going to school and home, that's it. Got it?"

"Yes." He bit aggressively into the last slice of pizza. "Are we done?"

"Yes."

He slammed his dishes into the sink and then walked out of the kitchen up to his room.

THIRTY-NINE

The next day, Chance got up and and got ready for school, saying absolutely nothing to Holly at all.

"Straight home after school." She said to dead air as he pulled the keys off the hook and walked away silently. She watched him drive away, frustrated and sad that these curt exchanges were the extent of their relationship lately.

She didn't have much more time to consider it and was distracted at work until right before lunch when she saw a missed call from the high school attendance office. She punched in the numbers calmly to hear the voicemail tell her Chance never made it to school. Was he sick or at an appointment? Please call and let them know.

The first prickles of fear tingled in her stomach. It wasn't pretty, the last conversation they had, but to not show up at school at all? Where the hell was he? She pulled out her sandwich and texted Mick.

Holly: Is Chance with you?
Mick: Um. No. It's a school day.
Holly: I know that. He was a no show at school today.

Mick: That's not good. He's not here. If he shows up, I'll text. He's probably just blowing off some steam.
Holly: He failed a random drug test. THC.
Mick: It's just pot, Holly.
Holly: Jesus, that's exactly what he said. You are identical.
Mick: Stop overreacting. He'll come home.

Frustrated, she went back to class and tried to teach, distracting herself with teaching math and facts about rocks and moss for science class. Preoccupied, she ran through scenarios in her head. In every one, he was lying dead in a ditch somewhere. She was right back in that park watching that stretcher get loaded into the ambulance. Watching the clock was a painfully useless activity that she couldn't stop doing even if she wanted to. Finally, blessedly, the last bell rang, and with twenty more minutes to sit in fear and wait, she sat still, wracking her brain, looking for clues she might have missed. Things he said or did that were out of place, that pointed to what he was thinking, where he was going.

She texted his friends, one right after the other, begging for information, and no one had heard anything. It was a useless exercise.

Should I report the car stolen? Can I even do that?

It had been nine hours since he drove off.

Where are you, buddy? What are you doing?

The clock ticked painfully slowly as Holly gathered up all her materials, her notes, and her lesson plans and stuffed them into her backpack. She was just about to get up and leave when she heard a soft knock on the door. Dr. Remington's face made her stomach drop.

"I was hoping I could catch you and do your evaluation now."

Shit. Her timing is the worst.

Holly forced a calm, blank expression on her face. "I'm so sorry, there is a small emergency at home and I need to attend to it. Can we reschedule?"

"Oh? Is there anything I can do?" The older woman's comment should have been comforting, but it felt like an attack.

"Thank you for your concern, but no. It's one of those things only I can handle." Holly stood and grabbed her keys, hoping she would pick up the signal that she was in a hurry. "I'm sorry, please email me another time. I will make it work, but I must be going."

Holly walked quickly down the hallway, hoping each step would get her closer to finding Chance. She just knew that staying in that classroom for even one more minute would be impossible.

———

At seven that evening, Holly sat out on her front porch in a turquoise Adirondack chair and calmly dialed the non-emergency police department. The dispatcher said an officer would be en route in fifteen minutes. Any other day, a woman sitting on her front porch would be a normal welcome slice of Americana, but today, she was a terrified mother of a teenage runaway, desperate to have her child home and safe. She sipped nervously on a glass of water while waiting for the officer to arrive. Her mouth was so dry. Waiting on the porch ensured that Dillon might be spared from the interaction. He wouldn't hear the mechanical chatter from the officer's radio, and he wouldn't hear a strange authoritative voice in his house and come to investigate its origin. She prayed that the YouTube videos that consumed his life were especially engrossing right now because she knew the effect that a police officer coming to their home would have on her sweet, anxious son.

I can't protect him from the consequences of his brother's actions. Chance sets off a bomb and not only kills me and his dad, but his brother is collateral damage. I am tired of feeling out of control all the time.

She saw the squad car turn onto her street and was thankful when the officer parked across the street from her house. Almost instantly, she caught a flash of the curtain as her neighbors noticed the patrol car on their usually calm, picturesque cul-de-sac. Holly stood and smoothed her hair and met the officer in the driveway, waving him to the side of her house out of Dillon's eyeshot from her windows.

He was young, with a sharp blond crew cut and a physique that looked like it included lots and lots of pull-ups. He pulled a small notebook from the pocket on his chest, and she waited for instructions. She had never called the police before and wasn't sure how to proceed.

"Can you start with your name, please?" He stood like a bulldog thick and consuming space, poised with his pen.

"Holly Simon," she said obediently. "My son, Chance, took the car this morning and never showed up at school."

"How old is he?"

"Sixteen." She paused and then continued. "He has a history of mental health issues and was recently released from a treatment program."

"What's his DOC?"

"Pot and Xanax," she admitted, feeling the shame of the words on her tongue. She braced for his condescension, something that usually never came, but that she was mentally prepared for every time.

"Do you have any idea where he might go?" The officer

continued, "Does he have a phone or have his Snapchat location on?"

"No, I confiscated his phone and drug tested him." She looked down at her feet. "He failed it, and I grounded him. The next morning—that was this morning, he left for school, or at least I thought he did, but an hour later, the attendance office called and said he never showed up."

"In cases like this, the best thing you can do is reach out to his friends. Someone likely knows where he is and is letting him crash at their house."

Holly nodded. "I am concerned about him missing doses of his medication. It can have very adverse effects."

The officer considered the information and made another note.

"Can I report my vehicle stolen?" she asked. "Would that help?"

"Actually, it's a simple misdemeanor, operating without owner's consent. In parent-child relationships, though, it is going to be hard to find a judge that will charge him with that."

"So that's it?" Her voice rose an octave. "That's all I can do, sit and wait and hope he comes to his senses and comes home?"

"I'm afraid so, ma'am," the officer stated matter of fact and scribbled something on the back of a card he fished from his pocket. Then he folded his notebook back together and placed it in the same pocket, swiftly clicking the ballpoint pen to indicate the interview was over.

Holly was shocked. The powerlessness washed over her again making it hard to think.

"He'll likely come home. If he does, call this number." He handed her the card with his name on it. "The case number is on the back. In the meantime, I will file the report, and we'll be on the lookout for him and your vehicle. The best advice I can give you is to keep talking to his friends, any girls he's interested in. A kid without money will have to hunker down somewhere. Someone will know where he is."

"Thank you, Officer," she said and shook his hand; his grip was like steel. She turned and walked back up the steps to her house, but not before she saw a couple of her neighbors taking a little too long to drag their garbage cans to the street.

Nosy busy bodies. Messy, single mother over here, as always, happy to entertain you.

She walked inside the house, leaving the front door unlocked, hoping that sometime in the next few hours her beautiful boy would walk through it. She wasn't even mad anymore. She was just tired. So exhausted by this adversarial place their relationship had gone. She walked up the steps to Dillon's bedroom, thankful that he was fully absorbed into a gaming YouTube video that was making him laugh. She kissed the top of his head and said goodnight and then walked into her own bedroom. Her phone stayed glued to her hand as she willed a text to come in or the phone to ring. Staring at it, she texted all his friends and their parents one last time. Getting nowhere, she walked into the bathroom, brushed her teeth, washed her face, crawled into her bed, and snuggled into the down comforter, binding it around her body so tightly it felt like a cocoon. After two hours of fruitlessly checking and re-checking her phone, her body finally gave in, and she drifted off into an anxious, restless sleep.

———

The next morning, Holly checked her messages. None. Nothing. Even her desperate pleas to a girl that Chance had been dating had gone unanswered. Teenagers could be incredibly tight-lipped when they wanted to be. She drank coffee and contemplated her next move.

He can't stay on the run forever. He doesn't have any money. Eventually, a parent would notice he was still around and send him home, right?

But for now, she wasn't above eating crow. She dialed Anna's number, dreading every second. A clipped greeting from Anna relieved any doubt Holly had that Anna had gotten over their last encounter.

"Sorry to bother you, but have you seen Chance with Zach lately?"

"No," Anna said then probed further. "Wait… what do you mean, lately?"

"The last few days?"

"Days?" Anna said, dragging out the word, thick with judgment. Holly knew, if she could see her, her deftly micro-bladed eyebrows would almost appear to break free from their Botox prison.

"He took off with his car Friday morning, and I haven't been able to get in touch with him," Holly admitted. "Can you ask Zach if he's heard anything?"

"Of course," Anna said. "He's probably just acting out again, Holly, but I'll ask Zach and get back to you."

"Thank you," Holly said quietly and hung the phone back up.

"Hey, Mom," Dillon said, dressed in flannel SpongeBob pajama pants and no shirt. His eyes were sleepy and barely open.

"Hey, buddy." She pulled him in for a side hug. "Get dressed. We're going to your dad's."

"Really? Chance, too?" Dillon asked, instantly perked up at the prospect of seeing his dad.

"No, he's busy." Holly made an excuse. "It's just you and

me. If you get ready in five minutes, we can hit the Dunkin drive-thru on the way over."

"You're the best mom ever!" Sleepy Dillion disappeared in favor of donut-lover Dillon, who immediately raced up the stairs to get dressed.

After a dash to the donut shop where she was talked into getting a dozen because they were cheaper that way, she pulled up to Mick's house. Her heart dropped when the driveway was empty. She had been hoping to see Chance's car sitting in the driveway and that Mick had just forgotten to let her know. She knocked on the door, balancing the box of donuts and two cups of coffee in her hands.

"Hey there, Tiger!" Mick greeted when he opened it. For once, he looked mildly healthy, not nursing a hangover. "I've got a new PlayStation. It's all hooked up in the basement. Why don't you go play and let me and Mom talk?"

Dillon disappeared into the house, and Mick came out onto the porch and lit a cigarette, sucking on it as if his life depended on it, and then dissolving into a fit of coughing so loud and so hard she thought he'd never catch his breath.

"Might want to lay off the cigs," Holly retorted when he had regained his ability to breathe, his eyes drippy and his face red from the effort.

This guy would never change.

"Have you heard anything?" she asked, eager for any word about Chance.

"Not a peep."

"I filed a police report. This is getting serious. He's not taking his medication. We might have to do something more extreme."

"Like what?"

"Like going to the courthouse and filing a mental health committal."

"You're not serious," Mick appealed.

"I am," she said resolutely, sitting up straight in the chair. "That's the difference between me and you, Mick. I'll do anything to keep our kids safe."

"You're overreacting."

"He's sixteen, driving God knows where, not taking his medication. How come I am the only one who sees what a dire situation we are in?"

"Let me think about it," he relented and inhaled again.

"Think about it?" Holly said, exasperated. "There is nothing to think about. We need to *do* something."

"I said I would think about it," he said, irritated.

Holly glared at him and shook her head, frustrated. He was never the kind of guy to do anything, especially anything that was difficult. She stood and opened the door a crack, glancing at the mess inside before shouting for Dillon. "Dilly, it's time to go!"

She leaned against the house, waiting. Mick sucked on the cigarette again and again, saying nothing, coughing in-between.

"That shit is gonna kill you," Holly muttered, relieved when the door opened and Dillon came out of it, nibbling on an ice cream sandwich. She didn't even fight him on it. She was just too bloody tired.

FORTY

Two more days crept by agonizingly slowly. Sunday was the worst. She spent the better part of the day taking Dillon on "a drive" through New Hope and surrounding towns as she feverishly scanned parking lots for Chance's car. She distracted Dillon with gas station Slim Jims and old songs she used to sing the boys when they were little. She knew it was futile, but she had to do something. Sitting at home wringing her hands, waiting for him to walk through the door was excruciating. She just couldn't do it anymore. Dillon finally asked where his brother was, and Holly threw together a lame excuse about a class project that his ten-year-old mind accepted, but she hated the lies. Even little white ones that were told to spare the big feelings of an innocent child.

Her phone was silent, but that didn't stop her from checking it constantly, willing the incoming text bubble to appear. Something. Anything. The fear was choking her, every day growing stronger and bigger until, by Monday morning, it was all she could feel.

She was up at three am, sipping on coffee, trying to

distract herself with reading. At seven am, she was going to call the police officer and see if he had any leads. She already knew the answer, but she was going to do it anyway because doing things seemed necessary. Even if it was in vain.

She opened her phone and tapped on the photos app, scrolling through the photos in the Chance folder. Years of his life had been carefully curated and documented there. Holly had always been an obsessive picture taker. Now that they were older, especially since Chance was a teenager, her requests were met with groans and sighs of frustration, but she didn't care. She did it anyway.

She scrolled through her albums of precious photos, Chance with a sparkler when he was seven, a mischievous sparkle in his eyes, waving it around with glee. Twirling him on the makeshift dance floor at the cabin they rented every summer in Michigan, his flat-billed hat too big for his ten-year-old head. The birthday cupcakes she made for his fifteenth birthday, vanilla with maple-bacon buttercream. It had taken her two hours, but the smile on his face when he bit into one made it totally worth it. The full-on goth black wardrobe he morphed into when they first moved to New Hope. She thought it was a phase and gave him the room to explore it, and now she wasn't sure that was the best idea. Tears started to gather at her lashes.

Where are you, honey? Why won't you come home? Just come home.

At precisely seven, she dialed the number on the card from the officer and was told there was no new report. Officers were continuing to look for him and the car. She was told to update them if he came home. Holly swallowed the rest of the cold coffee at the bottom of her cup, then called for Dillon and drove him to school on autopilot. If a gun was put to her head and she had to repeat what he talked about in the car with her or get shot, she'd have died. Her mind was preoccupied as she drove, mumbling, "Uh-huh," now and then for Dillon's benefit while she endlessly sifted through all her past conversations with Chance, one by one, looking for clues to his whereabouts. When Dillon popped out of the car and then turned back to wave at her one more time, she waved back and then was crushed by pangs of guilt from not being fully present for him.

Poor kid deserves a better mom than me.

————

She drove the mile to her school, parking in the lot that was just starting to fill up with faculty cars. Gathering up her books and backpack, she walked into the school, looking at the friendly mural on the wall but not really seeing it. She walked into her room and deposited her things on her desk then beelined to the staff lounge for coffee.

Stacey flashed her a bright smile that faded with concern when she saw Holly's face. Stacey walked closer and looked around before asking quietly, "Nothing yet?"

"No," Holly confirmed and sipped the coffee, biting her lip to stop the tears from forming.

Not at work. I cannot lose it at work.

"They are going to find him." Stacey squeezed her shoulder gently. "They will."

"I know, but the waiting is killing me. He's been off his meds now for four days. It's not something you can stop and start or miss doses on without adverse side effects."

Stacey nodded in agreement. That was what Holly loved about Stacey. She didn't try to fill the space with chatter about mundane things. She was physically and emotionally there and empathetic. Never blaming, never shaming, she radiated quiet strength. "I love you, you know."

"I know, and I love you, too."

"And you're a great mom."

Holly's voice cracked at the compliment from burning shame, and she let out a small wounded sigh. She didn't feel like a great mom, and the evidence clearly confirmed she was a shit show. One teenage runaway and another son so anxious he was going to need years of therapy to undo the damage that had been done.

"You are," Stacey whispered and squeezed her shoulder again. "Anyone would break down under the pressure you've been under. You have been given these kids because you are the only one who could mother them. I am so proud of you."

The tears she was holding back broke loose and fell fast down her face. She wiped them away quickly. This wasn't the place to cry. The door opened, and Dr. Remington walked through it. Holly stepped back and turned away quickly to wipe the rest of the tears away, trying to maintain control of her emotions.

"Holly," Dr. Remington said curtly, "I'll be in your classroom today for observation."

Holly's stomach dropped.

Today? Why today? Of all the days she wanted to phone it in, this was the one and now she couldn't.

"Certainly," she finally answered. "I look forward to it."

———

Dr. Remington sat stiffly in the back of her classroom, writing copious notes on a legal pad, and Holly was aware of her presence constantly. Her stomach rolled, and she found herself talking too fast. She was having a hard time taking in a full breath, and the shallow, quickened breaths left her feeling weak and light-headed.

I just have to make it to lunch, then I can relax for a minute and eat something. I'll feel better after I eat something.

She heard her phone vibrate in her desk drawer. Her heart leapt into her throat. Chance? Was it Chance? Her fingers itched to open the drawer and make sure it wasn't anything important. She slid the desk drawer open nonchalantly and glanced quickly down at the phone there, a missed call and a voicemail from a number she didn't recognize. Nervousness surged again through her body. Holly glanced at the clock, she was on pins and needles counting the minutes until she could listen to her voicemail. She looked down at the phone longingly, and then met Dr. Remington's penetrating stare. The older woman was like stone, emotionless and stoic; the only clue that she was alive was the never-ending scribbling of notes.

"Okay, friends, gather around and pick out a square," Holly told the kids. All the students knew it was time for a story before lunch, so they scrambled into a haphazard line by the stacked carpet squares in the corner.

"Does this look like a good example of a straight line?" Holly asked them, and her students immediately adjusted, snapping into a much straighter line at her request. "Very good, friends," Holly praised. "Thank you for having your listening ears on."

Holly pulled out a low stool and centered it in the middle of the room. She walked to the bookshelf and trailed her fingers down the thin spines of easy reader books to choose one, stopping at the Magic School Bus sight word books. When her boys had outgrown them, or she should say, when sentimental Dillon was finally able to part with them last year, Holly had donated their entire collection to the school. She pulled one out where the bus shrinks down to nearly microscopic size and drives into the bloodstream. It had always been Chance's favorite. A fresh pang of sorrow hit her heart, and she swallowed hard and then composed herself. She settled down on the stool, watching the children jockeying their carpet squares on the floor.

"Criss-cross applesauce," she called out, and the students folded their legs and rested their hands on their knees. "Your square is your own little island," she reminded them gently. "You should not be so close to your neighbor that you can touch their island."

She opened the book and started reading. The children stared up at her with wide eyes from their patches of carpet, and she was transported to Chance's little twin bed. Lying down next to him, his soft thick hair was clumped into damp ringlets smelling like the lavender baby shampoo she had used on him since he was a newborn. She'd read it cover to cover. Then he'd beg, "Again! Again!" and she'd start all over again. He could listen to that story over and over and never get tired.

"Maybe he'll be a doctor!" she had told Mick, who by that time was barely around to hear it. He was traveling and playing guitar at the end of his semi-professional career, before the booze had numbed his skills too much to be taken seriously as a musician. She didn't mind that he traveled. He was doing something he loved, and it provided enough income for her to be at home with their boys. To be honest, it was refreshing to have him gone because, when he was home, he was getting harder and harder to be around. He drank more to quell the fears and insecurities that seemed to be ever-present and gathering strength the older he got. Mick was talented, but he was also fragile. The slightest bit of criticism could send him reeling, either into rage or booze. And out of the two, she slightly preferred drunk because at least he was a happy drunk.

She knew the story by heart. It was easy to re-tell it without thinking while she walked down memory lane. Back to before, back to when the boys were innocent and sweet and life was simpler. Back to when Chance laughed more than he cried, bounding around with endless four-year-old energy, asking why nearly constantly.

I wish I had savored that part more.

Just keeping up with the kids' day to day obligations without help was exhausting. Most nights, she fell into bed wishing she had cooked a healthier meal or taken them to the museum for an educational experience, instead of parking them in front of Teletubbies while she took a break.

Holly finished the book and smiled at her class. "It's lunchtime, friends. Gather up your squares and stack them neatly, and then we will go to the bathroom and wash our hands."

The excited lunch murmurs cued up. "Voices level one," Holly gently reminded them.

In the back of the room, she saw Dr. Remington look down at her walkie talkie and walk out into the hallway quickly, and Holly breathed a sigh of relief. Being in the white-hot light of her intense scrutiny was hard to handle for longer than a few minutes. Holly ran back over her performance in her mind, looking for missteps or errors that would come up during her one-on-one with Dr. Remington later in the week. Even if she performed flawlessly, the principal was notorious for never giving a perfect score. There was always some little stupid criticism she would dole out nearly glee-fully. Praise from the woman was few and far between.

Dr. Remington opened the door again and walked toward

Holly. "There has been an incident with your son. He was arrested," she said in a low voice. Holly was thankful the kids were so focused on lunch and the coming recess that they didn't hear anything.

Holly felt instantly sick. Her stomach lurched and then dropped to the floor. "Arrested?" she squeaked out, wishing desperately that she didn't have to have this conversation with her boss. The woman had enough reasons to criticize her already.

"I have already put in and approved a half-day for you. You need to pick him up at the police station." She said the words matter of fact, with a wisp of scorn. "I'll see the children to the lunchroom."

"I'm sorry," Holly mumbled. "I need to get this sorted. Thank you for taking care of the details."

She gathered her things, her hands shaking as she searched for her keys and her phone, and nearly ran down the hall. Swerving to miss meandering students, Holly was completely preoccupied with worry and deeply entrenched in fear.

Arrested? I can't believe this.

FORTY-ONE

It was pouring as she ran out to her car. She should have waited for the rain to slow, but she physically couldn't. The urgency to see Chance with her own eyes drove her panicked out into the deluge. She hurried to the car, holding a folder over her head. Jumping in the van, she shivered and tossed the soggy folder to the side. She was cold and cranked up the heat and the windshield wipers. Looking in the rearview mirror, her fingers swiped at the black smudges under her eyes, and then she put the van in park and peeled out of the parking lot.

She texted Mick on the way over, and as usual, no response, so she drove straight over to the police station and parked the van, waiting for the torrential rain to subside.

Arrested?

She felt nauseous. This wasn't just a misstep; this was an actual chargeable event. Finally, the rain subsided enough, so she gathered her purse and the little bit of wit she still had left and walked quickly to the door. The thick glass of the door in the vestibule was coated with a network of bulletproof wires. She pressed the intercom button next to it and was buzzed into the station. She walked up to another glass-encased window where a secretary waited for her to speak. "I'm Holly Simon. My son Chance was arrested." She hated saying the words out loud and felt dirty as they hung in the air. She wanted to take them back. She wanted them to be wrong.

"Officer McCoy will be with you in a moment. Have a seat." The secretary motioned to the empty chairs lining the room.

Holly walked to a chair and ran her fingers through her damp hair absentmindedly. She checked her cell phone, but there was still nothing from Mick.

The door buzzed, and an officer came out in full dress uniform. The gun in his holster immediately reinforced the seriousness of the matter. "Mrs. Simon?" he called out.

"Ms.," she corrected and jumped up, offering him a hand. He was solid, over six feet tall, and very intimidating. His blue eyes intently looked deep into her own.

"Follow me," he ordered, and she walked behind him quickly, trying to keep up with his long legs. He led her to a small cubicle and offered her a chair covered in blue polyester industrial fabric.

"Can you give me some details?" Holly asked.

"We got a call about a kid sleeping in a car behind the bleachers at the stadium. When we arrived, your son was witnessed buying drugs from an acquaintance on school property. There are legal ramifications, but the school will be in contact with you for their consequences separately. Normally, it's a suspension of some sort."

A stab of pain seared Holly's heart. "An acquaintance?"

"Yes, Chance will have to fill you in. The other boy is a minor, so we cannot divulge any more information. Chance had marijuana in his hands and backpack and three pills in his pockets that we believe to be Percocet. We'll know more when we get the lab results back. Does your son have a prescription for Percocet or any other controlled substances?"

"Vyvanse for his ADHD," she confirmed. The officer scribbled a note on the file.

He shoved papers in her face with court date information. "Sign here and you can take him home. He will need to be present for juvenile court. The dates are listed here where he'll likely get put on probation. Chance will be assigned a probation officer and will be subjected to random drug tests. He might be put on house arrest. It really depends on the judge." He looked down at the papers. "I see he was reported missing four days ago?"

"Yes," Holly admitted, feeling like a kid getting punished in the principal's office. "I reported him as a runaway and drove around looking for him. I texted his friends, but…" she trailed off. "I am not trying to make excuses. He needs to deal with the consequences of his actions, but it's been a long few days." She sighed. "I can give you the case number if that helps."

"I can look it up." He handed her one more carbon form. "Sign here and I'll release him into your custody."

She scrawled her signature across the paper and then followed the officer to the reception area. "Wait here," he said curtly.

Several minutes later, Chance walked toward her. His head hung low, his clothing wrinkled and dirty. Holly stood up and watched him, not sure how to react, so she just opened her arms and accepted him when he fell into them, sobbing and holding on like he was drowning. His entire body shook and trembled as he tried to catch his breath. Holly's heart broke, the agony twinged with tenderness seeing him in this condition. Cracked wide open, tormented, and defeated.

"You scared me," she admitted, whispering her fears into

the hollow of his neck. "Let's go home." Her voice broke. He nodded, seeming so small. The events of the last several days, instead of aging him made him more childlike. He was someone who needed help, who needed to be taken care of again. Instead of lecturing and screaming, she led him to the van and opened the door quietly. Without getting angry or giving him the itemized list of his offenses, she stayed silent. There would be plenty of time later to give consequences and punishments. Today, she was driving her broken son home. Today, he was safe, and that was good enough for her.

"Aren't you mad?" Chance asked quietly.

"Of course, I'm mad," she answered truthfully. "But more than that, I am so relieved to see your face. I'm so grateful you are in one piece."

"I messed up, Mom."

"Yes, you did."

"I messed up really bad."

"That's true." Holly reached over and squeezed his arm. "Want to tell me where you were or what happened?"

"I knew I messed up when I failed that drug test, and so I didn't think I had anything to lose," he explained. "I just drove until I ran the car out of gas."

"Where did you go?"

"You don't want to know," he muttered and looked out the window morosely.

"I think I need to," Holly whispered. "Honestly, Chance, I won't even get mad anymore. I just want the truth. Just tell me the truth."

"I was stuck at a gas station, and a woman filled my tank. She said she had been where I was before and wanted to pay it forward. She gave me twenty dollars and a cheeseburger," he admitted and then hesitated. "Then I Snapchatted Zach. I wanted some bud to help me relax, and I just wanted to forget about what happened and chill out. Everyone knows he can pretty much get anything."

Stunned, Holly was silent for a moment. "And it didn't occur to either of you that conducting that kind of business on school property was a bad idea?"

"No. We didn't even think about it. He does it all the time."

"All the time?"

Chance laughed wryly. "It's hard to believe the golden boy is the plug, but he is. Everyone at school knows. He makes me sick. I'm the one who gets sent away, yet he's the one who's supplying the entire school. It's not fair."

She felt a little tingle of self-righteousness rear its ugly head after learning this information. She couldn't help herself; it was going to be fun watching Mrs. Perfect fall off her high horse since she had to have gotten the same call from the police department. It was one thing for her to ignore Holly's accusations; she couldn't ignore the police.

She pulled into the garage and turned toward Chance. "You made some bad choices, but you're not a bad kid." She let that sink in. "I guess we'll have to see what's next with the school and court and then make some decisions after that. I love you, and I am happy that you are home, but this acting out has got to stop. You're so impulsive it scares the hell out of me. If you had just come home, none of this would have ever happened."

"I don't know why my mind is like this." He smacked his temple hard with the palm of his hand. "I don't think like normal people, Mom. My mind just goes and goes. I just want to shut it off." He bashed his head again, this time harder, punishing himself before she had a chance to. Holly grabbed his hand and pulled it down while making a soft shushing noise.

"We will go see the doctor again."

"That doesn't help. I just feel numb."

"Then they need to try something else, honey. There are lots of options. They can even do a swab now and prescribe medication that works best with your body chemistry and makeup with a DNA test."

"Nothing ever works for me."

"You're depressed. It is easy to think things will never get better when you are depressed. You just have to trust me. You have to tell me what is going on with you, what is happening inside your head. I can help you if you'll let me."

His body shook with sobs as he cried in the car, and she wasn't sure if she was getting through to him or not.

"You have to open up more and let me in. I am not the enemy, Chance. No one loves you like I do."

"I don't even know why you still love me. All I do is screw up your life."

"Hush now," she whispered to him. "I don't ever want to hear you say anything like that ever again." She started gathering up her bag. "Dillon is home, and I have to go inside or he will worry. Take some time out here to get yourself under control, but don't come in the house until you're calmed down, honey. Dillon is walking on eggshells. All of this stress has been hard on him."

"Okay, Mom." He blew out a long exhale. His breath hitched and sighed as he tried to calm down. He hiccuped and blew the air out between his tight lips. He scared her, a shell of the funny little boy she had raised who saw friends around every corner. When he was four-years-old, he would open his window to shout hello to anyone walking down the street, or across the street for that matter. "Hey, Katie!" He'd repeat himself louder and louder until their neighbor heard and responded with a wave. The sweetness in his face and voice was gone. He was all long, lanky planes and angles. Everything was sharper and harder—his chin, his jaw, his hip, even his personality.

"You're going to be okay. I promise. Even if it doesn't feel like it right now." Holly gave him a smile and then walked into the house where Dillon was oblivious to it all, playing his game, laughing into the headset, and smack-talking his friends. Holly crinkled her nose at the smell of his dirty wet socks. She busied herself with unloading the dishwasher. Gathering plates together with her fingers four at a time, they clanged together. The noise must have roused Dillon, who wandered over.

"Hey there, smelly beast." She pulled him in for a hug. "Any special requests for dinner?"

The door opened, and a more subdued Chance walked in.

"You're home!" Dillon ran over to his brother and hugged him tightly. Chance couldn't help himself. A smile broke out over his face as Dillon continued, "I was so worried."

Chance looked over at Dillon's abandoned game on the TV. "Wanna play Roblox?"

"Really?" Dillon's eyes got big. "You never want to play with me anymore." He ran over and grabbed a controller, then ran it back to Chance before he changed his mind.

"Who wants peanut butter cookies?" Holly asked.

"Me!" Dillon rang out.

"I wouldn't say no to that," Chance offered meekly.

"Was thinking we'd just order a pizza from Roselli's tonight."

"Are we celebrating something?" Dillon asked.

"No, silly, just wanted to spoil my boys a little if that's okay with you."

Chance looked up at that and smiled a small wan smile. Holly yearned to see the real one. It had been so long since she had. A smile so big it spread across his face like a sun breaking through the clouds chasing away the sadness that seemed to fill every corner of his mind lately.

Holly pulled out brown sugar, eggs, and vanilla and listened to the boys talk to each other. Dillon's still slightly babyish sounding voice contrasted with Chance's deeper one that would still crack occasionally. She memorized the way they lilted up and down and teased each other with a stunning array of boy insults, and for one moment, it felt normal. Like everything was alright. They were a family of three hanging out at home together on a typical Monday night. She made the cookies because she was tired of fighting. Tired of fighting for her son to see his worth, tired of fighting to keep him safe, and tired of always being on the defensive and suspicious. She just wanted one night where none of that mattered. Where she didn't have to be the bad cop. She didn't have to lecture him and hold him to a standard. She could just let him be a kid playing video games with his brother.

FORTY-TWO

H olly had gotten up early and laced up her purple running shoes, the ones she bought to run the 5K Bubble Run that she had optimistically signed herself and the boys up to run when they first moved in. They never quite made it there, mostly because the kids would have rather poked needles in their eyes than run a 5K, even if it was through bubbles. She signed up because that was what families did in New Hope. They ran marathons and volunteered at animal shelters and hosted block parties and bunco nights.

But today she wanted to go for a long walk. Get some exercise and think about how to handle Anna. After listening to Chance's side of the story, she had an obligation to report what she learned. She was already skating on thin ice with Dr. Remington. She knew that if she didn't come forward with the truth to her superiors, it would not end favorably for her. Anna was a true spin doctor. Stacey called last night in a panic to fill her in on the latest neighborhood gossip, and she was horrified but not surprised to learn that Anna had thrown Chance under the bus. There was no way Holly was going to let Chance take the fall for a crime he had not committed.

The autumn air was cool on her face as she started walking faster on the endless trails that weaved through her development. Initially, it was one of the things she loved most about upgrading her neighborhood. On the website, beautiful glowing families of four were depicted dragging their toddlers behind them on elaborate bike-trailer set-ups. Everyone had looked so blissful and healthy. Shiny families with perfect teeth and angelic chubby babies attached at their hips were out living their best lives. It was a façade, but at the time, she was desperate to buy into it and clung to the fantasy. She wanted to believe that her children's brokenness after the divorce could heal in New Hope, that they could join those other happy families on the trail. Holly was convinced that if she just worked hard enough, some of those warm family moments might be hers, so she invested in the lie that the right neighborhood would be the answer. The right school system would give her boys the best opportunities. The right kids would become their lifelong friends and insulate them from the riff-raff on the south side. That bubble had burst, and now she saw everything with fresh eyes. She saw the posturing and manipulation for what it was, a neighborhood full of people whose self-worth was tied to the houses they lived in and the cars they drove. Concerned only with posting photos on social media that showcased their successes.

She walked faster, pumping her legs and arms, trying to get her heart rate up to at least keep up with the thoughts racing through her head.

Anna is in total denial. I have to talk to her, but she is not going to like what I have to say. I'm not even sure she is going to believe me. And what if she doesn't? It doesn't make the fact that her son is a drug dealer any less true.

She walked up a hill as her calves burned and saw the wilted coneflowers among the prairie grasses. They were slowly dying, like everything did the closer it got to winter. She walked and walked, partly wishing she could walk away from her life. From the never-ending stress and pain that came from raising two teenagers who struggled with mental illness and trauma. From a job that she loved, but a critical boss she hated. From all the obligations and responsibilities that weighed down her shoulders, crowding out even the tiniest glimmers of fun and ease. Everything had gotten so heavy, and living on the edge was wearing her down. She yearned for a do-over, for a reset, for a complete re-boot, but she had no way to get it. She was locked into this life, working hard to keep all the plates spinning in the air and covering all the bases for herself and everyone else in her life. She let out a long sigh and walked faster up the hill, her shins protesting and her heart racing. The cold air hit the back of her throat, making it hard to inhale a full breath. The tears were at her lashes, heavy and hot, but she pushed them away, biting the inside of her cheek to keep them from spilling down her face.

Ahead of her, a dad was stopped on the trail giving a pep talk to his daughter who was learning how to ride a bike. He ran alongside her and then let go, and she pedaled and swerved, careening down the path while jerking the wheel back and forth. She slowed down, leaning dangerously to the side, an unrecoverable tip that was going to result in a crash that was narrowly avoided by her father reaching out at the last minute, grabbing her handlebars and steadying the bike. Crisis averted.

There wasn't a strong, capable pair of male hands that reached out to protect her sons. The truth of that burned. She had tried to be both, but she couldn't cover all the bases; that much was obvious. She hated Mick for avoiding the responsibilities of fatherhood. He was the un-father, completely sucked into his own selfish life, unwilling to sacrifice any of his precious time to be there for his kids. He pursued his hobbies ruthlessly and desperately clung to any shred of pseudo-celebrity he could. The praise from strangers meant more to him and motivated him more than his desire to be a father. It was a role he had never wanted it in the first place.

She thought that when he saw his boys for the first time, he would change. He would settle down and step up to become the father they needed. He was so excited when she got pregnant, but the excitement wore off quickly when the workload and responsibilities that came with being a father were revealed. It was something he didn't want at all, and he found endless ways to shirk his duties while she begged and pleaded. But eventually, enough of those cries fell on deaf ears that she finally understood he was never going to make his children a priority. He was never going to show up and be a father because he wasn't capable. He just couldn't do it, so she did the thankless work of both parents, and allowed Mick to bounce in and out of their lives when he had nothing better to do.

Holly walked farther, finally seeing what part she played in the destruction of her family. She made a fundamental error, choosing the wrong teammate, and realized they were doomed from the beginning. Even though she had tried her best and put in so much effort, it was never going to work. The most difficult part of that realization was forgiving herself for being so distracted by Mick's charm and her own neediness, desperate to fill the void her father left that anything was better than being lonely. It was as much her fault as it was his, and that truth was a hard reality to swallow.

FORTY-THREE

That night, Holly tossed and turned, looking at the clock on her nightstand that mocked her with its red numbers ticking by mercilessly. She had a rough day on tap and decided to kill three birds with one stone. She had appointments with Dr. Remington, Chance's principal, and Anna just a few hours apart.

At four am, Holly gave up the good fight and walked to her coffee pot, pushing the strong button. To be honest, there wasn't a button strong enough to make the next twenty-four hours more tolerable. The ominously thick envelope from the District Court lay on the counter. When she pulled it from the mailbox, it felt heavy and official and gave Holly heart palpitations just seeing the return address. It sat there unopened because she wasn't ready to face the contents the night before.

What the hell? Might as well make this day epically shitty.

She swiped it open with her finger and winced as a sting from a paper cut appeared on her forefinger. She yanked the thick stack of official documents out of the envelope while sucking on her finger.

Court dates and a court-ordered evaluation at a hospital over an hour away. She would have to apply for a public defender to appear in court with Chance. More obligations and more having to accept ugly realities that she didn't want to accept. Her fidgety brain cued up a repetitive loop of destructive thoughts swirling through her head. Deciding she needed a brain dump, she turned to her computer, tapping away at the keys to drain some of the craziness from her brain. She gave her worries identifying characters, line by line, filling up pages and pages of text. When she was finished, she felt clearer, tired but more intentional and ready for the confrontations she would face that day.

Holly ran the flat iron through her hair, taking extra effort on her appearance to summon confidence. She dressed in the suit she wore when she interviewed for her job at New Hope Charter, hoping that Dr. Remington wouldn't realize it was the same one. It was the only one in her closet, a binge purchase she made, justifying she had to look the part at her interview. It was a gamble that had paid off at the time.

Knowing what I know now, I'm not entirely sure I would have accepted this job in the first place.

Walking into her closet, she studied her limited footwear options. She had two pairs to choose from that would work with the suit. Grabbing the basic leather heels, she slipped them on and then settled in front of the mirror again to actually apply makeup. She was going to battle, and her armor was polyester and a killer eyebrow arch. The physical transformation did spur on more of an internal one. She listened to "Eye of the Tiger" on her Bluetooth speaker and ran over the points she wanted to make, mumbling to herself. Saying the words out loud, trying out voice inflections and wording selections, she tricked herself into thinking there was a perfect way to arrange the vowels and consonants to have a successful but delicate discussion about Zach's small business with Anna. Mouth agape and winking, she leaned toward the mirror and carefully applied two coats of basic black mascara to each eye while running over her remarks in her head.

The transformation from disaster to put together mom was finally complete. In the living room, she gathered her bags and yelled up the stairs, "Guys! Move it! The van is leaving in five!" She walked to the kitchen and switched off the coffee pot and paced the wood floors, her heels clicking across as she continued to run through her talking points in her head.

The boys ran down the stairs and pulled their shoes on, grumpy and tired, but said nothing as she drove them to school.

"I'll be there at four to talk to your principal and counselor," she hollered as Chance walked away.

She dropped off Dillon with a hug, reminding him to ride home with Sarah and then pulled into the parking lot at her school. Pulling together her laptop and backpack, she began the walk to the school, dreading every step and every word of every difficult discussion she was going to have this day. Relieved when Dr. Remington wasn't in her office, she slunk toward the teacher's lounge.

"Wow, woman!" Stacey exclaimed. "What is the special occasion?" Stacey was dressed in her usual uniform of brightly colored maxi dress with sleeves and comfortable shoes. Her blonde hair was pulled back into a loose braid.

"Had to put the war paint on."

"Are you going to war?"

"Unfortunately. Meetings with Dr. Remington, Chance's principal about his suspension, and Anna."

"Sweet Jesus. Do you hate yourself that much?"

Holly laughed. "I must." She put her fourth cup of coffee

that morning to her lips and took a long sip. "Just thought it would be easier to get it all over with at once."

"You look great." Stacey smiled. "Don't let them intimidate you."

"I won't. But I'll be so glad when this day is over."

"Want to come over for a post mortem?"

"I won't have the energy. Been up for hours, and this is the only fuel in the tank." She hoisted her mug full of coffee toward Stacey.

"Okay, love. But if you need to talk, call me anytime."

———

Holly's day of instruction dragged slowly. Her eyes fixated on the clock as the minutes crept by, and when the final bell eventually rang, she released her class to the parent pick up volunteers and gathered her things for the long trek to Dr. Remington's office.

She hoped that she would have a second to calm her hammering heart and slow her rapid yet shallow breathing before her inquisition, but those hopes were dashed when she caught a glimpse of the older woman through her office window. She was engrossed in a document in front of her when the secretary knocked on the door.

Dr. Remington waved her in and continued to read, blissfully giving Holly a few extra minutes to control the panic in her belly that always surged through her when being judged. She smiled, her lips pursed together as she waited. Breathing in through her nose, she tried to calm the nervousness in her stomach, steadily walking through her talking points in her head.

"Thank you for waiting," Dr. Remington stated as she shut the folder and focused her eyes on Holly.

"Yes, I wanted to speak to you about an incident that happened at the high school," Holly began.

"The one involving your son's arrest for buying drugs on school property?"

"Yes," she answered simply, startled by the woman's harsh response but continuing anyway. "He's got a dual diagnosis that we have been working hard to treat. Last weekend, he made some bad choices, and I wanted to be forthcoming. He was arrested for buying drugs from another student in the district, and I wanted you to hear this from me before the rumor mill started up. It's important you know the facts."

Dr. Remington looked at her over her reading glasses. "Obviously, you have been dealing with some behavioral issues at home. I am sure this is a very trying time. It is unfortunate that this event happened on school property, as I am sure you already know. The penalties and consequences are more severe."

"Yes, I am aware of that. He made a grave error," Holly agreed, "one that he will pay for, for a very long time, but he is just a kid."

"That is no excuse."

"I agree."

"In strictest confidence, I will tell you that this is not the story we are hearing from the other party. Her position on the school board and high standing as a donor to the school and community have given her a rather large microphone and a captive audience. If it happened like you say it did, you have to be aware that is not the story she is telling."

Of course not.

"But it's the truth."

"Unfortunately, it doesn't seem to matter. What matters is what people believe, and the ongoing history of substance abuse and treatment is going to make him look guilty, even if he isn't. The other party says Chance was selling the drugs."

"You have got to be kidding me."

"Look, Holly." Her voice softened. "She is very well connected; her roots go deep in the community. You are going to have a hard time convincing anyone that your son is innocent."

Why is she being nice to me?

"You're an excellent teacher. Parental feedback is exemplary, but maybe you should consider a leave of absence to take care of your problems at home."

"I can't do that. I'm a single mother. I have a mortgage to pay and kids to feed."

"You definitely are in a rough spot." She said nothing else and folded her hands back together in front of herself, sitting back in her chair. "Sounds like you have some challenging decisions to make."

"Decisions to make?" Holly's voice sounded pinched and tight as she shook her head, unable to hold back her words any longer. "This is what I hate about professional women. You expect us to drop everything to be a mother, but then cover all the bases at work, too. Instead of solidarity, it is shame and condemnation. I wish I had other options or people I could lean on in my circle, so I could… How did you so succinctly put it? Oh yes, take care of my problems at home. But I don't. You're absolutely right, I *am* a good teacher, but I am also a good mother who is navigating an incredibly intense mental health battlefield right now and the stakes are high. I should not be asked to sacrifice my children's lives in order to secure my paycheck, especially when you agree that I am an excellent teacher. I am doing the job I was contracted to do. What happens outside of that should not even be part of this conversation."

Red splotches appeared on the principal's cheeks. Holly boldly and out-of-character engaged in a staring contest with the older woman.

Holly continued, "The fact that you are even suggesting it is ludicrous. I will not have you force me out to keep up appearances."

It felt so good to stand up for herself. Adrenaline coursed through her body. Her blood was pumping from strength instead of fear this time like she had unlocked a secret superpower.

"I felt it was my duty to inform you of the situation. I have done that, so I believe this meeting is over." Holly stood and walked toward the door, but then stopped and looked over her shoulder. "One last question. Would you have had this conversation with any of the male teachers here on staff?"

Dr. Remington said nothing.

"Exactly," Holly said wryly. "Good day." Then she held her head high and walked out of the meeting to her car. Drunk on her own power, but finally feeling like the gloves were off and she was no longer the timid little reactive bird. Today, she was an eagle, soaring and swooping. A new Holly was born.

———

At the car, she turned over the ignition, laughing at the song on the radio. Twisted Sister's *"We're Not Going to Take It"* screamed through the minivan's speakers, crackling and popping and throbbing with the bass. She scream-sang the lyrics, cranking it up to maximum volume, and tapped her hands on the steering wheel. With Holly, good music always came with a lead foot. Driving fast toward Chance's school, she made it there quickly and parked the car, squared her shoulders, and then walked into the building ready for round two.

Chance was seated in the principals' office when the secretary ushered her in to sit next to him. She squeezed his hand and waited for the older man to speak. His hair was thinning and combed haphazardly across his scalp, and his eyes were small behind thick glasses.

"Thank you for coming in today, Ms. Simon. We have come to a decision regarding Chance's consequences for the events that transpired on Monday. He will have a three-day suspension and can return to school on Friday."

"I assume the same consequences have been doled out to the other student involved?"

The principal was taken aback and didn't say anything.

"It's just that, according to the parent handbook, the school code of conduct has a zero-tolerance policy in these matters, and since Zach was actually the one who was selling the drugs, I would think that his punishment would be at least equal or more likely harsher."

"I am not at liberty to discuss another student's violations."

"Chance made mistakes and is paying for them. I am only asking that the same opportunity to right the wrong is given to Zach. Are you aware that Zach is one of the biggest dealers at this high school?"

Chance's eyes widened, and he pursed his lips together and sat up taller in his seat.

"Prescription drugs, weed, molly. Apparently, anything you want, he can get," Holly stated fearlessly. "I've gone through Chance's Snapchat and IMs. Zach's been running a very lucrative enterprise right under your nose. So many kids here that have too much money and not enough parental supervision makes for a thriving business model, don't you think?" Holly couldn't stop now; she was on a roll. "You do not get to use my kid as a scapegoat. I have seen with my own eyes what is going on here. I spoke to Anna but got nowhere, and I have heard the story she is telling you about it. I know this institution has a long track record of looking the other way, especially when a key donor's kid has a behavior hiccup—but this is more than a hiccup." Holly paused then continued, her voice steady and in control. "I have done my duty and informed you of the problem you are facing. I'll bet that someday in the near future, some other child will get caught up in this mess. It might not have a happy ending where everyone gets to go home safe to their families like this one did. The next student might have a fatal overdose. Are you willing to take that risk?"

"Let's not get hasty, Ms. Simon."

"I am tired of playing this political game where you stumble all over yourself to kiss their asses to keep the donations flowing. I am done with this. Chance will accept his suspension and pay his debt legally. If Zach isn't held to the same standard, we are going to have problems. I have evidence of the discussions, and I will get a lawyer and subpoena the video footage of the incident. There is no length that I will not go to, to ensure justice for all the parties involved and that the blame gets shifted to the appropriate shoulders."

The man was silent for a very long time, considering Holly's words carefully like men in the business of public education are forced to do. "I think we can come to an understanding," he finally offered.

"Fantastic." Holly smiled. "Is there anything else?"

"No, Ms. Simon. Thank you for your time."

Holly waved to Chance and jumped up, and he followed

her out of the office. She felt invincible, tough as nails, strong and competent.

"Oh my God, Mom, that was sick!" Chance was excited, his energy cagey and bouncing like a boxer's was before stepping into the ring at a title match. "Did you see his face?" Chance morphed into a caricature of the prim and proper principal, mocking his voice. "I think we can come to an understanding, Ms. Simon."

"Dude, you probably shouldn't be gloating. I mean, you did just get a three-day suspension."

"I know. But, Mom, that was awesome."

"I meant it, Chance. I am not going to sit there and let them blame you. Zach was at fault, too, more at fault than you were. He should be held to the same standard. It's not okay for people with money and power to get to play by a different set of rules."

"You're different."

"I am," Holly agreed. "There was a time that I would go along to get along, but no more. I will fight for what I believe in, and when someone goes after my kid, the tiger will be unleashed. I am done playing their games."

———

She dropped Chance off at home and told him to make hamburgers for Dillon and then drove to her final showdown. She felt different this time, pulling up to park in the circular drive. She looked in the rearview mirror and refreshed her lipstick and then walked up the curvy sidewalk to the front door. She pressed the bell and didn't have to wait long until Anna opened the door.

"Holly," she mumbled like a statement, leaving the door open behind her as she turned and walked down the hall.

Holly followed her in, seeing the house was in shambles, not the professionally cleaned perfection of the last visit. Dirty dishes littered the sink and soured the air. Anna herself was disheveled, her dark hair in a loose messy bun piled on her head, wearing a fitted sweatshirt and tight black leggings. Anna looked distracted and a little deflated as she pointed at a stool.

"No thanks, this won't take long. I just met with the principal. Chance got a three-day suspension, and I encouraged him to give Zach the same punishment. I am not going to let them railroad Chance. He will accept the consequences for what he has done, but nothing more."

"Of course," Anna acknowledged.

Confused by her reaction, Holly pushed it away and pressed on. "Zach is engaging in some really risky and illegal behaviors. I have evidence from their messages, and I fully intend on subpoenaing the video footage from the campus cameras of that day."

Anna nodded. "I understand."

This was a different Anna. Quieter and humbled. It was throwing Holly off, detaching her from her anger. "He needs help, Anna," Holly said softly, hoping she could get through to the other woman.

"I am starting to see that," she admitted softly, on the verge of tears. "His father and I seem to disagree on how to best handle it."

Anna's hand shook as she pulled a crystal glass of water to her lips. Holly had never seen the other woman so weak and without lipstick. A sliver of empathy invaded her heart and softened her voice.

"I am sorry this is happening. Sometimes, teenagers engage in behaviors that don't reflect the family values."

Anna met her eyes and licked her lips, considering her words.

"It's like I don't even know him anymore." Her voice broke, and she started to cry.

Holly pushed her anger to the side and reached out. "He'll come back to you. There are options for treatment and therapy that can help, especially when you have the financial means."

"I know." Anna wiped her tears away and exhaled. The room settled into an uncomfortable silence. "I owe you an apology."

Holly was shocked and didn't know what to say.

"I looked down on you and your family. That was a terrible thing to do, and I hate that I was that person. I guess it took a stumble like this to show me what a monster I was. I wasn't ready to see the truth, and I was quick to blame Chance." Anna's eyes were filling again as they locked on hers. "I am truly sorry," Anna offered quietly.

"I appreciate that," Holly said.

"This whole event has shown me that I don't have any true friends. Everyone in my life has disappeared. They blackballed us."

"That is typical in this type of school system." Holly shifted from one foot to the other. She was empathetic but didn't want to feel responsible to comfort the woman. They weren't friends, and they never were going to be. Anna made her bed and would have to lie in it.

"I can send you some resources for you and Zach that I've used to navigate this," she offered, unable to stop herself from helping someone who was obviously in extreme pain.

Anna nodded slightly. "I don't deserve it, but thank you."

It was harder walking out of that meeting. This time, she wasn't drunk on power and self-righteousness. This time, she was leaving a woman who was suffering, a torment so fierce and exhausting it had almost killed Holly herself. She knew that ache, the destructive place it led, and the absoluteness of it. The fear that was all-consuming, the anxiety that ratcheted up every emotion combined with the loneliness of being ostracized from people she thought were friends. She understood the quiet that came from the isolation from her community, finally acknowledging how fickle their attention really was. She didn't feel good about it at all. Walking to her van, she wiped away her own tears, intimately knowing the levels of suffering that another mother was being asked to endure and not enjoying it at all.

FORTY-FOUR

Chance was picking at the rip in his dark skinny jeans, his elbow propped up on his knee, waiting for his name to be called for his court-ordered evaluation. He wore an aqua colored Thrasher skater sweatshirt and black Vans.

"Chance Simon?" An impossibly thin woman with long frizzy hair that was so long it swung across her bottom called out. Chance popped up and shuffled to the plain woman dressed in scrubs who was holding the door open with one narrow hip, and Holly followed behind him, hating how low his pants were sagging and resisting the urge to tell him to pull them up. Even skinny jeans hung off his thin frame.

Once in the office, the woman introduced herself, "I'm Jane." She sat down on a giant round exercise ball that was crowning on a short metal base, slightly bouncing up and down while she tapped at her computer. "Have a seat." She indicated the institutional polyester chairs next to her. For the next several minutes, she ran through Chance's history, tapping their responses carefully into the computer on her desk.

Was he a full-term baby?

Did he meet all the normal developmental milestones?

Did she smoke or do drugs during pregnancy?

Is there a family history of mental illness or substance abuse?

Holly and Chance took turns answering them all, and then Jane turned to Holly.

"The next portion of the evaluation is to be done without the parent present."

"Oh, okay," Holly said, slightly offended, and went back out to reception and sipped on a weak cup of scorched coffee. She sat in the stiff chair, waiting and waiting, watching daytime TV. Fluffy filler that she never had the time to enjoy in real life. A cooking segment, followed by a rundown of the top ten tech Christmas gifts, and a studio audience trivia game. It went on for another hour until, finally, Chance came through the door with Jane right behind him.

"Why don't you sit out here? I need to talk to your mom for a bit."

Chance sat on the chair and looked bored, and Holly followed Jane back to her office.

"Have a seat." Jane waited for her to settle in and studied her for a moment as Holly shifted in her chair. "Chance admitted some alarming behavior."

"I know," Holly said. "He's been struggling with his anxiety for a long time and trying to self-medicate."

"Yes. He admitted to that," Jane answered. "But he also disclosed that his father allows him to drink and smoke in the garage at his house." She stopped and studied Holly's reaction, then continued, "He said that Mick taught him how to smoke dope without getting caught. There was some long, convoluted story about using a toilet paper roll and covering it with wet paper towels to mask the smell."

Stunned silent, Holly felt everything come to a screeching

halt. She gulped at the instant lump in her throat and heard her heartbeat in her ears, a soft increased thump-thump-thump. She heard the clock ticking on the wall as Jane's soothing voice continued delivering alarming information, but she stopped comprehending after the words, *his father allows him to drink, his father allows him to smoke.* Jane's voice was so far away like she was in a tunnel, and she lost track of the words. Holly struggled to accept the truth, plucking the pieces from the foggy ether, realities that were still impossible to string together. Surely, she was going to wake up from this nightmare and laugh at herself for having such a dramatic mind, sighing in relief that it was only a dream.

His father allows him to drink. His father allows him to smoke.

The phrases were repeating on a loop in her brain. Circling and circling. Each time, she was gutted by the revelation.

The fluorescent light flickered, and a fly was trapped against the window, slamming into it over and over. Holly watched the futile attempt with a full understanding of his predicament. Bashing himself into the glass... into the glass... into the glass.

What in the hell? That couldn't be right, could it? He didn't. Did he?

The back and forth was screaming in her mind as she struggled to comprehend what Jane was revealing about Mick. The truth tore her soul in half. She tried to reconcile it in her mind, to fathom a circumstance where that would be acceptable.

"Ms. Simon?" Jane asked again, concern flashing across her face.

"I'm sorry. I... just... I'm speechless," Holly stammered,

trying to mentally regroup. "Are you sure he isn't lying? Lately, Chance has had a problem with the truth."

"He's believable. The details are very specific, and his delivery shows no sense of deception or deceit."

"No, Mick is many things, but he'd never do that." Holly's voice was pitchy and questioning. She was asking the other woman as much as she was asking herself.

He wouldn't. Would he?

"I wouldn't be so sure."

The question gripped her tightly in the pit in her stomach, transforming into a tiny seed of knowing. There was a distilled essence of the truth there that sickened her.

"I don't know what to say," Holly said. "I feel totally steamrolled. I will get to the bottom of this." She shook her head, trying to clear the words away, but they remained as the truth always does. "This is unacceptable. Mick is an alcoholic and has had limited contact with the kids. But if this is true, he will never see them again." She paused, considering the information again, trying to make sense of it but unable. "Honestly, I am floored. I have no words and had absolutely no idea this was happening." Holly's voice cracked. "I wish Chance would have come to me."

"It's not unusual for a teenager with an addiction to identify with and want to be with a parent that struggles with addiction as well. He might see him as a kindred spirit, or that his dad is the only one who truly understands him."

Jane turned back to the files and wrote down several more notes. "This will be part of my report that I send to the judge. I will submit it electronically, but I wanted you to know what Chance disclosed so you can address it. I was able to breach patient confidentiality in this instance because of the safety aspect."

"I appreciate the information, even if it is so difficult to hear." The words sounded wooden and robotic as she felt them leave her mouth.

"You will get a copy of my report from Chance's attorney."

"Okay." Holly sat still in the chair, running through her mind, looking for hints from the visits with Mick, trying to discover something she had missed. The guilt pierced her heart. It was sharp and punishing.

I willingly sent my boys to learn at the feet of their alcoholic father. What a fool.

For the rest of the conversation, she was a ghost. The knowledge had wrecked her, destroying her beliefs in two little sentences. She didn't remember gathering the papers, saying goodbye to Jane, or driving Chance home. The only thing that filled every corner of her nervous mind was the horrific truth and the nausea that accompanied it.

FORTY-FIVE

Holly didn't even ask Chance about it; she dropped him off at the door and drove straight to Mick's house to confront him. She needed to see his reaction and hear him say it with his own words. The only way to ensure she would get the truth was to ambush him.

She pounded on the dirty door, over and over until she heard footsteps and his gritty voice through it.

"Jesus, what is the urgency?" he asked when he stepped out onto the porch, immediately lighting up a cigarette. "Is it the kids?"

It took everything inside of Holly to hold her back from the intense desire to bash his head in for what he'd done. She took a deep breath. "Yes."

He perked up, a little more interested in what she had to say. "Have a seat."

"No." Holly searched for the words, but in the end, she couldn't find them. The right words to accuse her ex-husband of such a grandiose failure that was actually considered child abuse escaped her.

"We learned some very brutal truths at Chance's evaluation."

He met her eyes with uncertainty, and she watched as his hand shook. She wasn't sure if it was because he was afraid of what she was going to say, or because he was jonesing for a drink. Both of these possibilities turned her stomach.

"Chance disclosed that you have been allowing him to drink in your home and have gone so far as to teach him how to smoke dope without being detected." She waited, watching the emotions wrestle their way across his face. He swallowed hard, unblinking. Mick's eyes flashed back to the door longingly like he wanted to run back through it. His shoulders dropped, and he rubbed his hand across his mouth while she waited. She didn't even need to wait for a response. She knew. After spending a decade and a half with this man, she had learned all of his tells. He was firmly in the mitigate damage phase now and was scrambling to find a place to shift some of the blame.

"Tell me the truth," she demanded. Even though she already knew what it was, she needed to hear him say it.

"Holly, you have to understand..." Mick began, reaching out to touch her arm. She stepped back out of his reach immediately, and her stomach dropped.

"There is nothing to understand," she spit back at him.

"I was trying to be his friend, to get close to him, so I could find out what he was doing."

"Do you even hear yourself right now? You make me sick," Holly hissed. "All this time, I thought we were a team, that you had your shortcomings, but at the end of the day, you had my back when it came to the kids. But this—I am disgusted. This is the biggest betrayal of them all. How could you do this?"

"He was going to do it anyway. I just thought he'd be safer here."

"Safer?" Holly screeched, and laughed mirthlessly, shaking her head in disbelief. "It is illegal activity, you piece of shit. He is sixteen years old!" The tears gathered at her lashes. "I trusted you to take care of our children while they were in your care."

"Holly," he begged and looked down in shame.

"Shut up," Holly muttered and then continued, "This is what is going to happen. At Chance's hearing, when the judge gets the report from the evaluation, you are going to be present and admit to what you have done."

"No way, what if they arrest me?"

"You selfish bastard. *That's* what you're worried about." She shook her head in outrage. "Our son is following in your footsteps, and you are not only lighting up the way for him, you are leading the expedition. You will not have any more visitation with the kids until you, yourself, have been through a fully accredited in-person treatment center. I will have my attorney draw up a new custody and child support agreement, and you will sign it. Do you understand me?" Her voice was an octave higher and she was shaking.

He took a long drag on his cigarette and nodded in defeat. "I'm sorry," he finally said.

"That's not good enough. You don't get to be sorry." Holly's voice was cold now. "You have changed who they are and who they will become. I hate you."

He said nothing, seeming to shrink into the chipped metal chair he was sitting in, wrinkled and disheveled in dirty khakis and an old concert t-shirt. Holly got up and walked away from the porch and drove away. She got six blocks down the road when the avalanche of tears let loose and ran ragged down her cheeks, obscuring her vision so much she had to pull over. Her breaths came faster, and her chest felt heavy. Rage filled the van and her body as it built and erupted. She pounded on the steering wheel until her hands were red, and she screamed at the top of her lungs in the car to release some of the pain. It was a long thirty minutes before she was under control enough to drive home and put on a happy face for her boys.

Mick had crossed a line that he could never come back from. It was a death in a way, a loss of innocence that Holly could no longer ignore. Equally cathartic as it was an instant awareness that she was alone. Single motherhood had a whole new meaning. She was solely responsible for her boys. She was on her own.

FORTY-SIX

Holly was emotionally drained and took the next two days off work. She sent the kids to school and then took to her bed, only getting out to eat junk. Handfuls of Doritos chased by fistfuls of dark chocolates. Around noon, she ate half a carton of ice cream, but she couldn't eat enough junk to fill the hole in her heart. The sum of her terrible decisions stuck thick in her throat. The total regret she felt was like a heavy boulder she had to push away with all her might to keep it from rolling over her and her children. It was endlessly exhausting and physically depleting, but obligatory. She slowly combed back through her memories, one at a time, searching for clues carefully with a comb, like you do when your child has lice. Hair by hair, interaction by interaction, she searched and searched for the truth. Surveying each moment for the precursors that would have given her the clues that she was going to end up here. At forty-two, single-handedly parenting two high-risk children, and scared to death.

Mick, he was the epicenter, the source of all the current devastation. She wished she could cut him completely out of her life and erase all existence of him. Cauterize the wound or, better yet, never even get the wound in the first place. If she had never gone to that bar seventeen years ago. If she had never seen him on stage and felt an instant pull, if she had never bathed in the warm sun of his charisma, things would have been vastly different.

It was easy to blame Mick because he was an addict. He had faulty DNA, and he was the one who crossed the line with his weak standards and rules. She hated him. She punched her pillow, she muffled her screams with it, and in the end, she made herself an appointment with Susan, who thankfully had a last-minute cancelation and could see her tomorrow.

She was peopled out, drained and exhausted, and tried to take care of herself the best way she could. She ran a long bath and opened up one of the myriads of books that had taken up permanent residence on her nightstand. Books she planned to read one day when things slowed down. She laughed at that thought. Instead of slowing down, things had ramped up full tilt on a terrifying merry-go-round to hell.

She tried to get pulled into the story, but the happily ever after endings mocked her. Nothing was perfect like this in real life. Real life had plot holes that didn't get sewed up in two hundred pages. The cut and dried formulaic stories felt cheap and flimsy now that she knew intimately what plot twists her real life had in store. Setting down the book, she reached for her iPad and opened up Pinterest.

I want to run away from my life. I want to get in the car and drive as far as I can until I run out of gas.

She tapped on a pin screaming, "Top ten cheap vacation destinations in the US." She wandered through the options, adding hiking in Utah, a treehouse you could rent in Oregon, and a Yellowstone National Park seven-day travel itinerary to her Places I Want to Go board.

She walked to her closet and pulled a bottle of premade margarita from the mini-fridge, twisted it open, and hungrily sucked it down nearly in one gulp. Then she pulled out a second one and settled back down on her bed to peruse more escapes, to discover more places she could go and hide. The west had always called to her. Cowboys and horses. Wild, open, and free. She had been there only once when she was seven and on a family vacation. She remembered whitewater rafting and how icy cold the water was, so bitterly cold when it splashed up and hit her chest, it took her breath away. She remembered camping in the park and being scared that a bear would eat her in her sleep. She remembered the campfire stories her dad told, the way his face was lit up from the flames. A pang of sadness hit her heart. She missed her dad.

I would give anything to be able to call him right now.

He'd been gone so long there was scar tissue on her heart. Mostly, she thought of him fondly, choosing to erase the truth that he was gone for most of her teenage years. He had left such a void in her and left her hungry for male attention. The desperate, immature craving of a fifteen-year-old who needed male attention so badly she was willing to sacrifice parts of herself to get it.

Fifteen. What was it about fifteen that had the power to forever change the trajectory of a person's life? It happened with her, with Chance, and with countless other nameless, faceless victims she'd watched on *Intervention*. Studying the series like a class so she could pick up on the signs and understand why people self-destructed. It hadn't helped. Fifteen seemed to be a fork in the road for so many. A time of reckoning where normal, happy children can get off track if left unattended. She saw it now, so plainly, wishing she could go back and pay more attention. She would have been more vigilant and watchful. She might have been able to save him. The power of that thought crushed the air from her lungs, threatening to pull Holly deep into an undertow and drag her out to sea. The regret came in waves—powerful, soul-crushing waves that left her choking and gasping for air.

I should have paid more attention. I should have done more.

FORTY-SEVEN

The next day, Holly drove to her appointment with a dull headache. Sleep had been fitful, and she tossed and turned. Just getting the boys up and driving them to school used up all her resources. She sat in the waiting room and leaned her head back against the wall, pressing at her forehead and her right eyebrow at the tension that was lodged there. She inhaled the lavender scent and tried to calm her mind.

"Holly?" Susan asked like a question.

Holly's eyes opened. She pulled herself from the chair slowly and followed the woman into her office.

Susan sat in the chair across from her and waited.

Preemptively, Holly pulled two tissues from the ever-present box on the coffee table. The tears were at the surface. Tight and unyielding, it was all she could do to keep things together while driving the kids to school. She didn't want them worrying about her.

"I'm so lost," Holly started, and the first tears spilled out onto her cheek, causing Holly's hand to shoot out to mop them up.

"Chance's evaluation shined the light on a serious issue. Mick has been allowing him to drink at his house, and he was even teaching him how to smoke dope and hide the smell. I feel sick."

"That would be very difficult to hear."

"It's such a betrayal. I thought we were on the same team. Sure, I knew that we had our differences, and I didn't agree with the lifestyle he was living, but I never in a million years dreamed he would do something like this. I'm in shock. I've taken two days off work. I can't focus on anything. This pain is so deep. I just sit and eat and cry. I have never felt pain like this." She wiped at the tears that were coursing down her cheeks and tried to swallow the lump in her throat. Her mouth was just so impossibly dry. "My principal told me maybe I need to take a leave of absence and get my family problems under control." She laughed grimly. "No shit! I'd love to be able to do that, but I have a mortgage. I have kids to feed. I can't just take time off work." She wiped at the tears that just kept coming. "I had to confront the neighborhood busybody with the truth of what her son was doing. I wasn't going to let Chance take all the blame. That conversation was brutal. I just feel like I am in a war zone, and every day I get up and gather the few resources I have left and figure out how to fight my way through another battle."

"Let's take some deep breaths together," Susan suggested. "I'm going to teach you the 4-7-8 method. Inhale slowly through your nose only for four. Hold your breath for seven. Exhale through your mouth, making a whoosh sound for eight."

Holy felt stupid but did it anyway, and after two minutes had to agree that she felt calmer and more relaxed.

"You have been traumatized," Susan continued. "You have been blindsided and betrayed, and this brings up rounds and rounds of devastating emotions that weaken your system. Whenever you feel overwhelmed, try that breathing exercise. First and foremost, safety is important. The kids cannot be around Mick until he has significant sobriety."

"I told him he wasn't going to see them until he had been through treatment."

"That is a good first step, but I would suggest longer," Susan said calmly. "He will need to earn back your trust, show that he can maintain sobriety in the real world, not just inside the controlled bubble of treatment."

"I agree. I have already contacted my attorney to change the formal custody agreement and arrange child support."

"Good." Susan added, "You need to let go of him and his problems and focus on yourself and your boys."

"I'm trying, but the guilt is so draining."

"Guilt from what?"

"Everything, from letting the kids spend time with their dad to marrying him in the first place. Looking back, I hate the decisions I made," she muttered. "And I see how they led me here. It's my own fault."

"You can't wallow in regret like that. You need to let that kind of destructive thinking go. There is only today and right now." Susan stopped for a moment. "Do you hear what you say to yourself? It's my fault. Taking all the responsibility is another insidious form of codependency. It is not all your fault. You have to forgive yourself for the part you played on the path that got you here."

Holly considered her words carefully.

"What would you say to a friend who was walking the same path?" Susan probed. "Would you tell her it's all her fault? That she's an idiot?"

"No," Holly answered weakly.

"So, why do you do it to yourself?"

Another deep truth that resonated. Holly plucked it from Susan's tree of knowledge and took a big bite.

"You're absolutely right." The first ripples of peace tingled through her.

"You have done everything you can to support and protect your children in a healthy way. When you found out the truth, you immediately took steps to correct the situation. That takes courage and strength, Holly. You should be proud of yourself, not beating yourself up."

The sob broke free, and she shattered into pieces, fracturing and splintering as the pain cracked her heart wide open. She let herself fall apart for all the things she lost and all the things she sacrificed. She sobbed huge weighty tears for herself, for the little girl who had tried to do everything right for everyone else and who had gotten completely lost in the process. She sobbed for Chance, the sweet little boy who lost his way and searched for something to take his pain away. She sobbed for Dillon, her peacemaker sweetheart who was forced on this hellish journey simply because he was born. The tears were cleansing and powerful. Years of pent up anger and fear coursed down her face and were soaked up by tattered tissues. When she finally slowed down, her breath still hitched, her throat hiccupped, and she looked at the other woman with fresh eyes.

"I think we are done for today," Susan remarked. "You did a very good job. I am proud of you."

Holly was proud of herself. She walked out of the office to her car, feeling lighter and freer. Bigger ripples of peace coursed from her center to her arms and legs. She drove home and slept deeper that night than she had in a week.

FORTY-EIGHT

Chance was calm as he drove Holly to his outpatient rehab appointment. She wasn't quite ready to give him access to his car again. He had to earn the privilege back, and he accepted it instead of fighting her. Holly's newfound stability and removal of Mick's chaos from their lives was giving him a safe place to heal. He knew what she expected, and he knew that he wasn't going to get away with anything. The last several weeks had been easier and calmer with just the typical teenage skirmishes that popped up from time to time. With the boundaries and expectations clearly defined, and Holly's complete consistency, order was restored for the boys and it felt tentatively hopeful. When she asked Chance about it last week, he even said, "As much as I hate it, I know I need structure and consistency if I am going to make permanent changes in my life."

He sounded so old when he had said it, like a teenage Yoda. Wise beyond his years, the truths he had discovered had been hard-won. He was quieter. Calmer. Holly was beginning to let her guard down, and this shift permeated everything. Dillon was happier, work was easier, life was simpler.

"Only seven more sessions and I'll graduate," Chance said. "I'll still have to check in with Cody and go to meetings, but it will look good when we go to court next week."

"I am proud of you," Holly praised, knowing that Chance's love language was words of affirmation. That he lived and died by the words people said to him and they were seared on his skin. Addict, Disaster, Waste, Loser. They would always be there. Scar tissue would form over them and lighten them, but they would never disappear fully. She was trying to build him up by using words like strong, smart, mature, and capable as often as possible. She was willing to do anything in her power to help build him up into the man she knew he was capable of becoming.

Holly was learning things, too. How to stop her first reaction to jump in and help. She was dealing with the guilt that prickled down her spine when she waited to respond. She was clamping a hand over her mouth that was ready to riddle off solutions and advice and letting Chance figure it out himself. It got easier and easier the more she did it. The first few times, though, were painful. She knew exactly what he needed to do but sat on her hands, uncomfortably waiting for him to arrive at a decision himself.

"Are you worried about court?"

"Nah. It is what it is," he said, resigned. "I have no idea what to expect, so I am just going to see what happens."

"That's a good approach," Holly agreed.

He's schooling me again. I need to let go of the anxiety around this. He's better at facing his consequences than I am.

Chance pulled into the parking lot and grabbed his red folder. "Love you, Mom."

"Love you, too, buddy. I'll be back at eight."

She opened the door and got into the driver's side, then drove back to her house.

FORTY-NINE

The following week Holly sat in the courthouse next to Chance in a pew that looked more like it belonged in church than a judge's chamber. She searched the room for Mick and was not surprised when she didn't see him.

At the last minute, he walked through the antique double doors, skating on a cloud of nicotine that made her nose wrinkle.

"Hey, kid," he said to Chance. It was awkward. He was trying to figure out his place in the pecking order again since his dressing down with Holly.

She had expected for court to be more formal, but it was a little more like *Night Court*. She was surprised by how informal and laid back it was. People sat in the waiting room and then were whisked into the judge's chambers case by case. It was a sea of broken humanity covering the benches. Holly noticed that, more often than not, race and economic stations were the criteria that determined if you were sitting in those pews waiting for a summons or not.

Chance's attorney, Linda, was a simple woman in a basic black suit, with her hair slicked back in a knot at the base of her neck. "We're the next case on her docket." She looked over at Chance. "Are you ready?"

Chance nodded anxiously.

The bailiff escorted Holly, Mick, and Chance to the judge's chambers, a room nearly completely encased in honeyed yellow oak.

Holly sat stiffly on her hard, wooden chair with her hands in her lap. Chance's knee jiggled up and down next to her, and Mick even sat at attention next to him.

Judge Sowers read the documents silently, stopping every few minutes to confirm the information she read. "Who has custody of the minor?"

"We have joint custody, but I am refiling for full custody, Your Honor," Holly answered.

"Based on what I am reading in the evaluation, Mr. Simon, this is very troubling."

Mick shifted in his seat. "Yes, Your Honor, it was a mistake."

"A mistake?" the judge asked him. Holly enjoyed watching him squirm under her scrutiny, feeling justified. Finally, someone saw what a train wreck he was. "A mistake is when you make a bad turn or wash something red with your whites. Your actions are unconscionable and bordering on abuse and neglect." She read further, finally setting aside the file. "Mr. Simon, I am ordering you to twenty-eight days of inpatient treatment, or I will be encouraging the district attorney to file charges against you for child endangerment and contributing to the delinquency of a minor."

Judge Sowers locked eyes with him as she demanded a response, and finally Mick nodded.

"As for Chance, how do you plead?"

"Guilty," Chance stated and waited, then nervously added, "Your Honor."

"I am entering your plea of guilty. I see you are nearly complete with treatment. I am hereby putting you on probation for six months and ordering you to complete forty hours of community service. We will meet in sixty days, and if there are no further incidents and you have completed the community service, your case will be closed. I suggest you pass all your drug tests and work your steps. Let this be your wake-up call."

Holly squeezed his knee, encouraging him to respond.

"Yes, Your Honor," he said timidly.

"See you in sixty." She scribbled in the folder and handed it to her clerk, then dismissed them quickly in a clipped but professional tone, asking for the next case.

Holly walked out of the courthouse onto the lawn with Mick and Chance. Mick instantly lit up a cigarette in frustration. "Rehab? That's a bunch of bullshit."

"That's what you got out of that?" Holly asked. It never ceased to amaze her the way his selfish mind worked.

"Look at what you've got me caught up in," Mick said, trying to shift the blame.

"You don't get to do that." Holly fished her keys from her handbag and handed them to Chance. "Go start the car, buddy. I have to talk to your dad."

He walked away quickly, relieved to be freed from the imminent showdown between his parents.

"What a bitch. Drunk on her power. She doesn't have the right to tell me how to live my life."

"Actually, she does." Holly countered. "The second you decided to break the law, she had every right to intervene in your life. She could have put you in prison. You got off easy."

"Easy?" Mick said. "Having to go away for a month and sit in a circle of crybabies bitching about how their mamas didn't love them enough is not getting off easy."

"Grow up, Mick," Holly hissed. "Your sixteen-year-old son is more mature than you are. I have cleaned up your messes and made excuses for you for the last time. Get your shit together. You have a problem. Fix it. Be a man."

"I don't have to take this from you."

"You're right, Mick. You don't," Holly said evenly and walked away from the man she had always worked to save and let him flounder in the mess of his own making. She was done wasting her breath on a man who fought against her, drowning her to save himself.

FIFTY

A few days later, Holly sat in Dr. Remington's office again, but this time she wasn't worried or anxious. She was fully in control of her emotions, and it felt like she was acting a part in a play. Like she had stepped into the body of someone else overnight.

"Hello, Holly," Dr. Remington said evenly when she breezed into the room and then settled herself behind her desk, waiting. "You wanted to speak to me about something?" she prodded with her hands clasped on the gleaming walnut surface.

"I wanted to inform you that I am planning to resign at the end of the school year. I have loved being part of the staff at New Hope Charter and have cherished the students that I helped shape here, but it is time for me to put my own children first and do what is right for them."

Dr. Remington nodded thoughtfully.

"Just between us—you, the school board, and Anna had nothing to do with this decision. I fully expect that to be reflected in my file. I am not sure what is next for me professionally, but I know I can be sure that I can count on you to tell the truth, so if I decide to pursue another position in education, I will be free to do so. And I know this goes without saying, but I wanted to confirm that none of the private information that I have shared with you will be part of my performance review."

"Of course," Dr. Remington confirmed. "You are a good teacher. I would never try to take that away from you."

"I appreciate that." Holly stood and shook the older woman's strong, yet bony hand and walked out of the office, flying high. She smiled wide and felt like she was soaring. For so long, she felt stuck in the wrong places. Now, she had cut herself free from everything. Her future was wide open without any strings. There was nothing holding her back anymore, and she felt like she was finally able to breathe.

———

Later that day, she met with a realtor. He was tall and slick and drove a Mercedes, and he gave a dazzling PowerPoint presentation that had culminated in her signing a contract with him to put her house on the market. She knew it was the right thing, but she was sad. It was the first and only place she had earned completely on her own. She had lovingly painted the entire house the week she got it. Fueled entirely on coffee and Coke zeros, she slaved away, crawling up ladders to cut in along the ceiling. She pushed herself to complete it, only allowing the boys to help paint their own rooms when they begged to be part of the process. She had wanted the kids not to see the new, smaller house as a downgrade. It had been a week of sleeping on the floor and ten-hour days of removing old carpet, but in the end, it looked fresh and new and was the perfect place to start over. She thought all their problems would be over the day she brought her boys home to it.

Looking back, she could now see that she was so naïve, thinking a house would fix things. That rafters and drywall would be the answer. Things were simpler back then, before the days of drug tests, and phone surveillance, and standing in front of a judge. She was ready to walk away from it all, to leave it all behind. She craved simple and easy. She craved distance from the overprivileged world of New Hope that had more money than values. She craved a fresh start to build a life with her boys away from Mick, who she could never trust to do the right thing. He loved the boys, but his love was destructive and sick. Addicts don't know how to love because, on their hierarchy of needs, the substance comes first and everything else takes a back seat. She couldn't wait anymore for him to mature or fix himself. The best course of action was complete surgical removal of him from their lives, and she knew that the only way it would be successful was to be a thousand miles away from him.

FIFTY-ONE

New people, new places, new friends.

The first time she had heard those words from Adam, she felt stuck. She didn't have the luxury of starting over; she had things like a mortgage and her sons' father to think about. This time, she didn't have either, and she was going to follow his advice to the letter.

If you want a different result, you have to do something different.

At first, she felt like she was in free fall. No career to fall back on, no job, no co-parenting to consider. The world was her oyster, and it was overwhelming to think that she wasn't tied to anything anymore. She could pick a place and just go. Anywhere.

It was a movie that first put the idea in her head. She stumbled across a documentary about Montana. Its incredible landscape and vast wide-open spaces called to her heart in a way that was impossible to ignore. It was the only place that seemed relatively untouched in America anymore.

She craved room to breathe. The events of the last few months had made Holly feel like she was trapped under a magnifying glass. That every movement she made and everything her children did were being studied and judged. She heard some of the gossip through Stacey, but she was just as sure that Stacey had kept the most painful parts to herself. Holly craved fresh air and space and peace.

It was just a random Sunday afternoon when she stumbled onto a Montana real estate website and found a remote little cabin near the north entrance of Yellowstone National Park. It was an acreage. At first, that word was daunting. Acreage.

I can't take care of an acreage.

But the seed was planted. She didn't exactly know how deep until she found herself looking at her retirement accounts and calculating how much she could afford to pull out and still have a chance at survival in her seventies. At first, it felt like a crazy dream that would never come to fruition, but she kept returning to it, again and again. She had twenty-four more days to research it, to find a place that was safe to start over when Chance was released from treatment and his responsibilities with the court. A clock was ticking, and she was hastily gathering the information she needed to make a good decision.

The only soul she told was Stacey. In the sunroom, sipping at a Chardonnay, Holly told her the day before the sign went up in her yard.

"I'm moving the boys to Montana," Holly said plainly like she was talking about taking them for ice cream.

Stacey coughed, choking briefly on the wine in her own glass. She held up one finger while she recovered, finally croaking out, "You're what now?"

"I'm putting the house on the market tomorrow and relocating to an acreage in Montana. I put in an offer yesterday."

Stacey's eyes widened in shock. "Oh my God, woman. That is huge!"

"Am I crazy?"

Stacey considered it for a moment. "No. I think a fresh start is what you all deserve."

Relief flooded into Holly, and she exhaled. "I think I've been holding that breath in for a month. At Sienna, Chance's counselor kept barking, 'New People, New Places, New things,' and last time I didn't listen. I felt like we were stuck here. Now, I have nothing holding me here."

"Nothing?" Stacey pouted her lips and mimed a tear falling down her cheek.

"You know what I mean, smart ass." Holly laughed. "The *only* thing I have holding me here is you, but it's not enough."

"I know." Stacey squeezed her hand. "Selfishly, I hate to see you go, but I think you are doing the right thing for the boys."

"I think so, too." Holly finished her glass of wine. Stacey refilled their glasses with the rest of the yellow bottle. "To your new life." She raised her glass and chimed it against Holly's. "Tell me all about it."

"As long as you promise to visit," Holly stated.

"Deal."

"It's in a small town called Garden Brook. They have a small country school and not much else. We could have chickens and sheep. It's so close to the north entrance of Yellowstone National Park that I think I could do pretty swift business as an Airbnb. There's a cabin on the property for us to live in, just two bedrooms, and then there are two smaller cabins I could rent out, and also an outbuilding."

"That's the perfect set-up. You know I'll be hitting you up when I need an escape from this madhouse." She hiked a thumb toward her own adorable house.

"You are welcome to visit anytime and to stay as long as you like." She went on, "I have to take a pretty big chunk out of my 401K to finance it, but I think, if I do it right, I can actually turn a profit in about a year."

"It's risky."

"Not any riskier than staying here and subjecting the kids to Mick," Holly said wryly. "I think having fifteen hundred miles between our houses might be the perfect distance."

"Touché," Stacey agreed. "Sounds like you are way past the thinking about it stage. You're approaching it the right way, so what can I do to help?"

"I think I have everything handled. I'll let you know if something comes up." She looked down for a minute. "Thank you for being here for me during the worst summer of my life. I don't think I would have survived this without you in my corner. I'm going to miss you so much."

"The world is smaller now, sweetie, more connected than ever. We will stay in touch. When I make a real friend, they are stuck with me forever. And lucky you! You and I are the real deal."

Holly smiled and sighed. One step closer to her new life. Leaving the old one behind would be easy, except for the one little flower named Stacey.

———

The sign was going in the yard tomorrow and nervousness roiled in Holly's belly, bracing for the reaction from her sons. Taking them away from everything they knew and thrusting them into the unknown was a gamble, and she wasn't sure how they were going to react. After the plates were cleared from dinner, she said, "Guys, I have something exciting to tell you."

Dillon's face lit up at the word exciting. They sat at the dining room table, Chance tipped back on two legs in his chair, something she normally chastised him for, but Holly let it slide this time.

She thought about the right words she wanted to use and, in the end, just pulled up a website from Yellowstone National Park. "I have decided I want to be around you more, and I think we all need a fresh start. So, I have put an offer on a new place in Montana."

"Montana? Where's that?" Dillon asked.

She turned her laptop toward Dillon. "It's a beautiful state, right at the north entrance to this park." She scrolled through the photos while the boys studied the screen. "It's got mountains and waterfalls, geysers and hot springs, elk and buffalo."

They leaned in close, looking at the pictures silently.

"Our realtor is putting the sign in the yard tomorrow."

"You're going to sell our house?" Dillon looked panicked.

"Yes, honey, we get to start over in a brand new beautiful place. I am going to run an Airbnb there and maybe take on some tutoring. I'll be working from home, and we'll have a house with a couple of cabins that we get to rent to visitors. On the weekends, we can go to the park and explore. It's going to be awesome."

She was trying to sell it, and she knew she sounded too excited and too over-the-top happy about it. She thought Dillon was buying into it; he was easily manipulated into doing something that made his mom seem happy. But she couldn't read Chance at all.

Finally, he asked, "Is this because of me?"

"Not entirely," she said truthfully. "Your therapist did say new places, new people, new things would be best for you. But I think it will be best for all of us."

"What about Dad?" Dillon asked.

"He's got to get his life together, and when he does, he can always come to visit."

Dillon looked at his older brother for clues to see how he should be reacting to the news. Chance ruffled the hair on his head. "We can feed you to the bears!" He smiled a small smile.

"We'll feed *you* to the bears," Dillon tossed back.

"We can go horseback riding, zip-lining, and whitewater rafting."

"What's that?" Dillon asked.

Holly pulled up a YouTube video to show him. "It's so awesome. I did it once when I was close to your age with Grandpa."

"That looks sick," Chance said, warming up to the idea.

"It's so fun!" Holly enthused. "Such a rush, you guys are going to love it. I'll get to be around more because I'll be my own boss, and you two will have jobs to help me keep things going on the acreage."

"Will we get paid?"

"Of course," Holly said.

The prospect of whitewater rafting and earning their own spending money was enough to push the boys in favor of the move. Holly was relieved.

"I'm gonna go tell my friends," Dillon said. "Wait, will I ever see my friends again?"

"Maybe on Skype. Montana is a long way from Indiana." He sobered up at the thought. "But I'll be around more, and you'll make new friends." He ran to his bedroom to deliver the news, but Chance lingered. "Is there something on your mind, buddy?"

"I feel guilty. It's all my fault."

"You don't get to carry that burden," Holly said quietly. "I have forgiven you for the mistakes you've made, but it sounds like you haven't forgiven yourself."

Tears welled up in his eyes, and he shook his head to clear the emotion.

"I made the decision for us, and I want to start over as much as you do. We get to do it in the most beautiful place in America! How lucky are we?"

"It's always so hard to leave."

"It's bittersweet, honey, but new beginnings can be so beautiful if you let them. You can have a fresh slate in a brand new place where no one knows your past. You'll get to rewrite who you are. We all will. We're getting a second chance. Not many people get to start completely over."

"Yeah," Chance agreed.

"We're going to have an amazing life in Montana, honey. Trust me."

He got up then and walked up the stairs quietly. He was more reserved now, not the child who used to bound up the stairs two at a time. The past year had changed them all, grew some of them up quickly while others regressed. Holly was certain that Montana was going to heal her family. Long walks in the prairie grasses filled with wildflowers, hiking up snow-capped mountains, and the fresh air punctuated with the sulphury smell of geysers. Being outside would restore their souls, and she was looking forward to getting them all settled in their new home.

FIFTY-TWO

They sat on her porch on a perfect May day. Sipping slowly on the wine, Holly could feel the tug on her sentimental strings. She knew this was the last time they would sit in the sun so close together on Stacey's porch. She was never coming back. In her mind, New Hope, Indiana, was decimated, a desolate wasteland that had nothing left for her family. Last year, it was the stage for the biggest battle of her life, and she would never, ever come back. It hurt too much.

Stacey refilled her glass one more time. "I can't believe your house sold so fast."

"Me neither," Holly agreed. "But I'm starting to believe that things work out the way they are meant to, and there isn't much we can do to change it."

"Look at you getting wise and sage in our old age."

"It just feels like all the pieces are falling into place. Chance finished up his community service, and the judge closed his case. If he stays out of trouble, he will have a clean slate."

"That's good." Stacey said, "Definitely makes life a lot

harder when you have a criminal record." She looked thoughtfully at Holly. "And Mick?"

"He signed the custody arrangement, and I got my first child support check."

"What did he say when you told him you were moving so far away."

"He accepted it. I think a part of him was relieved." Holly marveled at how, even after all they had been through, and after going to treatment himself, that he still was so selfish. "He's drinking again. He lied to my face, but I know him. He's never gonna change."

"Probably not." Stacey offered her a lemon shortbread cookie.

"I need to get the recipe for these. Would be awesome for the Airbnb guests."

"Are you excited about your next venture?"

"Excited and terrified," Holly admitted. "It's going to be a massive change."

"You'll figure it out like everything else you do." Stacey was lost in her own thoughts. "I am going to miss you so much. Who am I going to confide in when Remington is on the warpath?"

"Me, Babe, it will just have to be over Skype." Holly finished the wine in her glass and set it aside. "I have to finish packing before the movers come in the morning."

The finality hit her then, and a lump formed in her throat. "I love you, Stace."

"Oh, woman, I love you, too." She leaned in and hugged her tight. "You look so good, Holly. The fire is back in your eyes, and I know you are going to go on to do great things. Your kids are watching you pick up the pieces and put them first, and that one act will heal you all. I just know it."

Holly's eyes filled. "Oh, God, I hope so."

"Don't you dare cry, because then I'll turn into a blubbering mess. No goodbyes, just see ya laters."

She hugged Stacey tight one more time, and her eyes closed tightly, containing the tears that lingered. Endings were always bittersweet, but this one was more intense than usual. As much as she looked forward to the future with joy and anticipation, it was difficult to do it on her own, knowing there was no safety net. It was just the three of them, and she was going to have to figure out whatever challenges came her way. Finally, Holly pulled away, swiped at her tears, and then walked to her car. Stacey gave her one more little wave and then wiped her own eyes, gathered up the empty glasses and plate of cookies, and walked into her bright house as Holly put the van in reverse and headed to her own home, that was only going to be hers for twenty-four more hours.

———

It had been a long day spent organizing and directing the movers, but the house was completely empty except for the stray dust bunny. Her steps echoed in the empty living room without her long purple drapes and thick microfiber sofa to absorb the sound. She swept up the last bit of crumbs and stretched out hair ties that had hid behind her sofa for so long and said goodbye to her house. Stacey had already picked up the boys, and she was letting them crash at her house so they could start the two-day drive to their new house in Montana in the morning after a full night of rest.

Chance was right; starting over was hard, and for a second, she allowed the terror to wash over her. Without the boys to witness it, she felt the fear of moving twenty-four hours from her home to a town where she knew no one, to start a career she didn't know she could succeed at.

What if this is all a big, miserable failure? Then what? Then you suck it up and either make the best of it or start over again, you whiny baby. Nothing lasts forever. The great things are fleeting, and the terrible moments eventually fade.

She walked through the house and said goodbye to each room, noting the imperfections in each one. She remembered intimately which ceilings she accidentally touched with the wall color and forgot to touch up. She knew which knobs had to be jiggled to close properly. Her fingers felt the slight depression that remained in the drywall that Chance had punched through with his fist. It had been repaired and undetectable to anyone but her now.

She turned off the lights and dragged it out, savoring the last look at the house that she had worked so hard to secure, certain that it would also secure her boys' happiness. It hadn't been the answer she hoped it would be, but she had been proud of her ability to provide for her sons on her own, and that was hard to walk away from. Making sure all the lights were off and the windows were closed, she walked to the kitchen one last time.

She pulled out the bottle of wine she had left and wrote a note to the new owner. She learned it was a single mother with two kids, and as a result, she didn't hold out for top dollar. She bent more than she probably should have because she knew what it felt like to work so hard to provide a better life for your kids on your own.

She pulled the notebook out of her bag and jotted a quick note.

Enjoy this bottle of wine in your new home. You earned it. I hope this home becomes a sanctuary for your family and you thrive here.

Holly

Then she left the keys on the counter and locked the door behind her, pulling it shut and checking the knob, just to make sure it was secured. She walked down the sidewalk and got into her car, stopping to look back one last time before she drove away. Tomorrow, after they had a great night's sleep, their new life would begin.

FIFTY-THREE

They drove all day and into the night. Holly was grateful to have Chance take a turn driving. She tried to sleep in the passenger seat, but she never could quite relax and trust his driving enough to be able to rest.

The boys were quiet but not fighting. In close quarters, they all got along and passed the time, putting the radio on scan and playing name that tune. Murph slept in between them and munched on small bits of beef jerky and popcorn the boys dropped near his mouth. There was so much time to reflect on a long cross-country drive. The farther west they drove, the hillier the land got, and then all at once, it was dotted with mountains and long waving grasses. The roads began to curve, and the wind whipped through the valleys as they drove even farther.

"Look! Mountains!" She pointed excitedly and shook Dillon in the seat next to her, who sat up and surveyed them for a brief second and then fell back in the seat with disinterest. The miles ticked by as thick sturdy rocks snaked between snatches of highway that had been dynamited to make room for the roads hundreds of years before.

A few hours later, when the boys had changed seats, she exclaimed, "Look, Chancey! Look how far you can see. It goes on forever."

"Look at all the milk pandas," Chance teased her with a southern drawl, pointing at the cows.

There was so much to see. The closer they got to Montana, the more beautiful the landscape became. Her mind drifted and daydreamed about the life she was driving to, the one that was filled with fresh air and new beginnings.

I can't wait to have my days to myself, being able to hike with the boys and sit around a fire pit at night. To be able to ski in the winters. I am going to make this move fun for them.

It was going to be a beautiful place to start over. She glanced over at Chance, who was bent over in the seat, sleeping at an impossible angle. His neck was crooked and mouth open, and in the rearview mirror, she noticed that Dillon had drifted off, too. Murph had curled up next to him on his back with his tongue hanging out, dead to the world. Barreling down the interstate toward their new life while her boys rested, she begged.

Please let this work. Help Chance find his way. Let this be the right step for my boys and let us find happiness here. Let us heal here. Please. We all need it. We all deserve a chance to start over.

The soul-cleansing tears coursed down her cheeks as she begged and pleaded for their fresh start. For the longest time, when things went sideways, she wanted to go back. Back to before the time when her son reached for drugs to fill his emptiness. She wished she could go back and see it more clearly, that she could have helped him find a healthier way to fill himself up. That she could have spared him from the pain of following his dad too closely down the terrifying rabbit hole of addiction. For so long, she beat herself up because she hadn't seen what was happening to him right under her nose. That she didn't know what Mick was capable of when she dropped her boys off at his home. She hated herself for being asleep at the wheel, caught up in the busyness and full speed of life that being a single mother means.

She wished she had a fairy godmother who could have waved a magic wand and taken it back. Taken back the blood-curdling fear she felt when she found Chance unconscious that night at the park. That she could go back to the little boy whose laugh was so magical and infectious it made strangers laugh in that waiting room so long ago. She wished she could go back to that sweet little blond-headed, sensitive soul who cried when he accidentally crushed a toad with the garbage can and who jumped down into the egress window well to save a bird with a broken wing.

But she finally understood. You don't get to go back. There is no before. There is only now. And she would never find happiness today while pining for things from the past. She saw how paralyzing that line of thinking was, and as she drove deeper into the west, with its boulder-covered streams, majestic mountains, and waving grasses, she exhaled the past. It left her lungs, the last of the stale and constricting air from Indianapolis. The sick aftertaste of judgment and bitterness of conforming to fit in and keeping up with her neighbors. She had been stuck in a life that didn't fit her or her boys anymore. A life that got in the way of living. She rolled down the window and inhaled deeply the damp freshness and green, and even the sour note from the manure made her smile.

The sun lowered and cast pinks and purples and peachy colored waves, culminating in the most breathtaking sunset she had ever seen. She resisted the urge to shake the boys awake, knowing their annoyance would follow, and instead savored the first sunset herself. Driving toward her new life, she felt peace slowly ripple into her body. The weight on her chest loosened, and she let it go tumbling down the highway behind her. It disappeared like the sun did a few moments later, finally succumbing to the horizon and ushering in the beginning of twilight that skittered across the trees, muting the colors and calming the wind. She couldn't go back to before, but now she didn't even want to.

Discover other books by Blair Bryan: https://blairbryan.com/

COMING SOON! THE SWEETEST DAY: A DELUCA FAMILY BAKERY NOVEL

Real love doesn't exist... or does it?

Pastry cream runs through Gionna DeLuca's veins. Forty-something, curvy, and content with her life, she makes extravagant wedding cakes to celebrate other people's love stories. Believing she will never need one for herself.

Surrounded by a long legacy of loving relationships in her family's bakery, a brutal heartbreak forces Gionna to shut down and build unscalable walls. She resigns to live her life fiercely independent and tries to find happiness and success on her own terms.

Until a younger mohawked sous chef walks into DeLuca's and challenges everything she thought she wanted. He pushes Gionna's boundaries and forces her to confront her fears and failures. Demanding she open her heart to the risk of love or remain stuck and unfulfilled in a life she is beginning to outgrow.

The Sweetest Day explores one woman's misconceptions about the existence of forever love and the danger and reward of putting your heart into the hands of another.

Available on Amazon, BN Nook, Apple iBooks, Kobo, Google Play.

Get more information at: https://blairbryan.com/also-by-blair-bryan/